The Queen of the Prisons of Greece

WORLD LITERATURE SERIES

Fiction

Nonfiction

OSMAN LINS

The Queen of the Prisons of Greece

Translated by Adria Frizzi

Dalkey Archive Press

Originally published as *A Rainha dos cárceres de Grécia* by
Melhoramentos (São Paulo), 1976. © 1976 by Osman Lins.

English translation © 1995 by Adria Frizzi

First Edition, 1995

Library of Congress Cataloging-in-Publication Data
Lins, Osman, 1924-1978
    [Rainha dos cárceres da Grécia. English]
    The queen of the prisons of Greece : a novel / Osman Lins ; trans-
lated by Adria Frizzi. — 1st ed.
      p.   cm.
    I. Frizzi, Adria. II. Title.
PQ9697.L555R313   1994   869.3—dc20   94-7326
ISBN 1-56478-056-2

Publication made possible in part by grants from the National Endowment for the Arts and the Illinois Arts Council.

Dalkey Archive Press
Illinois State University
Campus Box 4241
Normal, IL 61790-4241

NATIONAL
ENDOWMENT
FOR THE
ARTS

*Printed on permanent/durable acid-free paper and bound in the United
States of America.*

The Queen of the
Prisons of Greece

April 26, 1974—Many times during the past year, so grim and empty, I have mentioned here my intention of occupying my spare time, of giving it meaning perhaps, by writing what Julia—Julia Marquezim Enone—always so private about herself, told me about her life, what I saw myself, and what I managed to find out later. How many nights have I spent looking at the few photographs she left behind, hearing the indistinct noise of traffic rising to this room, now empty? I know her notes, not always intelligible, almost by heart, as well as the recording of a conversation we had. Our daily chats are lost; I have managed to reconstruct only fragments of them, with a sharp sense of their irrecoverability.

Yes, I'd have a lot to say about her negligent and vulnerable ways, by which she seemed to suggest that she knew she was fragile and that, precisely because of this, she chose not to protect herself. I hesitate, limiting myself to a few brief and random comments about our life together.

At the same time, a vague idea that I don't want to record just yet has occurred to me during the last few days.

MAY 1—The idea returns and takes form. Instead of writing about the woman, why not write a study of the book, hers, which I read over and over again? It's a more reasonable and profitable alternative. After all, much of what I could say about Julia Enone would mean something only to me, like family pictures. Lacking the skill and the energy indispensable to the art of narrating, despite the attraction I feel toward fiction, I'd run the risk of suggesting but a pale shadow of my friend. Even if I scrupulously stuck to biography, without any fancy for incursions into the realm of the imaginary.

Dealing with the book presents obvious advantages. The text will keep me from getting tangled up in cherished memories and images, a labyrinth still to be mastered. Add, to the existence of the text, its nature. Texts: in principle, a universal gift. If we discuss them or shed light on them in any way—if we allow them to grow within us—we're working on a collective heritage.

In Julia Marquezim Enone's specific instance, the text to be enjoyed, it's true, hasn't been published. Because of this, its quality of public good (or evil) is debatable. Its existence limited to the original manuscript, and thus not even available to anyone who might want it, does it already belong to everybody?

MAY 2—I'm inclined to think that it does. The work, even if embryonic, concerns the collective being—us—whose substance informed it. Besides, those who deal with books must always bear in mind, and I believe that a return to this protracted period is not entirely unlikely, handwritten reproduction. Finally, the almost legendary book by Julia Marquezim Enone, in which sensitive and informed individuals recognize, painstakingly concealed, bold explorations, is circulating among several readers and people interested in the art of fiction, thanks to the sixty-five copies I myself ran off on an obsolete ditto machine.

One problem is still holding me back. Even accepting without reservations the public character of the literary work, even if unpublished; and the fact that this modest reproduction saves the book from complete anonymity, I'm still hesitant.

What are the chances of finding a publisher for a study of a book almost unknown and inaccessible, for the time being, to the general reading public?

MAY 6—Let's hear, on the threshold of my possible study or mere commentary (who knows, on the other hand, where someone who's getting involved in this type of project is headed?), let's hear, half revealing and half enigmatic, the novelist's voice: "I've begun the book that was slowly taking form within me. Everything, at first, was preparation, expectation, plunder. And then? Then, it'll be Africa. As Rimbaud wrote, I will bury 'my imagination and my memories' and head 'for the port of misery.'" (Letter of 1/6/70 to the writer Hermilo Borba Filho.)

MAY 18—I discuss the project with A.B., professor at the Pontifical Catholic University, a man of great knowledge and somewhat ironic, who, since I'm fond of books, honors me with his esteem. What he tells me, even making allowances for some likely exaggeration, a tribute always to be paid to irony, worries me and, on the other hand, mitigates some of my apprehensions. A.B. tells me, with his shrewd ecclesiastical smile, what happens with some of his students and even well-known professors: if, for example, they know something about Madame de Volanges, de Danceny and the libertine Valmont, it's not because they have read *Dangerous Liaisons*, but because they're familiar with the explication published some eight years ago in the journal *Communications* of the novel by de Laclos, that connoisseur of fortifications and human weakness.

Nowadays, adds A.B., a publisher who brings out a literary study has a significant, eager audience, larger than the audience—real or possible—of the work analyzed, and who perhaps doesn't even deem it necessary to know it. He warns me, on the other hand, about the negative aspect of what might otherwise be an advantage: my intimacy with the author. The study of texts, claim the specialists nowadays, must ignore the hand that wrote them (charged, nevertheless, with history and obscure motives).

MAY 25—I see in the German magazine *Burda* an ad for Delft china, with this text in the midst of a selection of pitchers and other elegant wares: "Don't look at the bottom of the piece first. Avoid stereotypical reactions of admiration or trust. Delft products stand out for their beauty and quality."

Interestingly, this ad repeats what the Roman theorist Bruno Molisani says in a study of a Hugo poem ("Written upon the Glass of a Flemish Window"). There Molisani presents as something that was demonstrated, *a long time ago*, "the advantage, for the scholar, of not taking into account the author's name, which avoids stereotypical responses of admiration or trust."[1]

Thus I think it's necessary to ask—still taking into account what A.B. told me—if I won't be wrong in disregarding an idea endorsed equally by literary studies and Delft faience ads, in dealing with Julia Marquezim Enone (or rather, with her book), I, who not only knew and know her name, but also hear it repeated so many times within myself, since we were lovers. Won't my work be doomed from the beginning to partiality, to failure, since I must fall prey, due to my past circumstances, to "stereotypical responses of admiration or trust"?

MAY 26—I could still ask: since the author doesn't exist, was I nobody's lover?

JUNE 3—I thought about it long and hard and decided not to back off in the face of decrees that—objective and laudable as they might be—lack knowledge in the widest sense of the word. Let's see. A mere letter can be better understood if compared to others—earlier and maybe even later ones—by the person who wrote it. Repetitions and changes can point to so many things! How can certain intentions and shades of meaning be translated if not by contrasting them, by setting them against a certain tradition, that is, an *authorship*? The same verses are not the same verses if they come from the epigonous Etienne Alane rather than Hugo. This is what Jorge Luis Borges, an Argentine who knows about these things, tells us,

---

[1]"Le poème comme représentation," *Poétique* 4 (1970): 403.

in his own way, in the story in which Ménard writes Cervantes' novel word for word. The style of the *Quixote*, natural in its first author, becomes archaic. The comparison of the two texts, says Borges, "is a revelation": Ménard has enriched the art of reading with a new technique, that of "deliberate anachronism and erroneous attributions." Borges suggests, among others, the experience of reading *The Imitation of Christ* attributed to Joyce.

Besides, since I'm far from being—and from the desire of being—an academician, why abide by rules? Let us forge ahead.

JUNE 10—Yes. Why submit to the trend predominant nowadays? I remember reading, in the *Almanac of Thought*, I suppose, or in some old issue of the *Lionhead Almanac*, what the Prussian Fontane wrote, not very elegantly perhaps, almost one hundred years ago: "Whenever it comes to the organization of the work, philosophers make inane judgments. They completely lack the organ to pick up the essential signals." "The opinion of a perceptive layman is always valuable; a professional aesthetician's is usually worthless."

Even though I probably lack finesse, at least I'm a layman. In any case, Fontane, I'm far from being your professional philosopher or aesthetician, I'm even far from the literary circles, which makes me lean in the opposite direction, that of the not entirely obtuse aficionados of the novel. It's in this capacity that I dream of discoursing about my dead friend's book, visited so many times and still so full of secrets.

JUNE 12—I knew the author, we lived together, I don't hide the fact that I loved her. Love doesn't necessarily mean blindness and deception. The widower Middleton Murry is not wrong when he presents his Katherine Mansfield's *Journal*. My love for Julia Marquezim Enone will inevitably show in some pages—maybe even in all of them. Even if this fact were to lessen the study's lucidity and impartiality, and I trust that no injustice will be done to either, lucidity or impartiality, I have trouble admitting that this would invalidate my commentary. For which inflexible law would oblige us to conceal our ardor before a work of art as shameful? Just how coherent is it to willingly block out part of our mental faculties with regard to this object that appeals to the totality of our being in order to talk about it with a detachment it does not aspire to by its own nature?

I won't fall into the error of "discussing the poet and not the poem," by which I'll avoid lucid Pound's classic criticism. But I won't demand of myself voluntary mutilations in the study I plan either. Never. Only my restraint, if I don't overcome it, and a certain tact, will limit the frankness of the work—an analysis or, who knows, just a memoir—from which an elegiac note will certainly not be missing.

Oh Julia, who, in spite of everything, I won't call *mine*, since you were always headed for some mysterious region, invisible and uncharted!

JULY 15—Part of the month of June and half of the school vacation have been spent making plans for my essay over and over again, without choosing one: all of them, with their brackets and subdivisions, imitate the charts—so useful, after all—with which the Linnaeuses of this world try to order nature. I think today I found a solution.

Every literary essay, following a convention consolidated by authority, evokes a hidden narrator. Unavoidable, in both cases, the so called *personal* discourse—which clarifies the circumstances of the utterance. The essayist never addresses us in a definite time or place: atemporal and somewhat abstract, he only reveals to us, by the artifice of a text that in a way conceals him and thus deceives us, his readings (always commendable) and his ideas (never unfinished).

I will take another direction. I want an essay in which, abdicating immunity to time, and, as a consequence, immunity to surprise and hesitation, I will establish with the reader—or accomplice—a more honest relationship. What other option stands out more naturally than the diary in this case? This way I will follow the progress and the turns in the questions that occur to me day by day.

My disadvantage in comparison with the authors of fictional diaries imagined by Goethe (*Werther*), Machado de Assis (*Aires' Memorial*), Gide (*The Pastoral Symphony*) is apparent. They all dealt with women—Charlotte, Fidélia, Gertrude—

whereas my hero is just a book. At least the not insignificant circumstance that the book and I are real is in my favor.

Let's therefore go on to my essay, half intimate, half public, confidential, a book that is to be composed slowly and imprinted with the passing of days.

May I not irrevocably fall prey to solitude by trying to elude it. May I not have to complain, like Goethe: "here, as well as everywhere else, I always find both what I am seeking and what I am running from."[2]

July 17—Nietzsche writes, I don't remember where, that a philosophy is always the expression of a personality. Julia Marquezim Enone wasn't tainted by the fierce need to astonish that afflicts most contemporary artists. Discreet, cultivating an uncommon kind of elegance, an intimate elegance, invisible, full of modesty, she rejected all forms of ostentation—a glaring proof of arrogance, in her view. Obvious originality pained her.

How to solve the problem, if she, as honest as someone lacking imagination—she, who incessantly enlarged the world—would never stoop to taking the beaten path; if she looked at writing and natural things from a perspective not at all trivial; if she couldn't hide her ineptitude when faced with what's established?

She chose, and her personality thus engendered, if not a philosophy, a poetics, a novel apparently following closely the models of the past. Going deliberately against the most widespread and respected dogma of modern fiction, which looks askance at the plot, she structured *The Queen of the Prisons of Greece* around an uninterrupted chain of events centering on Maria de França, a moneyless mulatto heroine lost in the stairways, corridors and halls of the social welfare bureaucracy, where she struggles to obtain a certain benefit.

When everything would lead us to believe that we have a conventional work in our hands, the opposite happens. And it does so because the narrator strives to conceal her inventions. If this trait, fundamental in the author, escapes us, we will

---

[2]*Italian Journey*, memento of September 19, 1786, *in fine*.

assess the book incorrectly. Discovering in it what is elaborate and personal—and my discoveries in this area, until now discontinuous and undisciplined, barely allow a glimpse of all those hidden lodes—will be the main goal of my essay, or whatever else it might be called.

JULY 18—". . . when she noticed a very curious appearance in the air: it puzzled her very much at first, but after watching it a minute or two she made it out to be a grin, and she said to herself: 'It's the Cheshire-Cat: now I shall have somebody to talk to.'"—Lewis Carroll, *Alice in Wonderland*, chap. 8.

JULY 19—What's the use of a book's synopsis? A superficial practice, it spreads and resurrects the common idea according to which the story *is* the novel, not one of its aspects, among those that illustrate the art of narrating the least. Imagining desires, mishaps, reversals of fortune, capitulations, death or triumph, pertains to invention in its raw state. The novelist is born by the act of arranging these events and elaborating a language that could either reflect them or simply make use of them to exist.

Here, however, summarizing the facts narrated in the book we are to discuss is indispensable. Since it hasn't been published yet (I'll explain the reasons for this in due time), my readers would be left in the position of someone who finds himself at a debate he knows nothing about. Without further delay—I don't want to be the target of Montaigne's criticism of Cicero, whose speeches, he said, swollen with preparatory remarks as they are, "languish around the pot"[3]—I will therefore return to the novel and summarize it, so as to convey, without Propp's assistance—bound by other commitments—as faithful an idea as possible of the heroine's banal adventures, adventures which repetitions and variations turn into a nightmare. I will alter the order of the original where necessary.

JULY 21—Maria de França, the daughter of farm hands, loses her father when she's a little over five; the widow, who's origi-

---

[3]"Of Books," *Essays.*

nally from the city and hates working in the fields, moves to Recife. She hopes to earn more than she would digging in the dirt and has dreamed since childhood of a capital city full of "forts and bridges." Maria de França and her brothers go with her. (Julia Enone abstains from characterizing, naming or even specifying the number of these brothers she always refers to vaguely and who hover around the heroine like obstinate shadows, sympathetic yesterday, and aggressive, if not indifferent, tomorrow.) In Recife she rents a room in the suburbs in which they all pile up. She washes and irons clothes for well-to-do families.

Maria, who has begun elementary school, skips class whenever she likes, doesn't learn anything, and, "lost among brothers," stays at home for good. Her greatest pleasure is to observe the transformation of dirty clothes: in the widow's hands sheets and shirts become clean, smooth, "with a scent that could be grass or new bricks." She notices that rain and good weather, so important for farming, also affect the business of washing clothes in the city. Now sunny days, especially when it's breezy, are more welcome than the rain necessary for agriculture, but this coincidence prompts the following reflection in Maria de França: *We depend on things that aren't part of us and that we can't control.* Not only that. She glimpses an incomprehensible connection between the chore performed by her mother's hands and the world at large. The association evokes the connection between the laborious hands of the peasant and, for example, clouds.

Here, then, playing on the unpredictability of the weather and in the guise of a mere opening, is the allegory governing the subsequent episodes of the novel. The widow's move and the first five years in Recife, by the end of which—increasingly taciturn and distracted—she has made no progress at all, represent the introduction to Maria de França and her tribulations. Complaining of problems with the genital organs, with the left side of her body paralyzed, the mother is moved to the background, leaving the drama's protagonist, who has just turned ten, center stage. The change takes place in a coherent manner: as the woman's strength declines (she also begins to suffer from kidney problems), Maria de França, despite her age, finds a job as a maid in exchange for food, lodging, and paltry wages.

JULY 22—Many of those who leave the countryside, as we know, would return there if they could, so difficult is life in the city for them. There they join the ranks of those who form the "culture of poverty," characterized by the disproportion between the mental structure of the individuals and the complexity of the cities where they try their luck, which makes failure inevitable. "For me there is only one place," a desperate ex-peasant said. "It's six feet under ground."[4] Even so, the rural exodus is intensifying, giving rise to shanties like Coque—150 acres of swampland filled in with garbage in Recife—where 10,000 people live, 90 percent of them without permanent occupation, subsisting on clams gathered from the mud.

I asked J.M.E. why she had given less deplorable living conditions to the migrants in her novel. The level at which her characters' troubles took place—she answered—and the nature itself of those problems were inaccessible to people such as the inhabitants of Coque, whom she didn't know as well. In relation to this she pointed out that a study of the social classes based on the type of adversities peculiar to each would be of great interest. What do Oedipus' grief and Fabiano's struggle with the drought in *Barren Lives* have in common?

JULY 25—From under Maria de França's bed, a voice warns her every night:

—Watch out, girl. Someone in this house wants to destroy your life.

This voice follows her through her subsequent jobs, invisible, repeating this ominous litany until dawn. Later, Maria de França begins to imagine that a huge fish is growing under her feet, in the subterranean fire, that this fish one day will erupt out of the ground beneath Recife and head for the sea, thrashing about with its tail.

She begins to receive the visitations of a "spirit of light," Antônio Áureo, who was a barber during his former life. Stut-

---

[4]*Realidade* magazine, 7.74 (May 1972), special issue on urban life.

tering and melancholic, the visitor scorns mundane things, calls life "a walk through Coque" and discloses to Maria, in detail, the circumstances of her death. He even specifies where the grave will be, the exact time, and the weather conditions: "It won't be raining, but it won't be sunny either." Antônio Áureo doesn't know the voice clamoring from under her bed. He does see, however, the fish swimming in the earth's fire and discusses it with the girl. It's this invisible friend who announces the coming of "a vassal of Venus" in whom Maria de França can find something, but "the way someone finds a nice little bottle of piss in the garbage."

The first chapter ends with the dismal presence of the ex-barber and harbinger of bad tidings: lacking in events, which, on the contrary, fill all the other pages, it's charged with expectations, implanting the certainty of afflictions to come. So clearly, in fact, that perhaps it wouldn't be wrong to see in Antônio Áureo the personification, the *manifestation*, I might say, of this part of the novel. Thus, when Maria begins to work, at twelve or thirteen years of age, in another apparently respectable home (actually, as some details confirm, a disguised brothel, in spite of the pictures of saints in the rooms), we see child prostitution looming as in a melodrama.

JULY 26—The expectations I hinted at and with which I interrupted my synopsis yesterday seem to be confirmed when the character of Belo Papagaio—a truck driver as well as the uncle and pimp of one of the whores—appears, with his hook nose, round eyes, bow legs, and his way of walking with his upper body thrust forward. He's missing his right thumb, which he cut off to avoid the draft: "He says he's a man of love, dear listeners, not a man of war."

Othello the Moor talked to young Desdemona "of most disastrous chances:/Of moving accidents by flood and field,/Of hair-breadth scapes i' th' imminent deadly breach, . . . And of the Cannibals that each other eat,/The Anthropophagi, and men whose heads/Do grow beneath their shoulders," as I just verified after looking through my collection of Elizabethan works, with the intention of enlivening and enhancing this passage. Belo Papagaio talks about motorways, trucks falling into precipices, swollen rivers, bandits, describes the brawls he started and won in famous whorehouses of Bahia, Alagoas, Sergipe, the overturned card tables, the bullets, the flashing knives, falling from windows down into the street, women whose genitalia, due to their unusual shape, size, scent, smoothness and fire, fill any male with awe. In spite of his being over forty, he deflowers Maria de França and, before daybreak, vanishes into time.

This episode doesn't carry the consequences one might fear. All that remains of Belo Papagaio's passage in the victim is the habit of hiding her thumbs. The voice under the bed and the gloomy spirit of the ex-barber, silent during the five or six days during which the visitor hides in the brothel, dressed in women's nightgowns, perfumed, with lacquered nails, reappear when he leaves, follow her when she changes jobs, and stop only when Maria de França rises from maid to factory worker, returning to her sick mother and her suburban room, now less crowded: some of the brothers have left. Belo Papagaio and even the defloration vanish like a dream. But the ease with which the factory worker gives in to any proposition, giving herself in barren fields or backyards, confers upon this period a certain air of degradation.

The huge fish keeps growing underground, night and day.

July 27—Should I give page references when I quote from the novel? I don't think the few copies haphazardly dittoed justify such a concern.

It's also possible that I won't always situate the other quotations with the customary rigorousness. Precision in these cases conveys the writer's courtesy and above all his desire to earn his readers' trust. The essayist, even when he's harsh toward the world, aspires to the respect of the general public. I will honor the memory of the woman I loved if I make it clear that I don't want to be believed and that the respect of the general public leaves me, an obscure secondary school teacher, indifferent.

August 4—This is not the place to try to analyze the turmoil, the need to investigate (but investigate what?) kindled in me by a certain character, Rônfilo Rivaldo, known in the neighborhood as Moon Duster—he's tall and lanky—who appears in the third chapter. Wavering between social action, spiritism, frank superstition, and protestantism, he claims to have an astral guide, Albert Magnus of Titiville, "archbishop, inquisitor, Gypsy and martyr"; despite his archiepiscopal tendency he lets his little fingernail grow to cut bad luck and knows countless evangelist hymns by heart. He teaches them to Maria de França and enrolls her in the free school he has founded and directs, in spite of being illiterate and poor, with family obligations. At the textile factory, she cries with joy when she signs for the first—and last—time her receipt: she's fired shortly after, for having failed to complete the so-called period of privation. This is a turning point for the textile worker and the book. She resumes her work as a maid—an ominous retrogression—and begins to hear again the warning coming from under the bed that someone wants to destroy her. One afternoon, while she's watering the garden, she experiences her first violent fit of madness.

Upon leaving the asylum on Avenida Rosa e Silva, an old building surrounded by trees, which the people of Recife refer to, a bit familiarly, as "Tamarineira," the tamarind tree, and which is entered through two rows of imperial palms, after having walked through the wide iron gate (there is a certain pomp in the palm trees, the size of the nearly dilapidated building and the capricious design of the bars at the windows, behind which the lunatics scream), as she's leaving there, she's advised not to work for a few months. Other ex-inmates, in similar conditions, have obtained a temporary pension. Why doesn't she give it a try? The trusting Maria de França follows the suggestion.

At this point it's necessary to ponder whether I should simply suggest, or instead describe in detail, her comings and goings in the world—malevolent and despairing—she begins to interact with, made up of prorogations, official letters, denials, equivocations, archives, delays, protocols, stamps, lies, certificates, seals, arbitrariness.

AUGUST 8—The expression "period of privation" describes the span of time between the complete absence of a right and its exercise: at this point we take uncertain possession of something that in theory belongs to us but from which we don't profit yet.

Decree 72.771, of Sept. 6, 1973, published in supplement to n. 173 of the Union Official Gazette, Nov. 10, 1973, establishes in art. 41 the "privation," or requirement, of 12 monthly contributions in order for the welfare system to consider granting:

illness subsidy,
disability retirement,
life insurance benefits,
hospitalization subsidy,
maternity subsidy.

This provision doesn't include all benefits. For example (art. 42), retirement in the following cases is not contingent upon it:

leprosy,
active tuberculosis,
blindness,
mental illness,
irreversible paralysis.

The right to medical care, already precarious, is earned beginning with the first payment. Equally guaranteed is the subsidy for funeral expenses.

But there remains a point that calls for clarification. What's the advantage of firing an employee before he qualifies for all the benefits of the welfare system, if the acquisition of those rights doesn't entail any expense on the part of the employer?

Aquilino de Macedo Lima, a lawyer and an authority on labor issues, has a caustic hypothesis on this matter whose inevitable lack of supporting evidence is balanced by his cogent reasoning, unfaltering as a madman's. What we have here, Macedo Lima says, is a gentlemen's agreement. What happens when an employee in the "period of privation" is fired? Unlimited access to the welfare system by countless members riddled with problems is avoided, members who otherwise would be very onerous and who, inversely, contribute the least share. This stratagem lessens considerably the liabilities of the welfare system which, favored in this way, doesn't consider remiss some degree of flexibility in the controls of the businesses it's in cahoots with.

AUGUST 9—I said, close to a month ago, that repetitions and variations turn Maria de França's adventures into a nightmare. I was referring first of all to her litigation with something which for her is as bewildering as an insoluble riddle. A legislation, with its articles, paragraphs and items, compounds the entity the heroine is grappling with. Compounds, I said: it's part of the composition. I see the legal text, there, as a sort of unsafe vehicle, driven by inept and malicious engineers, who change pieces, invert commands, damage the vehicle, turning it into an obstinate monster—into something insane. Thus the character's mental imbalance has an ironic ring to it: there is, in her acts, in the goal she pursues, a certain coherence. The true madness reigns on the other side, in the defective machine. This ambiguous confrontation between the woman and this entity can only be expressed through a series of arduous as well as ineffectual responses to ceaselessly changing demands.

Nothing, therefore, would justify the decision of reducing to a sentence Maria de França's nightmare, by saying, for instance, that new difficulties arose from the ones she overcame; or that an unpredictable factor, just when everything seemed to be approaching a happy end, decreed the beginning of the cycle all over again. In a schematic manner, as in a protocol or a file card, I'll go through, in chronological order, the history of the various steps—all vain—demanded of the witless aspirant to a temporary pension. The movement and tone of the original will be lost in my synopsis. Whatever agile and attractive aspects are left in it are not to be attributed to me.

AUGUST 15—Familiar to those who visit Recife and those who live in the city both, the white and unusual building of the Grand Hotel is located on Avenida Martins de Barros. From the front windows the guests can see the small coastal ships, the Alfândega pier across the water, dark roofs and some church steeples, each element contributing to a suggestive and intriguing view. In the back wing of the building, sought out, in spite of the slightly discolored curtains and the soot stains around the doorknobs, by travelers of means, there used to be and maybe there still is—a fact unique in the world, I think—a branch of the welfare system, the Benefits Office.

There begins Maria de França's "descent" into the purgatory of bureaucracy, and across those counters several episodes of her drama take place. The first one is favorable: even though she worked at the factory for eleven months, she paid—she doesn't know how—for twelve, and is therefore eligible to claim the benefit she's seeking. She's given a form she fills out with difficulty and which she has to take to Rua do Riachuelo along with two or three certificates. However, since over a year has passed between the last monthly payment and the request for the benefit, her rights have ceased, unless she proves that she suffered the first episode of insanity before the end of that period. In this case her request could be considered by claiming that if she didn't ask for anything when she was legally qualified it was precisely because she was in the Psychiatric Hospital.

She goes to the Mental Hospital, explains her situation as well as she can and, to her astonishment, finds in her file declarations of her mother's, saying that she was never normal. Fine. A document is a document: she takes the certificate to Rua do Riachuelo. The functionary has trouble remembering everything, finally she does, but now she has changed her mind. For the following reasons: a) a certificate is a very vague thing; b) it doesn't have an addressee, you know what I mean? it's not addressed to anyone; c) it's valid only if the signature has been notarized. So she instructs the confused insured to get, if possible, a letter stamped and signed by the "Tamarineira's" head doctor.

Maria de França manages to get that letter as well. The functionary goes into a room and closes the door. She reappears hours later with a form that must be turned in to the Medical Department. Rua da União. Maria de França goes many times to the address given before she's attended to, and then she returns as many times, patiently waiting for her test. The doctor has either left early or has someone tell her to come back another day.

He finally examines her and assures her that a year's leave is possible, in her case. But don't take it for granted, he's not the one who makes the final decision. Then who is? The Higher Medical Committee. The time between this information and the negative verdict of the Medical Committee, one gathers, is long. Maria de França, while she waits, tries to find work in family homes and, between one attempt and another, helps her mother with the washing.

She receives, again in Rua do Riachuelo, a new suggestion: to appeal to the Legal Aid office, after having obtained a certificate of financial need. She follows the advice, descends the steps—she's afraid of elevators—the dirty steps, repeating it to herself. When she gets downstairs she has already forgotten it.

She earns some money by making rag dolls at home. Sometimes she guts them with the scissors. Albert Magnus' chosen one, who knows nothing of these deaths, nor of the anger that fills the madwoman's heart, sees in this new occupation maternal instincts and finds her the least appropriate job: nursemaid to two deaf-mute boys.

The deaf-mutes' mother spends her mornings out, leaving them with the maid, whose violent tendencies are ominously growing. Will there be a double infanticide? Will the innocent Dino and Lino be stabbed? The sequel, luckily, doesn't fulfill these expectations: her mistress notices a swelling in the maid's leg and wants to take her to the Hospital of Tropical Diseases. Maria de França resists. Having been an inmate of the Psychiatric Hospital, she says, where she was treated well and has good friends, she trusts only *her* doctors. Without understanding why, she's immediately dismissed.

Hired by a notions shop (without being registered in the employment book), her sales don't even reach the minimum required "and just because of that, dear listeners, they tell me to hit the road, they throw me out."

She spends the better part of the day away from home, without anything to do, talking to the neighbors, squabbling over trivial matters, and she conceives of an *ideal*, "to be a woman with an open door, that is, open legs, empress of prostitutes, whorelove, glory!" Painted, covered with bows and wearing a very short skirt, she talks to any man passing by and assumes provocative attitudes, like rolling her eyes, flicking her tongue, grabbing her "everready," without heeding the advice and deliberations ("that's a bunch of jive, old limp dick talk, someone who never was and never is") that the prelate Albert Magnus sends her via Rônfilo Rivaldo. When she goes home it's in order to devote herself to such practices as putting a cork in a glass of water and keeping it from surfacing with agile movements of her tongue.

Finally, convinced that the reason for her failure is her swollen leg, she goes back to the Psychiatric Hospital, where she exhibits such signs of mental imbalance that she's kept there. She undergoes, one infers, treatment with electroshock, and her leg is also taken care of—"now I'm really in order, a gem, a jewel"—and is discharged on a Saturday, at noon.

AUGUST 20—In this last reading I realized that the characters of the book are always forgetting: promises, events, recommendations. I leaf through the remaining chapters and confirm this anomaly. What does it mean? Until now it had escaped me and, accidental or arbitrary as it may be, it deserves closer examination.

AUGUST 30—Isolation is the main characteristic of the gloomy building on Avenida Rosa e Silva; in the following passage and, one could say, in all of chapter 4, communion reigns. Maria de França, free, instead of going home, wanders around aimlessly and suddenly finds herself in the city's downtown area. People embrace in the streets, in the bars, throw talcum powder and water at strangers, play improvised musical instruments. She drinks the remains of other people's glasses ("to forget my troubles, dear listeners, I join in the ruckus"), tells everybody that she's a millionaire, climbs on the sidestep of the floats creeping along with an open exhaust, joins in the dancing beneath the loudspeakers ("it's terrible, it's because of the noise") and finally joins the "Morning Flower" Carnival club. There she marches with a new character, singing the group's "hymn," in chorus:

> I had a bouquet made for my lover,
> but one made of four-o'-clocks covered
> with the gleam of the morning star.
> Farewell, my girl,
> beautiful morning flower!

The "Tower," a suburban soccer team without a future in which her new friend plays as center forward, loses one championship after the other. It pays its players a pittance—when it does pay—and the solution for the lineman is to waste his remaining energy as a night security guard while he dreams of making the national team. Nicolau Pompeu (his professional name, Dudu, is seldom in the papers) radiates a tranquillity that Maria de França couldn't even imagine. This in spite of his quick step, his bright eyes, his hat tilted back on his forehead, and his way—deceptive, in the end—of someone who "if he doesn't go through them, goes around them." He becomes fond of her, and this poor love manifests itself in the form of guidance through the welfare system. He hears from Maria, after the Carnival, the tale of her useless attempts; he insists that she try again: there has been a change in the by-laws; he goes with the ex-factory worker, again, to Rua do Riachuelo, where they're told that she might obtain the benefits if she provides certificates of health and curatel. Curatel? What the hell is that, dear listeners?

SEPTEMBER 2—"The resources I.N.P.S. (Instituto Nacional de Previdência Social—National Institute of Social Welfare) invests in medical assistance are insufficient, and its per diem inpatient coverage has been decreasing in relation to the average cost of per diem hospital expenses. Due largely to this state of affairs, 48 Brazilian hospitals have closed during the past two years, among them Good Hope Hospital of Itapecirica which, in spite of its name, operated for only one year and, with the addition of a few bars, was turned into a jail." (From a report published 1/27/70 in the daily *O Estado de São Paulo*. Clipping found among J.M.E.'s papers.)

SEPTEMBER 4—The game against I.N.P.S. begins again, but, with the Tower's center forward, the stubborn machine is set in motion, although this match is like playing an away game, with a crooked referee on the take scoring everything in the other team's favor. Dudu obtains copies of Maria de França's admissions to the Psychiatric Hospital; he takes her to the Legal Aid office with her mother. Counterattack: the papers

proving that she was insane are not enough, please bring certificates of health and financial need, and have the signatures
notarized. Dudu besieges the Legal Aid office: he comes up
against closed windows and absent functionaries, all on leave
or out of town or at a relative's funeral. Finally, after so much
effort and combativity (his team, in the meantime, does lousy
in the state championship), he's informed that the terms of the
health certificate are too vague and that he needs to get another one. He flies into a rage and makes a stink at the Legal
Aid office, applying pressure in all possible places, insis-
tently, when they suddenly accept the second health certificate and decide to turn down that of financial need. He makes
the police commissioner soften up, smile, and provide them
with a new certificate, after he yelled at them to get out of
there and no way.

All this persistence seems to be yielding results. The papers
are accepted (the office has run out of excuses) and later returned, to be submitted at the Court House. The center forward takes them to the Court House and from there to the
League of Mental Health, where a doctor—at last!—is to examine his friend.

On the scheduled day the obscure urban athlete is by her
side in the small and stifling waiting room. The psychiatrist
doesn't even come close to seeing her. He sends word that
somehow or other the papers got lost.

September 7—The disappointment is offset, in part, when
Nicolau Pompeu, at the bus stop, presents Maria de França
with a thin engagement ring. This gesture marks the climax of
a jubilant movement, which, so to speak, develops sotto voce.
In spite of the incompetence or the bad faith of the welfare system, or of the combination of both, everything appearing to
follow a conspiracy, an insidious plan, the erstwhile weaver
feels, in the active care of her friend—now fiancé—in synch
with the world, as if pouring over everything and everybody
the demonstrations of love she receives:

Nobody likes me? Nobody loves me? Love, yes. Hello out there in
Radioland, listen, you're far away, outside the Death Globe, but now

I'm going to open the steel door and go there, my man and angel says so, I go in a straw hat and enter the ring-around-a-rosy, crown of people, holding hands, I throw flowers on the roofs, in the river and in the streets of Recife.

Surely because of this she, so forsaken that after all these months she still hasn't obtained any of the things she seeks, takes under her protection a six-year-old orphan girl, anemic and slightly retarded. So we see the heroine, in absolutely no condition to justify such a commitment, standing in lines and engaged in long and useless confabulations, both in the offices she used to go to and others, like the Child Care Hospital, holding the girl she wants to help by her hand.

In the meantime, Nicolau Pompeu, whose motto on the field is "Don't let the old wives embroider the trousseau," strikes again. With Rônfilo Rivaldo, now his friend, he turns on the League of Mental Health and extracts from the doctor the astonishing declaration that he has found the papers and made a decision without seeing the patient. What decision? He can't remember. And where are the papers? In his private clinic. Can they go get them the next day? The two men go and find out that they've been fooled, that no decision was made, that all the papers are at the League, that the doctor went to a conference, where? in Rio, and when is he coming back? in about eight days.

The events take an unforeseen turn. Maria de França, even though she has little to eat, takes in the girl. Early one morning the police, looking for burglars, knock down the door and, shooting all over the place, storm into the house. Realizing too late they have made a mistake, they warn the occupants, watch out, keep your mouth shut, or we'll come back and this time it'll be no joke. They don't even seem to see, in the smoke and confusion, the madwoman's protégée writhing on the floor with two machine-gun bullets in her neck. Shortly after noon, before the girl's burial, Maria de França has a major crisis. Chapter 3 ended with her release from the asylum; this chapter closes with another hospitalization.

SEPTEMBER 8—Mr. Reinhold Stephanes, I.N.P.S.'s new president, is beginning to discover that the bureaucracy in his agency is "frightening." The file regarding an authorization for construction at the Rehabilitation Center of São Paulo has gotten so big that it can only be moved from one office to the other in a handcart. Another, more modest, simply intended to correct some dates in retirement manuals, traveled through twelve agencies, two neighborhoods, four buildings and forty days, returning to its starting point with twenty-two stamps, an equal number of rulings and no solution. (*Veja* magazine, 9/4/74.)

SEPTEMBER 9—The Mental Health League's doctor goes to see Maria de França at the Psychiatric Hospital where he finally writes a report, charging (legally?) extra. Nicolau Pompeu pays him and takes the papers to a notary's office in the Court House. The inexhaustible distrust of the welfare machine causes another doctor to interview the insured.

What for, doctor? To see, my girl, how the fibrosis and the infiltrative steatosis are doing, the progress of the morbid condition, the tussigene effort, the eclampsia, the clinical evidence, and to make sure that the report that's been filed isn't false.

OCTOBER 4—I have bad eyes, I who take so much pleasure in books. Any greater effort hurts them; my love of reading is spiced with risk. With my pupils a little dilated (I occasionally think, looking at myself in the mirror, that my corneas are about to fall into the sink), I look hallucinated and incredulous before the world, which is true. Well, anyway, on the morning of September 9 I had written half a dozen lines when everything—even my pain—took on an intense brightness and I, who live alone, could barely make it down in the elevator.

During the nearly three weeks I spent at the hospital, deprived of my reading, something happened. Immobile, plunged in darkness, everything confused inside, the inessential turned to dust—or became forgetfulness, or nothing, or darkness—and only a few images prevailed, isolated from everything else: the balance, I might say, of my fifty years, the blessed minutes, a modest balance and almost always consisting of nonmarketable things. Julia's contribution was predominant, even though our life in common hadn't lasted long—

three years and six months.

The book she had written and which I never perceived merely as a text became entangled with those images, completing them in a way that eludes me. Not that the text undid itself and became, in a manner of speaking, the things it names. Without ceasing to be what it is, it also presented itself as a world, and I was moving in it, halfway between carnal and verbal. A different kind of reading? A forgotten modality, already obsolete among us, of perception of narratives? I don't know. I record the two phenomena because they mirror the intensity of the presence, in me, of Julia Marquezim Enone and her book—and because they show how, also in me, she and her text cross over into one another.

October 6—Used to Alameda Lorena and its surroundings, I avoid venturing downtown whenever possible. People who move naturally in their own neighborhoods look half blind when they rush—determined, but in a sort of panic—down Quinze de Novembro or Sete de Abril, areas where the life of São Paulo clamors, intense—and this makes me dizzy: even though I don't live, like Chekhov's character, old Mr. Bielikov, withdrawn into my shell, I can find myself only when I'm still.

Because of this, even though I wanted to investigate the names of some of the characters in *The Queen*, I had been putting it off. And it was only today, in the afternoon, following up a decision made during the extended hospital night, that I went to the Public Library. I was heading for a revelation—or at least a hypothesis—due to mere chance (Julia M. Enone didn't take anyone into her confidence regarding her curious literary project), or, to be more precise, to the hints she disseminated and which in the novel have the same function of a clue in a game of charades.

The name Rônfilo, which I couldn't find anywhere until yesterday, sounded foreign to me. Most of the dictionaries and encyclopedias I consulted today don't record it either. (I can still feel the dust in my throat, my eyes burning and here I open up my writing, for a second, to the deafening noise of traffic rattling the shelves and the inclined desktops. I finally discovered a certain Ronphile, a chiromancer famous in the eighteenth century for having foreseen that Marie Antoinette, shortly before forty years of age, "would lose her hair and never wear earrings again." Could there be a Nicolau Pompeu in the same trade? Yes. Between the fourteenth and the fifteenth centuries, a person by this name, a combination of man of letters (there are books by him on goliardic poetry and courtly love), chiromancer and clairvoyant, since he embarks on long journeys to read the hands of princes, merchants and even prelates whose identity, he says, is revealed to him "by celestial tongues," eagerly travels the roads of central Europe, and the seriousness with which he discourses about the lines in one's hands doesn't keep him from reading, in the palms of women who excite his senses, an indication that they are joined by fate and must submit to it. At the end of his life the former Nicolau Pompeu reinvents himself as surgeon and printer both. I think I can recognize, attenuated, some of his traits, not in the book's namesake but in Rônfilo Rivaldo: the penchant for books, the magic, something of the charlatan about him. A third name extends this play of correspondences, Belo Papagaio's, pure and simple translation of a famous nickname, Pretty Parrot O. (what could this O. mean?), a figure with a marked presence in quite separate spheres of action and whose biography I've had in my possession without any relation between him and *The Queen of the Prisons of Greece* ever having occurred to me until today.

OCTOBER 7—Last night I read the story of Pretty Parrot O., until then one of those books we acquire and then let lie among others, for years and years, awaiting an unlikely and constantly postponed reading. In the small volume, written by a certain Ashley Brown, clearly an aficionado of magic and adventure,[5] two aspects that vaguely attract me work together: piracy and divination. Even so, I only leafed through it a few times, but clearly visible fingernail marks highlight some passages. They're not mine.

A chiromancer, Pretty Parrot O. witnessed, as a member of the ship's crew, the last voyages of Calico Jack, captain of the pirate ship *Trinidad*, and he mustn't have been too sure of him-

---

[5] *Parrot & Bonney* (Liverpool: Search Books, 1948).

self; in fact, when he was undecided in deciphering a cross or a star tangled in the lines—certainly scarcely visible—of the buccaneers' palms, he consulted with (and listened to) a parrot always perched on his shoulder. It fell to the lot of this reader of destinies, in a company so unusual to his peers, to read the hand of the aspiring pirates and even prisoners, all those in whom Pretty Parrot O. read ominous forecasts, such as Saturn's Ring or the Sign of the Gallows, being rejected, thrown to the sharks or abandoned on a rock in the middle of the sea.[6] This precaution didn't keep an English sloop from tearing the *Trinidad* to pieces, capturing Calico Jack and taking him to Jamaica, where, after a trial, he was hanged. Two of the survivors escaped the punishment: Pretty Parrot O.—chiromancer and not pirate—and a sailor the captain hadn't submitted to his scrutiny. The sailor, stripped of his clothes, reveals his true sex and identity: her name is Anne Bonney and, free of the silk scarf around her belly, she turns out to be pregnant. The child may be Calico Jack's or the chiromancer's, who, as he will confess, had known from the beginning, from Anne Bonney's hands, her real sex, in spite of her disguise and her skill with weapons. The two get together; Pretty Parrot, who didn't get a taste of plunder and the errant life without contagion, becomes a black birder,[7] and his ability to charm an audience with the tale of his adventures becomes legendary. Let us add that his end, as well as courageous Anne Bonney's, is shrouded in

---

[6]"Saturn's Ring is the most unfavorable sign that can be observed" (Cheiro, *O que Dizem as Mãos* [What Hands Say], trans. Antoine Boueri [São Paulo: Hemus Livraria Editora Ltd., 1971], 87. Italian title: *Che dicono le mani.*)—"The Cross that appears isolated and distinct on the Mount of Saturn (thus ending the line of fortune) indicates violent death. Actually, some chiromancers call it the Sign of the Gallows" (Jo Sheridan, *O Futuro em suas Mãos*, trans. P.S. Werneck [Rio de Janeiro: Companhia Editora Americana, 1971], 83. Original title: *What Your Hands Reveal*).

[7]This term designates a rare profession: "port is entered in a distant island, where the natives are befriended, so that they will eventually come on board; the ship casts off and the captives are sold in another island, for agricultural labor" (Gilles Lapouge, *Les Pirates* [Paris: André Balland, 1969], 73).

mystery, between one Caribbean island and another.

It can't be said that Julia Enone transposed this figure to the northeastern Brazil of a few years ago, even though, besides the name, at least one trait of Anne Bonney's partner survives in Belo Papagaio: his pleasure in recounting daring feats and risky predicaments. Her goal, I think, wasn't to recreate legendary characters, but, availing herself of onomastic clues, to prepare a sort of cyphered inscription which, when discovered, would widen the work's horizons.

OCTOBER 8—*The Queen of the Prisons of Greece* insists from its first pages—a fact that can be observed by any less distracted reader—on referring to the hand, almost a *leitmotiv*. Besides less conspicuous instances, such as Belo Papagaio's missing thumb and Rônfilo Rivaldo's little finger, with its long nail, an entire page, at the beginning of the book, is devoted to the theme of the relationship between hands that lave (or slave) and the sun, the rain, the wind, the world. The emphasis placed on this motif is also apparent, as will be seen, in the final page of the text.

I planned to comment on this fact, the expression of a frequent phenomenon in the history of literature: the presence, in works pervaded by the times in which they were written, of *errant* themes, issuing from a remote tradition, such as this connection between the hand and the world, which finds in mankind—sum of the cosmos—its intermediary. A vestige of a civilization preceding Sumer's, the clay tablet found in the region of Susa, which can be seen in the Lanciano museum, shows, from the top down:

> the famous star-studded World Map;
> a man with open arms;
> the spread hand of Oam, god of clairvoyance.

"He for whom the hand is diurnal, nocturnal are the stars. The hand mirrors man and man creation"—declares Eudoxus of Antioch.[8]

---

[8] *O Umido e o Seco na Tradição Velada* [Moistness and Dryness in the Veiled Tradition], trans. J.R. Viana (Porto: 1931), 112. When he uses the expression "nocturnal stars" Eudoxus is certainly referring to the fact that these are more visible at night. This edition, lavishly illus-

It wasn't by accident that I mentioned Eudoxus' name, in whom many see the unacknowledged master of Artemidorus, ancestral treatise writer of chiromancy. Based on the correspondence between the names of the three main male characters of the novel—Belo Papagaio (Pretty Parrot), Rônfilo, Nicolau Pompeu—and the names of eminent chiromancers, I'm inclined to believe that this art, or science, or hoax, presides over the construction of the book, divided (arbitrarily?) into five long chapters, thus evoking the number of the fingers.

OCTOBER 9—"The most serious problems of this organization— Mr. Reinhold Stephanes says—could be practically reduced to one: the National Institute of Social Welfare lacks a policy of social welfare and assistance." (Interview in the *Jornal da Tarde* [São Paulo] 10/3/74.)

OCTOBER 10—Calm and announcing to her "listeners" her complete recovery, but with a symptomatic rosary around her neck, Maria de França gets another job as a maid. Moon Duster, instructed by the archbishop and guide Albert Magnus, has bought an old dentist chair and performs extractions at no charge. The indefatigable Nicolau Pompeu, who let up on the people at the Court House, enduring all the prorogations and going there almost daily, manages to get the curatel, ready to be signed.

The mother goes with him and Maria de França, as if they were going to get married, she signs as best as she can, retrieves the file, takes it, with the center forward and her daughter, to Rua do Riachuelo, from which they are sent to the office behind the Grand Hotel. There, the office head finds it strange that a curatel would be sought "for this poor innocent": he doesn't think any benefit will be granted to her. He puts a series of instructions in writing (the telephone is out of order) "to those bums in Riachuelo." Nicolau Pompeu acts as messenger.

But he's about to be tripped up. Burglars break into the warehouse he's guarding and he spends the night at the police

---

trated, presents, among many curiosities, Ulysses' alleged hand and the "reading" of his destiny.

station, testifying. In the morning he can't sleep and it unnerves him even more to know that the Tower will be playing in the afternoon. Before the game he takes an elixir the magician Moon Duster gives him, plays both halves without stopping and, at the last minute, with an unassisted kick, he earns the Tower a victory over Santa Cruz, at the top of the ranking until that Sunday. Under suspicion of doping, summoned again to the police, his name appears in the sports page for a couple of days, at the center of a scandal as brief and mediocre as his life. The warehouse owner, already dissatisfied with the night watchman's dubious performance during the break-in (it's not clear whether he resisted or fled), fires him.

For want of something better, Dudu takes a job as a bus conductor, for lower pay; in order to save money and still eat, he sleeps in the buses in the garage; and then he begins experiencing sharp pains in his back. The driver of one of the buses is Belo Papagaio.

OCTOBER 11—And what about Maria de França? Her hands, never very nimble, become heavy, she breaks faucets, brooms, pot handles, doors: she's given the sack.

As for her dossier, after more formalities, expiations and legal ceremonies, it goes back to Riachuelo, burdened by a mysterious addendum: it's a case of hysteria. Nicolau Pompeu wants to know who signed the diagnosis; but the signature is illegible; and varied, aleatory, impossible to reconstruct the papers' journey through the nooks and crannies of the bureaucracy. He receives, however, an important piece of information: the old stock clerk, after inflicting one of his poems upon him, lets slip that, in every request for a pension due to mental illness, somebody will declare it's a case of hysteria, to make it difficult or even impossible to award the benefit. He secretly gives him the name of the doctor Maria de França needs to look for, present her case to, and ask for a review.

Nicolau Pompeu, confined most of the day at the bus turnstile, has little free time now. Even so, he arms himself with determination and confidently charges forward again, for the last time. Undoubtedly heavy-hearted, since his fiancée, at this point, wants nothing more than to stay in the backyard, trying, amidst fits of rage, to keep her body one step ahead of her shadow. The new doctor examines her and turns in his report to the Institute, with a categorical request for permanent disability. Based on this wording the pension, which everything up until now seemed to suggest was impossible, is then authorized.

That same night the "spirit of light" Antônio Áureo reappears. He shouts to Maria de França to believe in nothing, to hope for nothing, nothing, not to make deals with any sonofabitch and, should she find the world's fuse, not to hesitate one second: light it. She begins to rub her right eye with her hand "to get some dirt out." Besides, she doesn't feel safe, believing that the fish, which is getting bigger and bigger, is about to break out of the ground.

Suddenly there is an almost festive interruption in this conflict, with false underlying tensions I will comment on later: Nicolau Pompeu, a recent admirer of Belo Papagaio, accepts his invitation to go out for a beer and takes Maria de França along. The encounter takes place without the heroine (let's not forget that she's in charge of the narration) or her deflowerer showing the least recollection of what happened between them. Maria de França returns home with her fiancé. A big fight breaks out. Her mother, whom the brothers, always mentioned vaguely and on the periphery of her difficulties, have just informed that she "lost her cherry" long ago—Maria's madness doesn't concern her and maybe she's glad for her sickness, which might become a source of income—her mother gets carried away with lamentations and condemnations, disowns her, throws her out of the house.

Holey! Shame of the family. Holey? Me? Am I a flute? The pants of a ragamuffin? A guitar case? Holey how and where, I'd like to know, and what family honor am I besmearing and what smear did I make, me, bitch of blind alleys.

Her fiancé, devastated with what he calls "vile betrayal," breaks off the engagement; then he calms the old lady down and reconciles mother and daughter.

OCTOBER 12—Belatedly and disconnectedly, a question about the way in which, during the month of September, in my days of blindness, I saw myself *inside* the novel, moving in it, is beginning to bother me. Could this indicate my despair in not finding traces of myself in it? Such absence is definitely disquieting for someone who loved the writer so much (and still does, as much as we love the dead), and I could almost ask: "How do I know if I existed—if, at least, I existed *for her*— when, in her book, I can't recognize myself in anything?"

OCTOBER 13—The pugnacious Dudu—of whom, even through my colorless synopsis, someone might become fond—is about to exit the stage. The X ray the Tower periodically requires from its players reveals a lesion in the center forward's lungs. Registered at the TB Dispensary, he goes on to Pedra de Buíque, where he is to stay for some time. Before leaving, he cries like a baby on his friend's fragile shoulder and resumes their engagement. Time flies without him returning or the decision regarding Maria de França's pension becoming effective. She and her mother decide to go back to Rua do Riachuelo; to their astonishment, they are told that the curatel, established over a year after the period of privation—that is, more than a year after the twelfth monthly insurance payment —is not considered valid by the Institute. It will be valid only if made retroactive, going back in time. The solution, "legal and banal, a matter of a few months," is to look for the judge and ask him to do it. Once again, as in an endless nightmare, we return to the starting point, with the disadvantage that the impetuous Dudu is now sidelined on the bench.

In spite of this they manage, with great effort, to see the magistrate. His verdict: the curatel's retroaction is unfeasible. He calls his son, a young lawyer, and tells him about the case. The lawyer deems "dispensable, superfluous, sterile and useless" an appeal to the Court, it could take several years. The magistrate confirms this opinion. He instructs the young man, and the result is a minutely detailed petition appealing the negative verdict. Curatel, medical certificates, a record of the hospitalizations, and other papers Maria de França knows nothing about are sent to Rua do Riachuelo, making her petition that much thicker.

October 14—Nicolau Pompeu returns to the TB Dispensary. He was recovering very rapidly in Pedra de Buíque, but he started playing soccer, his condition worsened, and now he needs surgery.

Maria de França's petition travels through a number of offices, earns an equal number of rulings, and goes back to the same person who originally received it for review. The lawyer follows the unfolding of the case and goes so far as to turn to the Regional Representative. This authority calls up a public officer who Maria de França must see and to whom she recommends, with obvious ostentation, "a fucking speedier solution." This functionary, bilious, indolent and of obscure appearance (as we will see, he's reminiscent of a hero of the history of Brazil), assistant at the Rua da Praia office, limits himself to sending the unfortunate applicant to one more physician. The doctor, who is already familiar with her case, requests her entire file. He will attend to the applicant within eight days, together with her guardian and her lawyer.

Nicolau Pompeu, hoarse, his clothes hanging from his body, shows up in the neighborhood. He had been sent to the Otávio de Freitas Sanatorium to undergo a lobectomy, a word he repeats with a certain pride. But his disease has evolved in an unexpected way and now it has even spread to the lung that was healthy before. The operation, he confesses, is impossible. But he can't stand seeing dying people, so he split and nobody will make him go back. He's found dead one or two days later with a revolver in his hand. The revolver of his nightwatch days?

On the day agreed upon, Maria de França, unaffected by her fiancé's death, is in Rua da Praia, alone. Nobody mentions the recommendation that she come accompanied by her mother and the lawyer. The physician has examined her file and is willing to grant a favorable ruling provided he receives, in writing, an "Interoffice Memo" issued by a functionary from Rua do Riachuelo. Maria de França goes to Rua do Riachuelo. The functionary, using Maria de França as messenger, writes to the physician: he sums up the case (when the addressee has all the papers with him) and gives his opinion (when this is rightfully the physician's responsibility). The physician, irritated, mistreats the carrier and scrawls more instructions for the same petulant clerk, reiterating his request for an "Interoffice Memo."

Maria de França, who's in charge of this message, instead of going back to Rua do Riachuelo and delivering it (only to go back again and again and again?), wanders around Recife with the paper in her purse, aimlessly, unflinchingly sizing up the insurmountable space between herself and passersby. Ahead of her walks a man with a package wrapped in newspaper. She follows him from afar. The stranger turns into a side street, opens the package, takes a cobblestone out of it, puts his right hand on the curb and smashes it with three blows. He runs down the street toward her, speechless with pain, his hand bleeding. Immobile, face to face, they look at each other. Maria de França passes him and walks toward the stone lying on the ground.

This is how the manuscript ends, which justifies the hypothesis—erroneous—that it was left unfinished. Not another word about the underground fish.

OCTOBER 16—How deceptive, in its poverty, is the summary—a little cold or tedious—of the plot! One verifies once more to what extent the novel—verbal construction, cluster of allusions, laboratory of instruments, testing site of new as well as apparently obsolete materials—the novel, I say, purporting to be subservient to the tales it narrates, makes use of them to exist, to the point that one might say: he isn't telling a story, it's the story that's telling him.

It doesn't matter, however, that the synopsis I presented—the first stage of my plan—still says little about *The Queen of the Prisons of Greece*. On the contrary, this shortcoming underscores the importance of the project at hand, which aims precisely at demonstrating how Julia Marquezim Enone's book, under the guise of, let's say, a banal figurativism, conceals unusual solutions which affect, far beyond what the synopsis might suggest, the current vision of reality and of narrative processes, as we shall see.

I will point one out, to show how the novelist, without flaunting her purposes, indeed by concealing them, establishes deviations from the norm. Nicolau Pompeu, the center forward, takes pride in his reverse-effect penalty kick, which sends the ball spinning high, making it describe a pronounced parabola in the air. I believe the insistence on this skill is intentional: the main plotline (this phenomenon occurs again in minor thematic units) also makes use of "reverse-effect" solutions. The events follow a direction that in principle leads to certain consequences. But the novelist doesn't limit herself to eluding the expectation she has raised: she fulfills it, never when it was expected and always giving the impression—which, upon closer examination, turns out to be false—of not having any connection with previous events. A more artful variant of false motivations, the process, as Julia Marquezim Enone's poetics demands, is reminiscent of assonance, or even internal rhymes, silent and invisible for the distracted reader.

I unmistakably recognize this device in at least three points. Nothing happens to the children in the care of crazy Maria de França, who "murders" rag dolls with the point of the scissors; but the girl she protects is shot by the police. Belo Papagaio divulges nothing when he meets her and Nicolau Pompeu at the bar; the revelation takes place, nevertheless, by other means and causes the break-up of the engagement. It's to be noted that the encounter of the three characters and the disclosure, at home, of her loss of virginity, take place one after the other, so that this accumulation of events in the end seems a little heavy, clumsy even. In this way the writer wanted to forestall the supposition that Belo Papagaio, discreetly pretending not to recognize Maria de França, would later try to interfere in circuitous ways with the engagement, already not very promising. The return of the bohemian truck driver, viewed from a traditional perspective, is useless; but it allows Julia Marquezim Enone to perform the maneuver she has invented. It's not at all surprising, therefore, when the same device is found at the end of the book. Assonance or reverse effect governs the final scene under a new guise. Strictly speaking, it behooves the heroine, lacking a satisfactory, defined, and reasonable place in the working world, to destroy her right hand, her basic tool. The narrator, however, rejects the clarity of this articulation and introduces someone who acts from afar, in place of the ex-factory worker, an anonymous character!

OCTOBER 20—The paper from the day before yesterday (*O Estado de São Paulo*, back page) contains an extensive article about a fire at a house in the Parque das Américas section, in Mauá, caused by a leak in a natural gas tank. I record it here because it's already forgotten (today's papers, and even yesterday's, have nothing more on the subject) and because the casualties' living conditions are reminiscent of Maria de França's, with her many faceless and nameless brothers. The dwelling that burned down consisted of a kitchen and a bedroom. Fourteen people lived in the two rooms, twelve of them in the bedroom: six people were sleeping in one bed alone at the time of the explosion. The accident occurred at 3:00 A.M. and one of the occupants, who hadn't returned yet from work, told the reporter: they all came from the country, from Ubá, in the state of Minas Gerais; in São Paulo you make more money, but you suffer "worse than a donkey"; piled up in there with thirteen people he could barely see anyone and, because of this, he hardly knew the other occupants.

The article discloses other significant details missing in Julia Marquezim Enone's novel, whose story takes place a few years ago and in a state capital less affected by the chimeras of industrial civilization: in the house there was a refrigerator, a portable radio-phonograph, a TV and even a slide projector; in an obscure theater of the Brás section, "taking their first steps in show business," Lúcia and Maria do Carmo, among the casualties of the fire, rehearsed every night.

Because of an accident the social stratum, which—like sewers—we're always trying to cover up and which, perhaps in a less emphatic manner, appears in *The Queen of the Prisons of Greece*, comes to the surface.

OCTOBER 21—How much our perception of things and even the intensity of what we see changes with a new hunch or clue! Going through the papers Julia left behind I more than once have come upon a Xerox copy I never paid any attention to before and whose source is unknown to me. Now I look at this paper made worthy of notice by the hypothesis I've already mentioned. Hermetic symbols swarm over the open hand it reproduces: castles, minarets, moons, a horse, the fleur-de-lis, the cogwheel, spirals and other creatures of geometry. This much I always saw. But until today I hadn't noticed the red pencil marks, delimiting the protuberances consecrated to Mercury, the Sun, Saturn, Jupiter and Venus at the base of the fingers. The red lines, invisible before, have become bright in my eyes and betray J.M.E.'s interest in chiromancy.

OCTOBER 22—I'm delving into scarcely familiar texts. I consulted primarily the manual by J. O. von Hellwig, *Die Hand, Zusammenfassung der Welt (The Hand, Summary of the World)*.[9] I'm intrigued by this Hellwig, who was also interested in alchemy and wrote at least two books on the subject: *Hermafroditisches Sonn und Mondskind* (Mainz: 1752); and *Arcana Maiora* (Frankfurt: 1712). The Azteca, Mexico, anthology *Los Profetas de las Manos*, a collection of texts by Patrício Tricasse, Gaspar Peucer, Rodolfo Goglenius, by Captain d'Arpentigni, by Desbarolles and by others whose names I hadn't heard before, will give prestige to my essay with a showy simulacrum of erudition, indispensable ornament to the genre.

The epigraph of the anthology: "He [God] sealeth up the hand of every man; that all men may know his work," Job 37:7. I always imagined that the other quote from the same text with which Julia Marquezim Enone announces her story—"Oh that I might have my request; and that God would grant *me* the thing that I long for!" (6:8)—referred to Maria de França's struggle, mirroring Job's trials. But perhaps there's a less obvious intention there, since, alerted by the versicle in the anthology, I go back to the patriarch of Uz and notice that the hand motif appears in the biblical text too, with an insistence that simply can't be casual.

OCTOBER 23—I see in a documentary pictures engraved on some desert plain in Peru—a spider, a bird, a peacock—so

---

[9](Hamburg: Patrick Verlag, 1953). The original edition, which is dated 1740, was printed in Mainz.

large that we can only see them at a considerable height, from an airplane. Men can walk over those lines all their lives without ever supposing that they form a harmonious figure, carefully drawn. Did those who conceived and engraved on the rocky ground such perturbing images—and who, without wings, were never able to see them—want to convey that the absence of meaning, in works of art or in life, can be deceiving and stem from our own limitations?

OCTOBER 24—After a new reading all my doubts were dispelled: *The Queen of the Prisons of Greece* is constantly referring us to principles current in chiromancy, each of its five chapters corresponding to one of the five fingers and to what the art of the almost mythic Artemidorus sees in them.[10]

What makes the identification difficult in the beginning is the fact that the chapters don't follow the order of the fingers. This is not surprising. Does the reader know that each phalanx corresponds to a zodiacal sign? The forefinger's to the first quadrant (the thumb has no astrological value); the middle finger's to the last quadrant; the ring finger's to the second; and, finally, the little finger's to the third. Like the novel, then, chiromancy, too, alters the order of the fingers when correlating hands and stars.

Of course one can wonder whether the very special character of the terrain on which the structure of the work is set doesn't rob laymen of the understanding of the analogy—which I discovered only by accident, and then with effort—and, consequently, of the implications arising from such analogy. The answer is affirmative and points out to us, beginning

---

[10]Strange case, this man's, preceding the Artemidorus of the *Interpretation of Dreams,* who lived in the second century A.D., under the rule of Antoninus Pius. There are people who confuse the two, against which Fred Gettings (*Le livre de la main,* French text by Madeleine Othenin-Girard [Paris: Deux Coqs d'Or], 162) warns us not without reason. If we believe the tradition, the first Artemidorus, an illiterate, *knew* what the texts contain: a reading similar to the magicians', who master a man's innermost feelings before his face. The lines of texts, it was said, are for them as transparent as the lines of the hand. Not the slightest real trace of his famous book, written "in air," exists.

with the initial design of the work, the fundamental law of the art of the author, an art which can claim for itself the title of hermetic in the highest and subtlest sense of the word, not because it is impenetrable, but because it's an art that conceals itself. *The Queen of the Prisons of Greece*—here is one of its virtues—is much like those ritual gestures studied by anthropologists which for a stranger have a banal meaning and for the natives carry another, broader, significance.

OCTOBER 25—Chapter 1 evokes the middle finger, what the middle finger means to chiromancers. This choice seems logical when we read that the middle finger is set on the mount of Saturn, a planet harbinger of obstacles. Maria de França, representative of agrarian migrations to the urban periphery—a particularly destitute part of the Brazilian population—takes on, in spite of her poverty, the role of victim, beginning with the encounter with Belo Papagaio, in chapter 2. Everything, until then, is prophecies, expressed through auditory hallucinations and Antônio Áureo, "spirit of light." The thirty typewritten pages don't amount to this alone, there are many registers of an almost naturalist tone disseminated throughout, but, overall, this chapter can be identified as the one foreshadowing the heroine's wretched life. Antônio Áureo and the voice, to be sure, give substance to the prophecy. But it can be affirmed that the entire chapter is an implicit foreshadowing of ill fortune.

The missing thumb of Belo Papagaio, the character who occupies and justifies chapter 2, makes the identification, also confirmed by other motifs, easier. Consecrated to Venus, the thumb is linked to love, flesh and sinuosity. The synopsis of the chapter is enlightening: the milieu in which it takes place, the prostitutes, Belo Papagaio's stories and his short affair with Maria de França fit in this thematic area.[11] We mustn't forget that hiding one's thumb, a habit which the truck driver passes on to the naive brothel servant, denotes a tendency to

---

[11]"In chiromancy the mount of Venus, the protuberance at the base of the thumb surrounded by the Life Line, represents our inclination toward love and friendship and our appreciation of beauty" (Jo Sheridan, *op. cit.*, 160).

regression. The novelist is dealing with a closed instrumental universe, making do with what Claude Lévi-Strauss calls *available means*, "a set of tools and materials which is always finite."[12] But we have to admit that she practices *bricolage* with great patience and a highly developed sense of order.

OCTOBER 26—"Saint Afonso Henriques! Make a writer of me. But only that. No festivals, no contests (beauty or literary), appointments in so-called departments of culture, shrines, witty remarks. Free me from the fascination that so many of our authors nowadays feel for the society of the rich, the required adoption of their books in schools, the trips with all expenses paid. Make me proud of my condition as pariah and rigorous in my obscure job of writing." (From J.M.E.'s papers.)

OCTOBER 27—Salamander. Scolopendra. Caudate. Surinam toad. X-ray fish. What's the difference between real parasites and aerial parasites or *epiphytes*? What's meant by mutation? On this undecided Sunday, alternately sunny and cloudy, while I organize test questions and put my papers in order, I think that there may be a certain irony at the bottom of Julia Enone's debt to this area of human knowledge (or dream): projecting some basic principles of palm reading in her book can be a parody of certain capricious structures familiar to the novel of the twentieth century, albeit with countless precedents in medieval poetry—where the numeric composition, for example, borders on mannerism—and much earlier, in the Old Testament. For F. R. Curtius, the poet, proceeding in this manner, "attained a double goal: formal framework for construction and symbolic depth."[13] The numeric allusion stretched its bonds to the very edge of mystery and expressed, at least in its most illustrious examples, reverence before the world. The poem became linked

---

[12]*O Pensamento Selvagem* [*The Savage Mind*], trans. Maria Celeste da Costa e Souza and Almir de Oliveira Aguiar (São Paulo: Companhia Editora Nacional, 1970), 38 ff.

[13]*Literatura Medieval e Idade Média Latina* [Medieval Literature and the Latin Middle Ages], trans. Teodoro Cabral with Paulo Rónai (Rio de Janeiro: Instituto Nacional do Livro, 1959), 548.

to something that went beyond it by means of the numbers it obeyed and of which, because of this, it was the bearer: it carried them within itself.

Incredulous contemplator of alchemic practices and speculations, of inquiries into the zodiac and of those who read in hands the indecipherable chart of life as I am, my appreciation for this aspect of the human quest and inquiry is not any less. Through these explorations we establish numbers and stars in ourselves as well, we drench in eternity our ever so brief passage. Julia Marquezim Enone's project, even if we allow that it might be ironic, adds to her work, in its artifice, this amplifying and magical dimension.

OCTOBER 28—The impenetrable motives of the poet, maker of syntheses, attract—nowadays more than ever—analytical minds. We arm ourselves with separating instruments to unravel what is tangled.

I think: the text, once it's decomposed (in the chemical sense), deciphered—and if the complete decomposition were viable and probable, how to aspire to the total deciphering? —dissolves, in a way. Even thinking this way, I'm a man of my time and, like a swimmer carried by the current, I find myself drawn, in this commentary of mine, to separate, isolate, classify what in the novel is one. At this point I conceive of something unfeasible: a work that would present itself as double, built in layers and purporting to be its own analysis. For example: as if there were no Julia Marquezim Enone or *The Queen of the Prisons of Greece*, as if the present piece of writing were actually the novel by that name and I myself were a fiction.

If such a work were possible, what would be its fate? Would the creator who dared to venture, naked, in a foreign domain be condemned or absolved? But I'm digressing. I was only trying to safeguard myself, stifle a little the demon of separations within me before commenting on the part of the novel in which the incredible Moon Duster appears.

OCTOBER 29—In the same way in which the amputation of the thumb, in the light of chiromancy, signals Venus' influence in

— 45 —

the thematic cluster hinging upon Belo Papagaio, the grown nail of the little finger, bane of evil spirits and neutralizer of ruinous influences, is the sign of the symbolic connotations centered upon the figure of Rônfilo, its bearer or radiation point.

The more I try to uncover these connotations, the faster they escape me. I tackle R.R., then, certain that I will omit what's essential in my discussion of him. Founder and patron of a school, he moves in the orbit of the written word. If he knew how to read, this association wouldn't be so relevant. Being illiterate, his love for reading takes on a suggestive ambiguity: he divulges what he doesn't know, an act evocative of the poetic phenomenon, fruit of the tension between knowing and not knowing. This theme also becomes entangled with intuitions disseminated among mankind, intuitions whose subtlety doesn't prevent them from surfacing even in so-called primitive cultures. Among the Bambaras, studied by Dominique Zahan, words simply represent emanations of Wisdom, vivid in the tongue that articulates them. Hence the paramount importance attributed to this organ: beyond words, they believe, is Knowledge.[14] It has also been said that great religious leaders, Mahomet among them, were illiterate men and that this trait—whether it's true or false—doesn't connote ignorance, but is, in fact, interpreted as the other side of ignorance: "it expresses the immediate perception (the intuition) of supernatural realities, the freedom from the servitude inherent in letter and form."[15] Among ancient peoples, like the Celts, certain traditions must have been spread through oral transmission. Writing, being immutable, represented death.

The incursions into the invisible world heighten the figure of the illiterate Rônfilo. Unnecessary to insist on his powders, his amulets and, above all, on the protection granted him, in spite of his social class and lack of education, by Albertus Magnus of Titiville. This name, it is worth noting, reaffirms

---

[14] I quote: "c'est la Connaissance qui constitue la fortune de la langue" (Dominique Zahan, *Sociétés d'initiation Bambara*, quoted in *Dictionnaire des Symboles*, vol. 3 [Paris: Seghers et Jupiter, 1974], 118).

[15]Tufik Didron, *La Naissance du monde selon l'Islam* (Paris: Orient, 1953), 312.

Rônfilo Rivaldo's link with the word. Inquisitor and martyr, the imaginary prelate's attributes, are false clues. *Titivillus*, a familiar nickname among monks in the high Middle Ages, was the demon of inaccurate transcription: an idle spirit, he haunted the *scriptoria*, leading copyists into error. Not only this: his namesake Albertus Magnus, Saint Thomas of Aquinas' master, following in the tradition of a magic procedure originating in Egypt or even earlier, had supposedly built an automaton with human attributes, an android capable of giving intelligent answers.[16]

There's nothing arbitrary about the unsettling play of contrasts at work in Rônfilo, even though it's intentional. It's based upon the tradition of ambivalence surrounding the little finger, placed under Mercury's influx and called by chiromancers "The Wise One," in the same breath as its power to conjure up negative influences is acknowledged. According to the Greeks, Thoth, the Egyptian god with the head of an ibis who presided over magicians and the creating word with the same intriguing ambivalence (he also held sway over archivists and astronomers, a surprising association), corresponded to Hermes in attributes and powers. This avatar of Mercury will create the world with the power of the word. Four gods and four goddesses were also supposedly engendered by Thoth's voice. They sing and never stop, sustaining the course of the Sun with their endless song. Light and life depend on the voice of these singers. It's also interesting that such suggestive and important attributes would be ascribed to precisely the most fragile of the

---

[16]There are, incidentally, other examples of this phenomenon, which nowadays amazes us, among great figures of the Church. It is said that Paul III, the pope responsible for the Council of Trent, was a fanatical follower of astrology, to the point of delaying the signature of a treaty with the king of France until the stars reached a favorable conjunction between his horoscope and the sovereign's. We also can't forget Father Antônio Vieira's pages about comets, which for him were omens of "intemperances of the air, winds, storms, shipwrecks, draughts, sterility, famines, earthquakes, plagues and all of the other more than ordinary calamities to which our mortality is subjected" (*Obras Escolhidas* [Selected Works], vol. 7 [Lisbon: Sá da Costa], 10).

fingers and perhaps the least useful one from a practical point of view (Goglenius called it "the idle finger"), which thanks to this consecration takes on a meaning belying its frailty. Perhaps the connection between the little finger and the mind is meant to suggest the fragility of the spirit in contrast with practical tasks. In any case, we won't be too far from the truth if we see in the contrast a symbol of mental life, delicate and, at the same time, endowed with unforeseeable strength.

The importance of these remarks is emphasized by the placement of the chapter, the third of five which, containing adventures not in the least spectacular, make up the work: in the structure of the novel, the element evoking knowledge and language constitutes a sort of center, axis or summit. What could this privileged arrangement, more significant in a text governed by the number five, center of the nine numbers, possibly express? Julia Marquezim Enone's attitude toward the word? A certain idea of the literary text, linking it to exorcisms, to incongruence, to the invisible voices, possibly—who knows—to the stars and the archives? I'm in no position to risk an interpretation. This won't be the only thing to cause me perplexity on this earth.

OCTOBER 30—Grading tests, a slow-moving job—my eyes are burning—took up the whole day. Not to leave the book without a new entry and because this subject, in my opinion, adds to the picture of Maria de França's world, I will summarize the article that came out today in the *Diário Popular*. Ninety-nine minors, escorted by thirteen lawmen—some of them with hoods covering their faces—were taken by bus to the town of Camanducaia, in the state of Minas Gerais, and abandoned in the wilds, naked, at three in the morning (it was raining), after having being beaten with clubs and iron pipes. Rendered equal by this peculiar treatment, the young criminals, among them an epileptic, are charged with quite diverse offenses, ranging from participation in car theft, to the sale of cookies in Dom Pedro II Park without a license.

OCTOBER 31—Was Rônfilo Rivaldo clearer to his creator than he is to me? I wouldn't say yes, nor that this is indispensable. It's wrong to attribute to the poet the same laws that govern abstract thinking. It's in Lautréamont: "One idea exists for poetry. It is not the same for philosophy."[17]

NOVEMBER 2—Perhaps All Souls' Day is meant to commemorate long forgotten dead people. This is not so in Julia's case. Nevertheless, I took the bus, went to the cemetery, took a few flowers to her grave. I myself would have simply engraved the name we know and these dates: 1/6/40–3/27/73. Her prodigal brothers added a trite sentence that would have made her smile and which I resist transcribing. Even though banal, this sentence is perhaps excessive to describe the relationship between them and the deceased. I also don't believe they were as sorry as the sentence suggests: for a long time my friend had kept to a minimum her contacts with her family, who didn't accept her for what she was, to the point of . . . Never mind. Let's change our course.

On the grave there is also the enlargement—oval and sepia— of a photograph. For lack of a more recent picture, or obeying an obscure desire to deny in this way the grown woman, presenting to the casual observers of the small memorial an image of innocence, the face of Julia one sees there, framed by a diaphanous and flowing veil, is that of her first communion. The counterfeiters made a mistake if the unavowed intention of absolving her from lucidity was what really moved them. The face, even though it foreshadows the one I held in my hands and keep in my memory, is that of a child—and the black hair down to her shoulders, the way she always wore it, accentuates what's childish about it. Her eyes, though, bright beneath her still untouched brow and her veil, look straight into the camera's lens, go beyond the brief moment of the picture and seem to attain remote visions, beyond her age. Precocious, the same fearless look she had when she died keeps vigil on that morning of her childhood.

NOVEMBER 3—Nicolau Pompeu, the obscure center forward of the Tower, exemplifies a little known aspect of Brazilian soc-

---

[17]Isidore Ducasse, *Oeuvres complètes* (Paris: Le Livre de Poche, 1963), 376.

cer: that of the player without a future, who plays himself out on the fields before invariably empty bleachers, bastard child of a world as unfair as the one outside the stadiums, with the added burden that glory there is clamorous, and boundless the champions' scorn, their indifference to their obscure teammates.

Along with the social or documentary value, this modest character takes on a new fullness—projected against the backdrop of the world and not only of a city in the northeast of Brazil—because of the connection established between the chapter in which he appears and the ring finger, consecrated to the sun. Motifs of little relevance point to this relationship, mirrored, for example, in the engagement ring, in which the circle and gold, solar metal, are combined. But the main theme suggested by the Sun is that of unity among men, heralded by the opening of the chapter, the long Carnival sequence, the most unifying of Brazilian holidays. Also to be noted is the change of attitude in Maria de França, who, under the influence of this love as hopeless as her fiancé's athletic career, experiences a respite in her drastic break with society. This union is not static, and it manifests itself in the attempt to help the little girl, the expression of a trust which the protracted chain of defeats hasn't dissolved yet and which the outburst of police brutality will destroy, ending the solar period of the novel.

November 4—The policemen questioned about the minors abandoned in Camanducaia that night said that, because of a break-down in the jail-bus, the ninety-three prisoners started a riot, took off their clothes (is it more comfortable to run away naked?) and fled. The representatives of the law also claim that they acted with "the purest of motives in order to solve a problem without a solution" and that they were inspired by the "best intentions to serve well the community." In the investigation opened by the authorities, J.A.P., a clerk who has been suspended for thirty days, is identified as the only culprit (*O Estado de São Paulo*, 11/1/74).

November 5—Denunciation, accusation and expulsion, acts linked to the forefinger, Jupiter's finger, dominate chapter 5.

Maria de França's deflowering is divulged, Dudu is accused of complicity with the burglars, of doping, he loses his job, his fiancée is thrown out of the house by her mother and he, suffering from tuberculosis (the lungs, along with arteries and touch, are among Jupiter's areas of influence), leaves the Tower, leaves town and loses his place among the healthy, finally ending his life with a gunshot (the forefinger, trigger finger).

Denunciation, accusation and expulsion also work together in the book's final scene, when the unnamed man, a projection of Maria de França, smashes his right hand. By destroying his hand the man excludes himself, cuts himself off from the *useful*, productive universe of which he no longer wants to be part. His gesture indicts, in a sort of synthesis, the insensitivity of the ruling classes, expressed in Maria de França's struggle with the social welfare system narrated in the book. As for the right hand, in the general opinion it involves the idea of usefulness in work, and in the Christian tradition that of compassion, while the left—also called *hand of rigor*—symbolizes justice. The accusation, then, is expressed by means of an agent, the left hand, invested with the power of judging, by which it gains an even greater intensity. We can adduce that, in the smashed right hand, complaisance dies as well. Maria de França's final motion toward the stone, instrument of the execution, is not fortuitous: she is assimilating the nameless character's gesture, an individual answer to a structure that knows neither justice nor compassion.

NOVEMBER 6—Those who, reading this essay, also read the novel and superimpose upon the complex concatenation of events that make up Julia Marquezim Enone's book the scheme proposed here may be disappointed and possibly reject my interpretation: the formulas of chiromancy, integrated in the story's plan, almost dissolve in the crush of events. (It must also be noted that the synopsis presented in this essay (?) leaves out the novel's numerous and lively descriptions). That's because the concatenation of the various unities of action in it doesn't seek to illustrate principles of chiromancy but rather to mold itself to some of them. The book calls together a branch of the divinatory arts ennobled by its venerability, and we can't say that this impoverishes it. But we won't judge it fairly either if we only see its esoteric side. *The Queen*, like all novels of a certain scope, is a heterogeneous object. It's informed, in varying degrees, by mythological resonances, metaphysical anxiety, social research, vindicatory outcry, aversion to the institutional, attempts to analyze the psychology of the poor (encompassing their dreams, their myths and their nuclei of information), all tied in with formal problems of great contemporary relevance.

NOVEMBER 7—Weeks before finishing her book, begun in November of 1969 (she was to work eight whole months longer on the original version, revising it considerably),[18] Julia Marquezim Enone received a letter dated 1/11/72 in which a publisher told her there was no point in sending him the manuscript. The state of the market, scarcely interested in Brazilian books, imposed certain demands on him, "since a publisher aims primarily at making a profit." Another sent back the final version of the book: he claimed that they were not considering original manuscripts. This letter is lost. Maybe the author threw it in the trash. About three months after her death I queried a third publisher. In his opinion, he answered, the work was unfinished, for which reason he didn't think publication would be justified.

The fact that the novel is unpublished, a situation which I fear will endure, has other causes now. This book is all Julia has left. But, with an intricate biography whose consequences she never tried to correct, unmindful of the laws governing our ordinary life, with her death she gave rise to an absurd dispute, involving people who can in no way evaluate the manuscript— an inconvenient legacy for them—and won't agree to make it public out of fear, or perhaps family pride: anything rather than this humiliation. Having merely lived with the author and without any legal claim to her possessions (I even lost custody of the

---

[18]. . . "but the end of a work is so far away for those who see far!" The quote is from Goethe and I found it in the *Reader's Digest*, which, heedful of fairness and variety, quoted the author of *Poetry and Truth* next to Harry Truman.

original manuscript, whose creation I followed closely), I partly gave in to circumstance, doing what was in my power to keep her work from remaining completely unknown.

NOVEMBER 8—Having summarized the plot and corroborated, I suppose, some captious intentions in the general plan of the book, I suddenly find myself faced with a question that was definitely hovering over these journals and which I can no longer avoid: "What is the central theme of the book I'm discussing, and what is its relevance?"

This problem, concerning a specific case, actually bears upon the art of fiction in general, and perhaps I will never find a satisfactory answer to it. But isn't there maybe a trace of uncertainty hidden in all assertions, even the firmest? Could questions be the only means of *knowledge* really granted to us? What do you think?

I wouldn't answer that a literary work is a verbal articulation, constructed around a pretext: the theme or themes. The lexicon and the ordering of this arsenal, the shifts of meaning, the rhythms, there lies its essence, admitting also in such a select field—but with lesser and, I believe, declining prestige—the art of ordering events, of suggesting the time or playing with chronological levels, of regulating the crescendo, etc. Hence an entire branch of the novel devoted to formal experimentation, disdainful of plots and ideas. As we have seen, Julia Marquezim Enone's conception was different. (Every work of art fashions its own theory). In spite of everything, the inquiry I am faced with today still remains. More than ever, the world lines our path with nets and snares. I know this, I know and I'm always on my guard. This is why, distrustful, not particularly sophisticated, I ask whether the concept of literary work simply evolves, refines itself, or whether perhaps some breath emanating from power, insinuating itself more than ever, penetrates it. Perhaps here we have entered a changeable zone, where shades and reverberations also carry some weight.

The social welfare system is portrayed in Julia M. Enone's novel, while the newspapers are filled with letters and even articles pointing out the faults of this institution. Graciliano Ramos writes a novel about the victims of the drought. Why?

This theme is so old and commonplace! The way in which it was written, the artistic construction, that's the reason for the literary work and its identity. Is that all? I don't think so. When the narrator, in this diverse world, chooses his themes, he defines an attitude, and not only in relation to life: in regard to literature as well. He says, with his choice, to what extent he, *committed to the naming of things*, is also committed *to the things named* and what sort of commitment this is. Those who flee the drought (the artist is not in control of all the significations of what he creates) are, without his knowledge, man running from hell or fate, struggling to understand, all this—and much more—are those who flee the drought, but for all their being and evoking and detonating of ideas, they remain those who are escaping from the drought and there's no escaping that.

Thus, as much as a book's theme and the concepts it deals with represent the base aspect of literature, so inconvenient, I would be less than forthright if I ignored them. Even when the theme appears to have been chosen or conceived to comply with a formal ambition of the narrator. Who can assure me that this ambition was not engendered in the shadows of his machinery, imperiously, by something the author, in a way, doesn't know and that, however, already resides within him and longs to be written? Who can assure me?

The Queen of the Prisons of Greece, seen in a transcendent manner, evokes the human quests—for salvation? for his destiny? for understanding?—or perhaps all of these. But let's beware of transcendence and its seductions, my friends. It can blunt our awareness of the circumstantial, and there's a difference between Aeneas' peregrinations (or Ahab the whaler's) and Maria de França's. We can't forget the limitations of her desire—narrow-minded, miserly—and the character of the forces opposing it.

It's almost two in the morning, my eyes are burning and even the dogs are sleeping, but a clarification is in order, it's already formulated, all I have to do is transcribe it. What I recorded today resists any normative intention. Variety is exciting, I know that there's no single sanctioned route to the novel and I'm not even prompted by the desire to sketch out a theory that accounts for my friend's choices in relation to the genre. Besides, dogmatic stands when discussing art scare me (and, on the other hand, is there a busier imp in literary manifestos?). Only two things can explain such rigidity: combat strategy (combat excludes the middle ground) and man's natural limitations, which at times cause him to misunderstand the beloved object, of which he becomes a sort of blind and fanatical guardian.

As for "my" book, what will its subject be?

NOVEMBER 11—Around the year 1920 a man dressed in black got off his horse and walked up the steps of a narrow porch beneath the gaze of two tall women, mother and daughter. A recent widower, he thought it improper to remain in this state; he was coming to ask for the girl's hand. Sitting with his peasant's hands resting on his strong thighs, he tried to keep the conversation alive while waiting for the head of the family, who was inspecting the work at the farm. Emerging from the silence and shadows, the girl's younger sister burst onto the porch, her firm breasts still smelling of dolls. She held out her determined arm to him, then left and threw herself on her bed: audible, on the porch, the sound of the fall.

The man had come to spend the night and was planning to make his request the following morning. He didn't want to risk the embarassment of spending the night in the house were his request to be turned down; the return trip, even harder for someone carrying a no in his saddle, was too long to be taken in the dark. However, disturbed by who knows what and wondering at his own behavior, since his decisions generally seemed not to belong to him anymore, and he, Oton, an emissary of himself who only had to carry them out, he stayed one day and then another, even though he was aware that everybody knew the purpose of his visit.

His deceased wife had bore him a daughter and three sons (he kept a picture of the little girl in his pocket watch). He showed and told many other things, not to the tall girl he planned to marry, but to the adolescent who little by little was coming closer and inspecting him more boldly. Why? He got his answer when she, looking straight into his eyes, sprung upon him the line formulated the minute she saw him on the porch and perceived—she or her still tender womb—the gift that man represented and that, in the last forty hours, she had gained authority, while the widower listened to those few words as if they had been a revelation or a proverb:

—You ought to take a wife, you know? but it's me you should marry.

He muttered like a drunk, without any logic:

—Why?

—You still have to ask that, Mr. Oton? If you had already known me and had come here for that reason, there wouldn't have been anything strange about it. It happens all the time. But no! You knew my sister. She's not the woman for you. She was just the lure. You're here on my account. Because you never saw me or heard anything about me.

Incongruity and senselessness have passed for truth before; but rarely as much as on that day. Who could take care of four orphans better than she, Adelaide, a stepmother of such a tender age? Everything justified her purpose, not that she was cunning and insidious, but simply because here was the mate, the impregnator, brought to her by the designs of fate, thrown into her lap, it was then or never, but it had to be then, now. Pregnancies and childbirths pushed her on, go! this is the patriarch. At four in the morning, without having slept, the guest knocked on her parents' door and the girl's wish began to come true.

She had him bring the four future stepchildren; she took care of them all as if she were their mother; she kissed them one by one before the wedding, her fiancé still in mourning. No other adequate suitor ever turned up for her sister—men with means were scarce there—and Adelaide never received her in her house. She didn't visit her parents either, and didn't go see them when they died: in all of those years she didn't leave home for one single day, doing the housework without ever taking a maid, an inadmissible whim when we learn that she gave birth exactly two dozen times, Julia being the twenty-first of her children. Beginning with her firstborn, the formerly loving stepmother neglected her stepchildren, subsequently distributed among their deceased mother's relatives. In short, Oton Enone only saw his second family and rarely mentioned his first offspring. When Julia learned about them she was fifteen or sixteen.

In all this—the way in which the almost illiterate and inexperienced girl managed to have her way with a man who was headed in another direction, and in the kind of relentless rate at which she was to give birth to twenty-four children, none of whom died in childhood—my friend recognized, without irony or enthusiasm, an expression of genius, something outsized and ready to trample over anything in order to reach its goal. More: the courage to dare and the untiring readiness to carry out an enormous task. This exorbitant design swallowed her husband, reduced with the years to a servant or an instrument, estranged from the rest of the world. More or less well off and already occupying the six-room upper story of a house in Recife, he received a letter from his first daughter—the childhood picture had disappeared from his watch—inviting him to her wedding. He sent word through the person who had brought him the invitation (he didn't even bother to write to justify his absence): "I've been very busy lately. No time." When he died he was over seventy and had never looked for his four older children again, completely blotted out from his heart by the tribal genius of the now also septuagenarian Adelaide.

These facts, of course, were passed on to me by the author of *The Queen*, who may have infused the story of her family with a certain romantic flavor.

NOVEMBER 18—My readers might notice—and I am going to have more than one, I believe—that at times there are gaps between one date and the other in these notes. I actually pick up my notebook and write almost every day—not always for the same number of hours. Many times I scratch out what I have written, and just as often I keep the page as a record of my inadequacies, or because I know that there, amidst uncertainty and turmoil, lies the thread to be followed. I wouldn't burden my potential reader with this larval and despairing part of my book; but I don't want to be silent about it either.

NOVEMBER 20—This is me at eighteeen: night is falling and I'm reading a novel by Stendhal, oblivious to the light fading from the room.

Years passed. I thought about novelistic processes, studied them in illustrious authors, and once again I'm reading a novel, by Stendhal. The book is the same, *The Red and the Black*, but the readings diverge and this makes it different.

The comparison between novel and reader in our times, however, is not limited to a matter of age. The contemporary reader and that of the old days are different. The reader ready to *evoke* what he has read, seduced by processes the sum of which have resulted in a sort of magic he wasn't aware of, has been replaced by the suspicious, rebellious reader, not in the least naive, who seems to be saying, when asked: "I don't remember and I don't want to remember."[19]

What are the options for someone who, aware of this refusal, doesn't want to renounce the act of narrating because he considers it indispensable or exciting? No longer able to rely on docile memories to recall the world implicit in his novels, with a maneuver reckless and taut with unexpected events, he begins, by having been admitted to it, to operate in the center of the refusal itself. He swaps the position of trustworthy—and more or less disguised—deponent for that of declared false witness, less honorable and riskier. The modification of the text no longer occurs outside the bounds of its existence but takes place at the source.

---

[19]"Does the fictional text captivate our imagination by playing with actions and things? By almost always choosing the past tense it rather appears to be relying on some kind of memory. Somebody tells me about waking 'from a dream full of whips and lariats as long as serpents, and runaway coaches on mountain passes, and wide, windy gallops over cactus fields,' as in Dylan Thomas ('A Visit to Grandpa's,' in *Portrait of the Artist as a Young Dog*) and everything is as if it had happened to me (how long ago?) and now, primed in this way, I or someone inside me remembered" (Dorothy E. Severino, *The Reader and his Memory*, quoted by E. Bezerra de Souza in his thesis about imaginary memories, presented at the Second National Symposium of Psychology, held in March 1970, at the Society of Medicine of Porto Alegre).

The contemporary novel deviates from what was considered a point of honor in the past and accounted for so many more or less naive dissimulations (characters' confessions, manuscripts found by the writer), with the purpose of legitimizing the story and the "recollections" of the reader, ready to restore, prompted by the text (a hypnosis?), unsuspected portions of the world. The writer flaunts his artifices, highly regarded in the genre's new hierarchy. With this he asserts his presence and seems to say to each of us: "You don't believe me? So much the better. It's only talk and artifice."

Maybe this current phenomenon represents, in the last analysis and under a new configuration, the return of narrative to its origin and true nature. Did the King believe Scheherazade?

Don't assume, my friends, the aesthetic validity of all that is being sold as modern, a comforting and tacitly accepted fallacy these days. Supposing that the character of a work might negate the user's character is a mistake, admissible only in those who don't contemplate the fate of things. The cemetery of books forever closed (there are some even in my library) covers the entire face of the Earth, and singularity doesn't imply immortality—or a life any less shorter. Borges, in his *Book of Imaginary Beings*, reminds us that not all of the animals that were invented endured: they didn't find an echo in the heart of men. It must have taken a slaughter of monsters for unicorns and centaurs to survive.

NOVEMBER 22—The new relationship between novelist and reader emerges clearly in the elusive entity to which the narration is entrusted. When Natasha danced for me in *War and Peace*, when Cathy told me, the night wind galloping across the moor, over the heath, "I am Heathcliff," when Jude died alone in his room, in Christminster, remembering Sue, while the insufferable Arabella was having fun in the streets, in all those moments I remembered as if I weren't reading, the story obliterated the text. Now I know: narrative is a verbal event, and therefore it requires an agent to enunciate it; the role of the narrator, enigmatic being, is mysterious and diverse; contemporary fiction has been eliminating the interdictions that hindered its mediator and attempted, in their rigorousness, to impose the laws of the physical world, unchanged, upon the universe of the novel.

How much has been written on this subject! What passion, in the discussions on the absurdity of a narrator who knows everything! How many people, on the contrary, appear inflexibly opposed to the character-narrator, who would limit the possibilities of the novel! Percy Lubbock, Wayne C. Booth, Henry James, Mark Schorer, Chavignolles, Warren Beach, Friedmann, Spielhagen, Wolfgang Kayser, Stanzel, Sartre, Genette. Impossible and inappropriate to name you all, investigators of what is commonly called point of view, focus, narrative vision or perspective.

All the same, even the attentive and unsubmissive reader, for whom the novel doesn't contain bare facts, being above all an artifice, a verbal one, can't always identify the point of view nor does he have a clear conception of this device. No, I can't speak of a device. Narrating presupposes testifying—truthfully or falsely—and how can that be done without placing oneself in one given *point* or several? The point of view, then, is inevitable in the novel: the novelist experiments with it, conceals it, struggles with it, subverts it, multiplies it, effaces it and it always comes back. The choice is ample and the terminology varied. Here, too, as in botany or zoology, there are plenty of classifications and brackets.

November 23—Can I say that I am alone? I slowly search with my eyes—and my imagination—my rows of books, the ones I have read and the ones I haven't read yet, the ones I long to read. A phenomenon never understood in its entirety, that of those decipherable signs (how many?), resting among the pages like clouds of little butterflies that remain miraculously still. Is it true, as an apocrypha of Saint John assures us, that, on Judgment Day, all the words will fly out of books, even those of books that have been destroyed? Magical flock! The codex doesn't say whether, in books that narrate, the words will fly and the characters will walk the Earth: heroes, extras and animals. This time has already come many times for me, and the novels I have read open their sealed doors to some hidden corner of my soul. As for the others, they remain inviolable and I contemplate them from the outside, half frightened, half ignorant. What do they conceal? Will they reveal some secret to me? Could some essential sap be within my reach, just waiting for the simple gesture of picking them from that tree?

November 24—Drawback: hearing these expressions, nowadays current—point of view, focus, perspective or vision—we are indeed led to think of a point, an eye, coinciding with a character or moving in the imaginary world of the novel, isolated. Such an idea shares in what is generally meant by narrative vision, it's true, but it only represents its most glaring attribute. So I prefer Diderot's suggestion, sketched out for his "In Praise of Richardson" and not used in the definitive text. In this manuscript, published in facsimile by the British journal *Drum*,[20] where he takes up or anticipates[21] some propositions of the *Paradoxe sur le comédien*, such as the one according to which nothing in the novel happens exactly "comme en nature" and that dramatic poems "sont tous composés d'aprés un certain systéme de principes,"[22] Diderot employs the formula "mediation device," which is broader than the ideas in vogue today. Absent, there, the simplifying notion of a "point" which observes or from which someone observes. The author of *La Religieuse*, a forerunner also in this, had conceived the idea, more complex and certainly more accurate, of a minutely calibrated mechanism, with laws that never repeat themselves and resonate on several levels: this mechanism governs the narrative. The "mediation device," he writes, "does not merely observe events. It accounts for what is known and what is not known, regulates distances—between one character and the other, between character and world, reader and character— and it can even choose between impartial recording of events

---

[20]4.7 (Autumn 1973): 75-80

[21]Anticipates. The essay on Richardson came out in 1761, while the final version of *Paradoxe sur le comédien*, according to Assézat, is dated 1773.

[22]This postulate reappears, word for word, in *Paradoxe*, Diderot, *Oeuvres* (Paris: Bibliothéque de la Pleiade, N.R.F., 1951), 1034, and for this reason I transcribe it in the original.

and passionate interference."

Diderot seems right on target to me even in sketching out a typology for the "mediation device." In his classification the device whose structure is inflexible and clear is *rigid*; apparent arbitrariness rules in the *malleable* device, more open to the unexpected or to what Thornton Wilder, in our century, would call "the capricious breathing of the composition." We have encountered many variations of this last form, for example in novels that implicitly admit the existence of an angelic, mobile narrator of undetermined age, maybe even ageless, who—it's believed—knows everything. "We who, incorporeal, know everything and can witness all deaths" (Sérgio Sant' Anna, *O Despertar de Gregório Barata* [The Awakening of Gregory Roach]).

NOVEMBER 27—J.A.P., the clerk suspended for thirty days as the person responsible for Operation Camanducaia, incriminated several of his superiors when interrogated by the judge of the Penitentiaries, adding that his temporary dismissal, according to what he was told, was meant to appease the press. It would be dropped right away and, as a reward, he would have lunch with the Secretary of Public Security. He claimed that he had received the order to "keep the record player broken" (not say anything), if he didn't want to be found "with his mouth full of ants." This euphemism doesn't correspond to the mere idea of death, but of a brutal and disgraceful death, the corpse dumped on some roadside. It also suggests the idea of punishment and example, the mouth that wasn't kept shut transformed into an anthill.

NOVEMBER 28—The "mediation device" in *The Queen of the Prisons of Greece*, in which a character, Maria de França, takes charge of the narration, a typically *rigid* process, becomes *malleable* because of certain distortions. The discourse, of which a semi-illiterate woman is in charge, avoids any attempt at mimesis. It's marked by a stylistic orientation incompatible with the one who enunciates it. Here we come to a delicate point, which I will try to clarify; and very cultivated readers, or those who are not too interested in this subject, as well as those who would rather preserve the innocence of other times in their transactions with the art of the novel, won't miss anything if they take a break and skip these last days of November. But I recommend that they return in two or three pages. Many surprises await them.

There are two different ways of creating, and they don't always coexist: the cultured and the poetic. The former always reflects the author's readings, chosen in areas consecrated by tradition, and aspires to a certain elegance; the latter, inclined to explore what is unformulated and rough, mines the ore of popular culture on different levels and ignores the cultural heritage or fights against it. Reflection, which in the cultured mode becomes crystallized in the aphorism, as in Machado de Assis, in the poetic mode is not presented as a definitive result of rationality but as a provisional truth, formed in one's dealings with the world. Works such as *São Bernardo* by Graciliano Ramos and *The Devil to Pay in the Backlands* by Guimarães Rosa are aligned with this tendency.

São Bernardo, linked to certain realistic conventions, frankly presents itself as written, and by a man with a rudimentary education; consequently it attempts a diction appropriate to the character, an objective literarily impossible, since it is necessary that the book, while convincing us of its primitivism, achieve at the same time—surreptitiously, of course—a high expressive level; this conflict, troublesome for the real author and for the pseudo-author alike, rises to the thematic level. *The Devil to Pay in the Backlands*, free of the requirements bogging down Graciliano's project, appears as immediately unacceptable, affecting an orality that the text, among the most elaborate, even though not cultured, ceaselessly contradicts: fiction is openly established in the act of enunciation itself. The gunman Riobaldo tells his story viva voce to a problematic interlocutor, a story related in a 550-page volume whose falseness, openly assumed, is never concealed.

NOVEMBER 29—*The Queen of the Prisons of Greece* follows the latter course, going further in the sense of an admittedly imaginary enunciation; the discourse presents itself as not written and always constructed in the present tense. Anatol Rosenfeld, with whom I was able to discuss this matter, believes that this solution, frequent in the modern novel, aims at "eliminating the sense of distance between the narrator and the narrated world" or "at presenting the geometry of an eternal, timeless world."[23] He omits something important in his interpretation: the voice of the present, in this case, represents a radicalization in the direction of fiction. *The Devil to Pay in the Backlands* still imitates—a slight concession to common sense—the oral narration of events that have already taken place; *The Queen*, by making action and verbalization coincide, seems to constantly suggest that its discourse is false, unreal, fabricated, absurd, bearing no witness to a past: it admits to being a story and nothing more.

Julia Marquezim Enone pushes the intention to stress the literary character of her fiction further. Her "mediation device," centered on the first person, expands many times over into an illogical "omniscience," a conventional attribute of the anonymous, angelic narrator, external to the novel:

He's always looking at me and thinking that I'm crazy, asking oblique questions ("Did it rain yesterday?" "What side of the window is dirty?" "Do you like rice?"). He never asks me what's really on his mind, what makes him shudder at night, in the dark, when he muffles a cry—my name—in his bachelor's bed.

The character who makes use of this "I," Maria de França, is crazy, the reader will object. It's not surprising, then, that she believes she can read the intimate feelings of the people she knows and even of strangers.

With this we take a turn and re-enter the natural sphere, which invalidates in part the thesis of a "mediation device" that takes on the privileges of the imaginary without reservation. This objection, an appropriate one, would involuntarily bring to the surface again the essential trait of this discreet art, its propensity to disguise itself. It's not to study the psychology of a mentally ill person or, in the naturalists' footsteps, to expose a "social plague" that Maria de França loses her mind. This choice is part of the strategy of dissembling. The heroine's

---

[23]*Texto/Contexto* [Text/Context] (São Paulo: Perspectiva, 1969), 90.

madness, as will be seen later, allows J.M.E., apparently operating within the limits of tradition, to explore in her own way certain areas of the novel targeted by contemporary scholars. The treatment of space and time, for example, if we read on the surface, seems to mirror the maid and factory worker's sick consciousness. A close reading uncovers the mistake: space and time, marked, as in so many contemporary novels, by disorder and contradiction, actually correspond to a calculated choice punctuated with unforeseen meanings.

NOVEMBER 30—The book omits Maria de França's diagnosis and is a little vague about the symptoms of her madness. This omission, common in great literary works, has an importance that generally escapes us and is linked to a deeper understanding of things. Many times naming is a fallacy, a sign of blindness or immaturity: we deceive ourselves when we name something much larger than the name.

Lost in the 1500 pages of *The Man without Qualities* is an illuminating sentence by Musil. Speaking of Agathe's first husband, he says that he was struck by "what is called, in the language of the unenlightened world, an infectious disease." For the enlightened world an infectious disease is a trivial concept: behind it, above it, is suffering, pain, the deterioration of being, malignancy. The same is true of madness. There is, we mustn't forget, a thinking attuned to what is essential, a sciential—not scientific—thinking in the face of which preciseness is not precise at all: it's disfiguration of truth, mask, equivocation, illusion.

DECEMBER 2—I should have already said that, not exactly having planned on it, I escaped the "ambiguous and ill-defined role"[24] of teaching literature, such a common fantasy in types of my sort, and one that not even the excellent A.B. escaped. It was he who told me, a few days ago: "When, with the purpose of reconciling work and enjoyment, those who find in books a source of pleasure succumb to the temptation of teaching what for them,

---

[24]Jean Onimus, *L'Enseignement des Lettres et la Vie* (Paris: Desclée de Brouwer, 1965), 135.

as readers, is less a subject than a way of life, they're lost."

He's right. The teaching profession, to be properly practiced—and he's among those who do—involves one in the establishing of systems, condemns what is vague and intuitive, demands methodical studies, leads, in short, to a useful, orderly, solid, functional, respectable—and joyless—kind of knowledge. However, there's something errant in the frequentation of literary texts, and I don't regret having preserved in myself this blessed vagrancy.

What are the classes and courses I have referred to more than once, then? I am a vague and obscure teacher of what used to be called Natural History. Expounding on the variety of roots or, reacting to the triumphant pedagogy for retarded people in action in this country, demonstrating the ambiguity of amphibians, appeals to me. Besides, in a mineral city like São Paulo what I teach takes on a magical quality. Spiders and night moths, in the eyes of my class, are unreal and as absurd as the Texas pterosaur.[25]

But—different, in this, from those who occupy the chairs of the Liberal Arts—the teacher of botany or zoology doesn't succumb to the impulse of wanting to inoculate minds almost always turned in other directions with that which is the least transmissible: a passion. I've always dreaded this role, undesirable in the teaching profession and typical of madmen (or those who, since they love, remove themselves from among the sane). The art of letters, like history and geography, demands an incessant modernization of the teacher. Plants and animals, instead, form an immovable universe in their variety—like that of geometric figures. Thus some will surely find a certain tongue-in-cheek humor in my choice; actually, it allows me the disinterested fruition of the works that fill my house. My vulnerable eyes add to this fruition the merit or the value of risk. In addition, I have the advantage that I work only in a high school: I avoid many absorbing tasks—sterile, at times, A.B. admits to me—for which the gains of higher-level teaching, I think, aren't a sufficient reward.

---

[25] It's believed that the pterosaur, with a fifty-five-foot wingspan, was a carnivorous reptile: it fed on dinosaur carrion.

Not even writing was in my plans, except for these (personal?) notebooks, in which I've been discussing the books I read for over twenty years; this organized study represents an exception in my life agenda.

DECEMBER 3—The entirely fictional omniscience with which Maria de França's "I" is endowed is not restricted to reading the innermost thoughts of her interlocutors or those who happen to pass by. It encompasses, with a freedom not always granted to the impersonal narrator, the register of space, all of her senses dispersed all over Recife and thus freed from corporal reclusion:

You can't feel it, but this is the smell of mangrove and of the smoke of the 7 A.M. train, anthracite coal, heading for the dry Agreste area of bare rocky soil, the handrail of the Ponte Velha bridge, tarred iron, is beginning to get hot, the taste of mangaba fruit and fried needlefish from the Market Place enters my mouth, through the air, the big bells of the Carmo church and the Franciscans are pealing, the baby bells of the chapels, the sun is beginning to rise, rising tide, it's rising, hello out there in Radioland! look and see, it's flooding the suburbs and the center of the city.

Smell, touch, taste, hearing and sight, isolated, capture individual aspects of Recife on a summer morning. At times Julia Enone alters the process, accumulating instances of the figure of speech writing manuals call synesthesia:

Look, look, the waves crashing, soot-colored and shiny, breaking on the beach, is it pretty? is it pretty? children stretch their hands out the window (in Torre, in Aflitos, in Encruzilhada, in São José, in the hotels of Rua Vigário Tenório where prostitutes ply their trade), that taste of rain on outstretched hands, the Archbishop, barefoot, lifts his face in the middle of the garden, opens his holy mouth, see the spark of lightning on his sacred tongue, closes his mouth, his tongue dazzled, Dudu! my love, listen to the rain smell slowly entering through the half-open windows of the bus, a secret this scent of rain crossing the oil, the grease, the soot of the garage, in the Government Palace the King flares his nostrils, inhales, he doesn't move, he can't see, he inhales and proclaims, royally: "The rain is cold."[26]

---

[26]For Maria de França the superior authority is always a "king."

The appeal to all senses is, in a manner of speaking, obligatory in this type of description, so frequent in the book and exhibiting such variations that it would justify a separate study.

DECEMBER 4—The possible objection that space represented in this manner doesn't express omniscience, it being nothing more than a reflection of the way in which the character's imagination works, seems to be refuted by other parts of the text, unless we view all of Maria de França's narration as false:

The rain is coming in from the sea, it reaches the Wharf, moves over the city, it moves forward and crosses the bridges that anchor the islands to the solid ground, hello out there in Radioland, these are the rains of March, its left leg covering the airport, the other over Santo Antônio, its head in Várzea, it stretches its right arm toward Casa Amarela and soaks the hills, Recife is almost entirely covered by this rainy body, the birds, as big as dogs, take shelter in the trees, a monster canary comes screaming, makes it just before the rain's hand which rapidly advances down the hill and catches me still in the yard, I run inside, the doors slam, a dove alights on the roof and the house moans, can you hear?[27]

The *real* perception of the rain (the rain in the yard where the character is) confirms the *unreal*, fictional perception (the rain in distant parts of the city).

DECEMBER 5—"Alice waited till the eyes appeared, and then nodded."—Lewis Carroll, *Alice in Wonderland.*

DECEMBER 6—One should not think that Julia Marquezim Enone's device, by conferring a sort of spiritual vision upon the narrator-character, presents itself as a mere transference of one subject pronoun to another. It's to be noted that Maria de França's omniscience is open to errors and because of this broader than the impersonal narrator's. The latter cannot be wrong. What good would it do him, after all, to be free from

---

[27]There are other points deserving attention in this passage, like the human form of the rain and the birds' gigantism: in Maria de Franca's eyes they are all huge and fearsome—an aspect that intrigues me and for which I still haven't found a satisfactory explanation.

human limitations, only to incur their errors? Maria de França, on the contrary, is endowed with omniscience and at the same time is trapped inside an "I" encumbered by human restrictions. Thus, dangerous mistakes occur more than once: her imperfect omniscience reads, incorrectly, other people's reflections and feelings. Maria de França, faced with another character, begins to act based on what she knows—or thinks she knows—of his soul.

But the book's mediation device, which is not at all rigid, has even more surprises in store for you. Occasional schisms between the character's conscience as character and what it records as narrator occur. The effect is suggestive and disturbing. The narrating "I" tells us, referring to Belo Papagaio, that the truck driver has a destructive bent and that the tale of his adventures is nothing but a trap, "a cloud of indistinct sounds and confusion, to make me lose my senses, lower my guard," while the acting "I," deaf to the observations for which it is the mouthpiece, throws itself into the trap.

DECEMBER 7—Thus there is a coming and going in the book, an oscillatory and arbitrary movement in the relationship between the character who acts and its double who speaks even though they both use the same pronoun, whose nature becomes mutable. The reader—along with the critic—becomes embarrassed and insecure: he's faced with a completely unreliable narrator who works hard at not deserving his trust by dint of a game of hit or miss, of apertures and restrictions in her visual field, at times so limited that it borders on absurdity. The following passage confirms our observation:

I go down the stairs, come back in a week, I go up the stairs, your claim is not supported by any law, I go down and up and down, cross the streets, nobody knows what I see, what sounds I hear, nothing, nobody knows, I don't know, I don't know what I think and what I feel, I don't know what I say if indeed I do speak, where am I? in the street or at home? station identification and reference tone, end of broadcast.

The discourse, always anchored to this mutable and elusive "I," goes on, while the character gets lost, in a sense. In addition to this, the motif of the doubt regarding the real source of the enunciation emerges, even though without any emphasis: "I don't know what I say if indeed I do speak." Thus we find ourselves faced with an ambiguous solution, which incorporates the prerogatives of the so-called omniscient narrator with the traditional limitations of the character in charge of the narration, with mutual impregnations occurring between these two possibilities, here joined together. Add further to this device, flexible and fascinating for the observer, the occasional obstructions or losses of contact, where the text, adrift, knows nothing more of the world and questions its own existence.

DECEMBER 8—Precise figures illustrate Mr. Reinhold Stephanes' statements, reported today in the *Estado de São Paulo*, about the National Institute of Social Welfare (I.N.P.S.), which he says he wants to reorganize. According to him, in the I.N.P.S. there are 300,000 feet of files in the benefits area; four years elapse between the decision to build a new infirmary and the placement of the first post; numerous decisions have a history of 100 to 400 official rulings; hospitals and equipment are obsolete. Redundant, after all this, is the additional information, divulged by the aforementioned authority, that all sectors of this huge organization (16 million direct beneficiaries and a total of 42 million dependents) "are completely bureaucratized."

DECEMBER 9—I said that *The Devil to Pay in the Backlands*, written in the past tense, *still* suggests the oral narration of events already lived; and that *The Queen of the Prisons of Greece* rejects this small conventional shelter, preferring to eliminate the distance between living and narrating. But Julia M. Enone's equivocal discourse, too, simulates in its own way—as well as J. Guimarães Rosa's on quite a different level—a consecrated form of oral enunciation which, in its artificiality, imparts to the book a certain uncommon vitality not devoid of humor. Let's unveil, confirming the suspicions of the most judicious readers, this aspect of the text—playful and, perhaps, tragic at heart.

The sociologist Cesarina Lacerda, developing some of Lucien Goldman's ideas, of whom she was a student by correspondence, conducted a research in the working-class neighborhoods of Recife and verified, as it was to be expected, the absolute predominance of the radio as source of information and the nonexistent importance of newspapers. Less predictable is the difference between the world portrayed on the radio and, for those who can read, what the newspapers print. Newspapers reach the outskirts of the city sooner or later, as wrapping paper, brought by the poor peddlers who buy them by the pound to resell them, and even carried by the wind. A housewife, interviewed in 1968, thought that Getulio Vargas' suicide, which occurred in 1954, had happened recently. But the aspect Cesarina Lacerda seems to have been struck by, and to which she devotes a long chapter, is what she terms "the validation of existence." Marginalized socially and geographically, the man on the outskirts has few links to the city, and is not indifferent to this exclusion. The radio, addressing through the announcer an unspecified and always exalted listener, fills a vacuum. "It reaches the shanty dwellers on the hillsides and by the water as (at long last!) the voice of the city, welcoming and acknowledging him. Radio language, therefore, takes on a soothing and at the same time rewarding quality for him. The silence of the city represents a form of negation of being: in order to exist the city must speak. The radio message fulfills this role, validates a problematic existence and in the process takes on a privileged and, one could almost say, sacral status."[28] Cesarina Lacerda's interpretation perhaps explains the radio's attraction for the poor. In any case, it attempts to assess the significance of an exceedingly cordial kind of message, frequent in this medium and pleasing to the receiver, among the so-called C class. In addition to this and without knowing it, the essayist justifies from a sociological perspective Maria de França's discourse, which purports to address a radio audience—a solution apparent since chapter 2. The book is enlivened by the linguistic clichés common to radio announcers, including the news, employed with humor and effectiveness and involving the characters (including the narrator herself)

---

[28]*Falando para o Mundo* [Speaking to the World] (Recife: Edições "Flos Carmeli," Convento do Carmo, 1968), 120.

as well as world events, distorted by anachronism and other factors.

DECEMBER 12—How many times, since *The Decameron* and *The Canterbury Tales*, have more or less loquacious narrators addressed themselves to a small audience or a patient interlocutor (who later writes the story)? There is the privileged narrator and there is the encounter of narrators, in which an exchange of tales takes place or, possibly, contests: the best *author*, in Chaucer's book, would be rewarded with a dinner. The insistence on this device and its variants is not fortuitous: it represents the phenomenon of fiction fully—here is the narrator, the story, the audience and even the inviting locale—and it can be affirmed that its charm stems from this coincidence. This evocation, at times, is emphasized to such an extent that the tale is no longer improvised and someone reads to the others a text, almost always of mysterious origin. Thus the "Novel of the Curious Impertinent," left at the inn, along with some books, by someone "who might return" and read aloud by the priest in *Don Quixote*: Thus, three hundred years later, the "faded red cover of a thin old-fashioned gilt-edged album" read to the guests of an old house by Douglas, in Henry James' *The Turn of the Screw*. Chaucer's pilgrims tell some of their tales at the lulling pace of their mounts, but the natural places for these encounters are the inns, where each guest is a still unopened book. Almost always at night, Boccaccio's ten young Florentines tell their tales sitting on the grass, when "the sun is high and the heat is great." "The Man of the Hill," on the other hand, spends an entire night telling Tom Jones his story and Henry James' Douglas more than one to read his strange manuscript. Charles Dickens describes in detail the Peacock's commercial room, where Mr. Pickwick and his friends are staying, shortly before "The Bagman's Story," also told at night.

With time the inns become hotels and restaurants, they leave traveled roads for urban centers, something adventurous begins to fade from the narrators in transit and their benevolent extras, who no longer arrive on tired horses or by mail-coach, are familiar with the washbasin, appear formally dressed at times, but the basic situation—the tale, the narrator, the listener and the shelter—remains unchanged:

A small lamp with a shade sat on the table. An itinerary, an almanac, the inkwell with a pen, and half a stick of sealing wax were on the mantelpiece. He had asked for two double cognacs with coffee and sat hunched up in the armchair. The strange feeling of intimacy radiating from the soothing and quiet rooms of the Plaza Hotel enveloped us.

—Would I bother you if I told you this story? It happened to a friend of my uncle's, eighty years ago.

The quotation is an imaginary one, made up of fragments from Dickens and Maugham. What novelist, however, doesn't recognize in it the art of telling, the alliance with the reader and the keen desire to be heard away from the tumult of the world?

DECEMBER 17—When Julia Marquezim Enone expands upon this formula, multiplying by thousands the four or five people that a long tradition offered to the narrator in inns, hotels, coaches and ships, she knows that such expansion has its price and that it will involve a loss. She accepts it: this, as well as others that art faces in our times, is a significant one. The narrators who in so many narratives of the past tell a group of listeners a story, or even those who read aloud a manuscript whose author is unknown, in a way choose their audience, who is never indifferent. Would the author imagine distracted listeners for these projections of his desire?

But Julia Marquezim Enone's artifice, if it evokes and alters a consecrated device (perfecting it, since the novel's audience is actually invisible), no longer reflects a yearning of the writer but acknowledges his irreducible isolation, the incessant monologue, the lack of response.

DECEMBER 18—Does reflection lead man to truth? I'm assuming, of course, the existence of a lucid and practiced mind. Without this, thinking is like driving a car without a steering wheel: the result is always catastrophic. But even if I possess the instrument and have instilled it with knowledge, will I be free from error? No. If I imagine, however, I am never wrong: imagination is autonomous and soars above all changes. For Anaximander of Miletus the wind, trapped in a cloud like wine in a wineskin, breaks loose with violence during the storm, and it is this rupture that produces thunder and lightning. Anaximander's ratiocination brings him to this absurdity. But the absurdity is no longer such if I stress the real nature of this hypothesis. Focusing his quick and powerful mind on the problem, the Milesian thinker, certain that he was hearing other voices, found an answer in his imagination, so enduring that even today it is not difficult for us to accept the idea of large seeds of air bursting from the clouds with rumbling and lightning.

DECEMBER 19—What I wrote yesterday seems to skid over what I'm trying to say. I will attempt to modify the text, clarifying and expanding it.

Does the mind bent upon solving a problem (I'm assuming that it's experienced and endowed with resources) always come up with appropriate answers? When I write "appropriate" I don't necessarily mean right answers; but, for example, abstract answers to abstract inquiries. The history of thought, at first, troubles us: how many times is the thinker deceived, accepting as a product of reason something engendered by invention? But is our uneasiness justified? Anaximander of Miletus, wanting to discover the reason for thunder and lightning, states—and this seems unquestionable to him—that the air trapped in clouds "like wine in a skin" bursts during a storm. Current knowledge invalidates this explanation. What saves it, however, is its *impropriety*. Appealing to reason to decipher and explain a natural phenomenon, the Milesian thinker inadvertently accepts a suggestion of his imagination. Precisely because of this, and because the imaginary soars above the transitory, some kind of life continues to animate his hypothesis and we can easily believe that clouds filled with air would burst like wineskins, with explosions and sudden flashes of light.

This digression is born of the doubts that at times have darkened my mood since I began to analyze *The Queen of the Prisons of Greece*. I focus on one aspect of the book and I'm not always sure of what I think I'm seeing. This is the case with some correspondences—for me fairly clear and affecting both story and discourse—which link Maria de França to the writer. Both destitute and crazy, removed from the areas of power and alienated from reality, they seek in the *city* an indemnification for their madness, with no success; the heroine's message, a broadcast in the void, evokes the drama of writers, many of whom live and die without ever experiencing the joy of a response; like the novelist and, even more, the poet, the central figure of the book bares herself, exposes to the indifferent world what is ordinarily concealed.

Look out! He's watching me with his blue eye, his face half turned sideways, he's still wearing his silk slip and I'm naked, he sticks his finger in my pussy, oh, what a scandalous finger, a big truckdriver finger, used to handling tools and changing tires on the road, he licks my ear, lifts his slip, what's this, dear listeners, sticking up in the air? come here, because it's now, it's now. And now for the time: it's exactly 10:31 P.M. in the capital of the Northeast. At this very moment I lose my virginity and become a candidate for prostitution.

The approximation I mention and illustrate is one example among many. Does it have a reason for being or did I make it up? The dilemma no longer weighs on me. I was bound to learn something from Anaximander's lightning.

DECEMBER 20—"Twenty-two police officers, including sixteen district chiefs, were indicted by the Magistrate of Penitentiaries and of the Judiciary Police for their part in 'Operation Camanducaia.'

"Public prosecutor J. B. Marques da Silva Filho, of the office of the magistrate of Judiciary Police, finished his report on the case yesterday, sending copies to the president of the Court of São Paulo, the attorney general, the juvenile court judge, the secretary of Public Security and minister of justice Armando Falcão.

"The principal suspect is R.A.L., chief of the State Department of Investigation and Apprehensions at the time.

"Police commissioner A. C. Lellis, of the cabinet of the secretary of Public Security, also completed the police inquiry into the aforementioned 'Operation' yesterday afternoon and subpoenaed twenty-three police officers—sixteen chiefs of police, three detectives, a clerk and a driver—*for offenses of a serious nature.* All will be prosecuted in an administrative court, which could result in their dismissal from public service" (*Jornal da Tarde* [São Paulo] 2/17/74).

DECEMBER 23—Trip to the resort town of Serra Negra, under heavy showers. My niece Alcmena, arrived from Espírito Santo to spend a few days with me and whom I last saw when she was fourteen, is now a young woman of twenty, slender, affable. She was always promising to come visit me and finally here she is, in the room next to mine, at the window perhaps, looking at the rain falling in the yard and on the hills, she, the unknowing harbinger of a brief spell of warmth and idleness in my routine, barely made tolerable these days by the authors I love.

DECEMBER 24, MIDNIGHT—Christmas dinner. The European tradition was imitated in everything: the music, the large illuminated pine tree adorning the back of the drawing room and even in certain delicacies: chestnuts, dates, apricots. This lack of authenticity irks the purists of customs, who demand a tropical expression of the Christmas celebrations. I don't know whether they're right and if a substitution is really possible. I'm inclined to believe that all this might even be more powerful, here, than in its countries of origin. Alcmena—her face glowed in the candlelight—kept raising her champagne glass, clinking it against mine or following the rhythm of the music. A time and space transfused with mystery by exoticism and rarity burst from the almonds, the walnuts, the illuminated pine trees (on which cotton balls simulated the most glacial of winters). Mankind is never immune—on the contrary, it is vulnerable—to spices, aromatic essences and animals brought from distant lands.

DECEMBER 25—Significant, this human need to celebrate holidays in the midst of abundance. Denying the limitations regulating our control over things and allowing us to pretend that we can enjoy the world without any worry, we ban penury, institute for a moment abundance and thus wastefulness.

JANUARY 6, 1975—Today would be Julia's birthday. Thirty-five years old.

Alcmena slowly raised her arm and brushed back some hair that was falling over her forehead with her long fingers spread like a fan.

—She never had children?

The room was almost completely dark and I could only see the wide-eyed gaze enveloping me.

—Yes, one. Almost your age now.

—Does she look like me?

—I never met her. I heard that she's a little . . . simple. Julia said it wasn't true. But she only saw her daughter a few times.

She waited quietly for me to explain. A star shone very near our heads. I informed her, evasively:

—She lives with an uncle, a brother of Julia's.

—An uncle like you?

She squeezed my arm, smiling, then she let it go and crossed hers, sitting back in the armchair, one of her long legs outstretched.

—Do you know how many times her mother got pregnant? Twenty-four: boys in the odd childbirths, girls in the even ones. It was Julia who inverted the pattern, at the twenty-first pregnancy. After her a boy came, then a girl, and finally a boy, the last one.

—Then she was born an exception, Alcmena exults.

—Marked. She broke the pattern!

—She didn't take any pride in it. She had an aversion to the idea of coming into the world marked.

The curtains stirred slightly. There was a light whisper and the life of things went on.

JANUARY 10—Alcmena, having planned to visit for a week, stayed three; and I believe, I don't know whether with reason or not, that she avoided looking at me when she got on the bus, clutching a little more tightly her guitar, protected by a green case. Her instrument, her youthful laughter, her heron steps will resonate here for a long time—and when I write *here* I think of the house and the book, this, which more than once I was tempted to show her. She insisted on reading *The Queen* and surprised me with a verdict: "I see you in the whole book." As I protested a little anxiously, she explained: "Not that I recognize you in any of the people. But you're here." She also observed that entire verses of Brazilian popular songs permeate the text from one end to the other, and she pointed out to me some examples. She sang one song for me, in her husky and melodious voice. Yes, a season of warmth and idleness, a respite, a pleasant and ephemeral summer, now come to an end.

I can't say that Julia Enone—older, quieter—and Alcmena are alike. How to explain, then, the atmosphere I breathed all of these past days, so much like that which reigned here at that time? Does a quality that could be called innocence, a clarity of spirit generally destroyed by maturity and which my friend was able to maintain until her death, render them identical perhaps?

JANUARY 12—Reading the novel, I had the impression of hearing in some pages a fleeting echo, a familiar ring (this, surely, the effect J.M.E. was after by introducing the lyrics of popular songs into the text), but without being able to discover what a young woman of only twenty saw on her first reading.

I had easily recognized in the Carnival sequence, when Maria de França meets Nicolau Pompeu, several fragments of Carnival lyrics included in the text, as in the following passage, in which those whose authorship I can establish are italicized:

Nicolau and me under a table, such a soft bed of confetti and paper streamers *that I'm even embarrassed*, the bar almost empty, what's the time? late at night? songs in my head, *oh gardener, what are you going to do, mandarin? I like to see you, baby, flying a paper kite*, perfumed ether squirters with beer are good, Nicolau gets up and gulps down left-over drinks, I cry from under the table that *there's no need to hurry* and he cries *"I want to see them burning coal, I want to see coal burning*, thirst is killing me, baby," I'm thirsty too, I'm thirsty and I have a headache, but what really hurts is the man at the piano, banging on it and shouting

"I already sang many a serenade
at an ungrateful woman's gate,"

the ungrateful woman a fat and patched-up prostitute, *banners in the wind*, a man in costume at the door, dancing like a puppet and shouting inside, "Look at the Gate of the World, everybody, the Gate of the World!," dawn, *a chorus* far away begins to sing the *return march*, the prostitute cries by the piano, rouge smudging her cheeks, a small heart on each side of her face, she wails to the man, *"This is really the way life is*, Hermilo, *I wish I could live happily,"* Hermilo sings pounding on the piano

"I don't know what to do
to keep my love from crying,"

Nicolau sings with him, bits and pieces of Sunday and Recife everywhere, *Rua Nova, Empress, Emperor*, Praça da Independência, me and Nicolau Pompeu *with our parasols open*, the *famous Carnival clubs, Club of the Flowers, Andalusians, Fireflies, The Futurist Hearts, Charmion's Lyre, the crowd goes with me*, the guy, now inside the bar, is shouting: "The Gate of the World! The Gate of the World!"

All the quotations—except for "oh gardener," from Benedito Lacerda's and Humberto Porto's march—are by authors from Pernambuco: Nelson Ferreira, Antônio Maria, Luiz Bandeira, the Valença Brothers and, mainly, Capiba, who appears at least seven times in this kind of collage. The passage "dawn, a chorus far away begins to sing the return march" alters (to avoid the anastrophe of its model?) Nelson Ferreira's verses in his "Recollection #1": "At dawn/the chorus the club's return march/began to sing." There also seems to be, in the series "famous clubs," in which homage is paid to composer Nelson Ferreira, an allusion to the famous "Values of the Past," by Edgard Moraes, who groups in this song twenty-five names of Carnival clubs, some extremely charming (Night Lyre, Golden Peacock, Magnolia Blossom), which, however, the novelist doesn't include in the text, surely to keep their accumulation from spoiling the suggestive mobility of the scene.

JANUARY 17—This is the time to write something I had already noticed before: Maria de França's speech (highly polished, as we have seen, in spite of its seeming artlessness and even ingenuity), becomes impregnated with various semantic fields, corresponding to the thematic areas invaded by the character. When she is with doctors, her "broadcast" is affected by a jargon half dry, half grotesque, taken from scientific books, directions for taking medicines and what linguist Dora Paulo Paes, in an essay filled with humor (an amazing thing among specialists, always full of themselves), calls the "stylistics of medicine pamphlets," pointing out very funny and pertinent similarities between the directions for taking tranquilizers and papal bulls.[29]

The door opens and I walk towards the center, therapeutic face this guy I'm talking about, sedative eyes, belladonna voice, tells the patient to sit down, are you doing OK? what do the listeners think? if everything were OK would I be here? Here?

—Take a breath. Open your mouth. Absence of crystals. Now say ahh. Open your eyes. Sclera and retin.

—Doctor! Does the passiflora respond to the mucous epithelium?

—Absolutely. From the rectum to the pulmonar axle. Take a breath. Spread your ass. Parasites present and uniform chromatin. Come back another day.

See also this example, in which the (half-crazy?) psychiatrist's self-assurance contrasts with the anxiety of the factory worker being examined:

—I'm a very good and competent doctor. Look at my diplomas on the wall. My graduation picture. The ring on my phalanx and my Rotary pin. I'm going to marry a healthy girl. What do you see in this card?

Once again the cards, spots, always the same, red and black, which haunt me and which I'll never decipher. Never. Life is sad, mister. A thorny path. Who can help me? What am I supposed to see in the card? Difficult if not impossible game. Recife is too big, the supply of things in Recife, I have thought of many, but I'll never tell, never,

---

[29]"As Bulas e as bulas" [Medicine Pamphlets and Papal Bulls], *Ciência* magazine, published by the Medical Association of Campinas, 3.7: 137-52.

what for, to give them what they want, and I always lose. Dyspnea. Shivering fit. Tachymetry. The nervous system. Posology.

—In this card I see . . . in this card . . .

—Bloo ay. Come back in a week.

JANUARY 19—Sophisticated instruments are also dispensable to grasp the caricatural intention of the passages in which the legal people—lawyers, judges or mere functionaries—interfere. The novelist explores here the heavy vocabulary of tribunals and, without relinquishing the general tone of the book, imitates the self-importance and the sophistical aptness of the sensible jurists, obliquely hinting at the fact that this language constitutes a trap.

It's impossible to convey the spirit of the original (overstatement and prolixity, essential virtues of the forensic manner, would be lost) if we only transcribed a few sentences of the passage in which Maria de França relates the Judge's prelection before he recommends, to handle her case, his own son, "protector and champion." This justifies the following long quotation:

If I am in front of the Judge and the Judge speaks to me, we may conclude, dear listeners, that the Judge has a mouth and I have ears. How could he speak, deprived of his emissory organ, to someone who, out of malice or in bad faith, had deprived herself of ears? Let it be proved otherwise. Therefore, it is not only proved that he is speaking, and that he is speaking to someone in the condition of receiving his judicious prelection, but also, so that the facts will not be disputed, or denied, and to avoid any attempt to misrepresent them *ab juris*, I broadcast far from the stamped and sealed windows of this select precinct his philosophy—wise, as it comes from a doctor—"that all and any law, my girl, if it's clear, works against the defendant, because there you call a spade a spade, and there are no possible loopholes or appeals. In the second instance, what would be the use of the Judge and the Roman Law, what would be the use of the Compendiums and the Appeals, what would be the use of the Gown and the Sword, what would be the use of the *Daily* and the *Journal*, the former *of Tribunals* and the latter *of Justice*, what would be the use of all this illustrious structure if laws were clear and could do without interpretations and therefore interpreters, it being appropriate to emphasize that the more arbitrary the interpretation the greater the margin for the transgressor to find a loophole, right? I will sum up all my doctrine in a brief sentence. It goes against the spirit of the law for the legal text to be a domestic book, an almanac like *Capivarol's* (the tonic for the entire family), or a catechism for novices, or *The Practical Handbook of the Can Opener*. This ridiculizes the whole deal. The law, ladies and gentlemen of the Jury, must be written in a lofty language, dead and buried if possible, unknown to the people, because if not it's no fun. The models for laws are the oracles and each servant will be an interpreter. This is why everybody is equal before the law and, without any reason at all, you can win your suit or be absolved, everything depending on us, its humble guardians and hermeneuts *uti possidetis*. Have you ever thought what a drag it would be, dear petitioner, if every bozo knew how much he had to pay every time he moved or opened his mouth? The natural sense of Justice demands that the people in general depend on a pleiad—us—because according to the first article, you, infringing upon the second clauses, benefit from the previous item, incurring the penalties inherent in the final paragraph, nevertheless within the use of the attributions conferred upon it by the related items and all provisions to the contrary revoked. Or, as treatise writers proclaim: *Ab hoc et ab hac.*"

JANUARY 22—This pompous tirade, "a brief sentence" for the Judge, is nothing but a grotesque paraphrase of a right idea presented upside down (note how involved the last passage is, a sort of trap, the living image of the specious language extolled by the magistrate—what it absolves or condemns no one knows any longer), and we won't be able to duly assess its importance if we don't compare it to the original it distorts so violently, which I believe is the opening of chapter 5 ("Of the Obscurity of Laws") of a classic of juridic literature, *Of Crimes and Punishments*, by Beccaria:

If the arbitrary interpretation of laws is an evil, their obscurity, which necessarily entails interpretation, is obviously another evil, one that will be all the greater if the laws are written in a language that is foreign to the common people.
As long as the text of the laws is not a familiar book, like a catechism, as long as they are written in a language dead and unknown to the people, and as long as they are solemnly kept like mysterious oracles, the citizens unable to judge for themselves the consequences their actions must have on their own liberty and patrimony will be

at the mercy of a handful of men, who are the depositories and the interpreters of the laws.

JANUARY 23—Yes, all of these whimsies had been revealed to me little by little. I hadn't realized, perhaps for having probed the tissue of the Enonian prose so closely, the novelist's large debt to the lyric writers of Brazilian popular music. Julia Marquezim Enone does with them what others did with proverbs, festivals or *cordel* popular poetry. She doesn't mention their names for two reasons, I think: she's always trying to hide her game; anonymity could mean a sort of consecration, the immersion of the individual product in the common heritage. It must also be considered, in some cases, that the writer, by withholding the authorship of the fragments of songs encrusted in her text, redeems them. Anonymous creations, inventions of the multitude, don't have an author.

This might be the reason why she prefers the lyrics in which the popular sources are most evident when selecting her material, as in Ataulfo Alves, "quoted" several times: "I stepped on my own toes" ("Samba Vassal"), "broke and busted won't build nothing" ("Broke and Busted"), "Never mind, alligator, summer is near, let's see if if the lagoon dries up and the day of reckoning comes" ("So Many Plans"), etc.

But it might also be that in paying homage to our popular songwriters by the systematic assimilation of so many of them, spokesmen of the humor, feelings and philosophy of the streets, in a book whose central figure is a woman of the lower class—who, in addition to this, is in charge of the discourse, a problem which has been occupying these journals for two months—the author wanted to indirectly express her rejection of the exasperated intellectualism reigning among specific segments of society, isolationist to the point of devising, by means of I don't know what mechanism, private codes, completely closed off to outsiders.

The kind of discourse consecrated by Maria de França, discredited and without any literary precedents, the radiophonic discourse in its most vulgar form, reaffirms, I believe, the author's aversion to impenetrable messages and all that's bookish.

January 24—I was writing, yesterday, when my right arm went to sleep and, at the same time, I couldn't remember the words *arm* and *hand*. I could see it and touch it, I could move it (awkwardly, yes), but it was as if it were a nameless ghost and the real arm were in another world, I can't explain how. This feeling didn't last long, yet it affected me deeply. Something like this happened in October with my name, also on a day when I had been writing for hours.

January 25—My friend never played her records when we were together. At those times she preferred others. (A night in July, the fog has enveloped the city to such a point that the farthest buildings have disappeared, we are listening to Vivaldi's *Winter* in silence). After she died dust gathered on her collection, from which I only listened to a few titles, even after I had been alerted. Yesterday I devoted the afternoon to the remaining ones and I verified that even the antiquated songs, of the kind you hear in decadent cabarets, interpreted by the stars of *sereste* and *samba compassado* music, and which prostitutes at the point of abandonment play until the early A.M. on the jukeboxes of the red light district, have a place in her book. Thus *The Queen of the Prisons of Greece*, for those who know it as well as I do, becomes, when we read it, more and more like walking through a festive neighborhood in which strains of music come at us from the shops and the side streets: the book resonates.

It's not surprising that we also hear the verses consecrated by shop assistants and the pale girls from the city's periphery. This fact simply confirms some intentions already identified in the novel under examination. There is a rhetoric ingrained, present in large segments of the population, according to which the highest stylistic virtuosity is expressed by sentimental clichés and which, because of this, makes liberal use of an imprecise, limited vocabulary, garnered a hundred years ago from the romantic writers and employed with absolute innocence since then. Deplorable and naive, it represents, however, a dissatisfaction with trivial language and the desire to aggrandize certain actions by means of an ornate style. We know that its use is obligatory in festive messages (anniversary cards, wedding speeches, etc.) and above all in love letters. This phenomenon, albeit lasting (one has the impression that it will continue, with the same intensity, when all folklore is dead) and in spite of its numerical importance (with lesser prestige and a sporadic character, it affects groups of average education), has been held in contempt by men of knowledge. What Brazilian fiction writer, besides Dalton Trevisan, whose attitude towards his characters is usually caustic, which distances him from them and the language they use, admits this linguistic vein in his texts? This makes more conspicuous the maneuver of Julia M. Enone, who—naturally or courageously? —by her deliberate choice of lyric writers in tune with the rhetoric of the people, joins them and, through them, a certain collective way of feeling and expressing oneself. Admitting only the composers who, mirroring the humor, the poetry and knowledge of the masses, represented a creative way of speaking would still express a bias of an intellectual nature.

At the same time, it is undeniable that many quotes, banal in the original context, transplanted in the novel, a more complex and connotative tissue, undergo a sort of transmutation affected by everything around them and become almost unrecognizable.

JANUARY 28—Watching Vicente, my barber, in the trade for over twenty years, sharpen the razor on the strop, I ask how long it took him to learn to do it.

—Ten years.

—Seven or eight weren't enough?

—No. Some barbers never learn.

—How do you know when the razor is sharp?

—I feel it on my hand. Even with my eyes closed.

Sharpening razors, then, resembles the art of writing: because of what it demands of the apprentice, in practice and patience; and because of the way the sharpened edge reveals itself, so similar to the way in which the writer, honing his sentence, feels (on his hand, too?) that he has achieved what he was looking for.

JANUARY 30—I've pointed out the popular applications of a certain rhetoric, limited but extremely widespread, and with an incredible capacity for survival. It's indispensable to adduce that it also manifests itself in a genre among the most highly regarded and one represented in *The Queen*, patriotic songs, a noteworthy fact in a country like ours, where the gap between the people and the dominant classes is wide. The entire Brazilian civic hymnbook respectfully abides by the laws of this style, so odd and, in a manner of speaking, enduring, even the national anthem, a perfect example of the genre, beginning with its adjectivation. In it, the (river) banks are placid, the cry resounding, resplendent the sun, worshipped the fatherland; and the sky, as if it were not enough for it to be beautiful, is also deep, limpid and cheerful (equally cheerful are the fields, including the barren ones), while the country, like a fabulous hero, rises fearless, beautiful, strong, without, for all this, ceasing to be—in this arbitrary and entirely verbal picture—a kind mother. Inversions are not lacking either, an obligatory rhetorical figure in this genre, like the famous "Of the Fatherland sons" with which the "Hymn of Independence" opens; and at least one antithesis, debatable from the logical and historical point of view, in which the future comes before the past. Finally, an event understandable only in the exalted universe of a rhetoric whose golden rule is to ignore reality, there descends to the earth, when the Southern Cross is shining, an intense dream (which?) and simultaneously a ray, a vivid ray—as this language distrusts things and worships attributes—a ray of hope and love, a ray.

I believe few decisions would be as disastrous as that of substituting the lyrics of this anthem of ours with more succinct or sober ones. With the substitution, advocated by many educated people, the only point at which the people and the official world possibly coincide in Brazil would disappear.

JANUARY 31—Let's put the finishing touches on the ghost of the mediation device Julia M. Enone, full of designs and subterfuges, introduced into her book, and which I've been trying to describe with caution and a desire for exactness.

Maria de França, fictitious agent of the discourse, wavers between sanity and madness: it's precisely because of the state of her health that she's determined to get a temporary or life pension. It wouldn't be surprising if the author, whose notion of this document is very peculiar—like an artist who, proficient in anatomy, alters figures—avoided perceptible notations in the text that might distinguish the lucid spells from those of mental confusion. The solution that immediately comes to mind is to populate the madwoman's mind with monsters and distortions and break up her language. Nightmarish images and a fragmented syntax would evoke the exclusiveness of her world and the horror of her isolation. Julia Marquezim Enone, who lived through the experience of madness and at times would tell me about the trash in the asylum, the bad food, the sale of corpses, with which she doesn't deal in the novel, sidesteps, with discernment and a tremendous capacity to renounce her own self, the confessional trap, which would divert her from the spirit and the governing principles of the book, choosing a more significant solution. Thematically, this solution is cold and, in a way, disappointing: the contracted, tumultuous and compact universe which is Maria de França's when she is lucid, is superseded by another, extremely banal, rarefied and devoid of mystery. Formally, it would be difficult to imagine a type of writing more limited and, at the same time, more clear: clarity saturated with ironic connotations.

FEBRUARY 1—Every morning the old man fed his birds, watered the flowers, disappeared and reappeared again among the trees of his yard, now part of the land occupied by a high-rise building under construction. It's not unusual for me to get up from my desk and stare at the point from which he was swept. I sit down again with a vague sense of menace and I see Julia's handwritten pages as if they were a salvation. But from what?

FEBRUARY 2—We have seen that *The Queen of the Prisons of Greece* is conceived as an absurd radio monologue: minute by minute, the character turns life into discourse (or institutes, through discourse, a simulacrum of life). The sequences of madness, significantly, disrupt this contact. Maria de França, cloistered in more ways than one, forgets the listener and no longer broadcasts her actions and cogitations. Besides, the action shrinks to such an extent that the character almost disappears; she's speaking from a dark area, in a cold voice. A disturbing coldness, which perhaps is meant to suggest another fracture: Maria de França, already disconnected from her *audience*, separates herself from her discourse as well. The extent of this divorce can be measured by what the tradition of this genre repudiates as a mistake or ineptitude—the discrepancy between psychology and language.

When I compared the learned and poetic forms in the preliminaries to the examination of the mediation scheme, I situated Julia M. Enone's novel in this second group. The hallucinatory phases, however, tend toward the erudite mode, of which they become a sort of wax model, ruined and vacuous. Fearful of ellipses, obscurities, images, this style wants to be precise at all cost, and in order to attain this it doesn't spare reiterations. Strangely, this aspiration results in nothing, and the world it wants to evoke with such objectivity lacks consistency. The syntax, dead, neuter like a dead man's face, doesn't engender the bonds of rhythm and still other imponderable links that impart to every felicitous sentence, taut with structure and word, a kind of murmur. To this ungluing, each term only apparently joined to the contiguous terms, like a mechanism whose parts someone pretended to assemble but are simply placed next to one another, corresponds a separation between discourse and things. The author, through meanderings difficult to follow, establishes, with a hand that is not only artful (a thousand intentions make her text resonate), the intriguing phenomenon of a composition which, beneath its apparent normality, expresses the horror of madness—and isolation. A perfect example of what I'm trying to fathom is the passage in which Maria de França talks about the fire that occurs in front of the hospital:

This is the first time I've ever seen a real fire, a completely new spectacle for me, and one that until this moment I knew only from descriptions. The fire is taking place in broad daylight (at ten o'clock, more or less) and right in the heart of a residential neighborhood, in Avenida Rosa e Silva, in front of the asylum, which is where insane people usually reside.

Many families are in the habit of closing their homes during the holidays to enjoy a deserved rest at the beach or other equally pleasant public parks. It is in these circumstances that a fire starts in the aforementioned home, during the absence, that is, of the owners and their hired help.

The fire is revealed by clouds of smoke issuing from the roof. This means that the fire has already reached the roof and therefore the flames are very high. [. . .] I and the other lunatics who, like myself, are watching the disaster, become very excited.

The brave firemen arrive, with their sirens on, and immediately get to work. After having connected the hoses, the valiant fire warriors climb onto the roof of the building and aim their hoses, whose water begins to gush onto the burning building. I will always be terrified of fires.

FEBRUARY 4—No reader will recognize Maria de França's voice behind what I have transcribed above: removed from *what she says*—from this burning house which never sets the text on fire—she appears to be equally distanced from *the way she says it*. On the other hand, no clues as to the reality of the fire are provided. What the character recounts or describes when she's out of her mind doesn't win our confidence; and no incident (this, too, leads us to the series of abysses which, similarly, express the theme of madness or of the isolation peculiar to madness in the book), no incident observed in the asylum has any connection with the remaining narrative units.

FEBRUARY 5—There is still a point to be appreciated here. All of the asylum scenes are undermined by brief expressions denoting the idea of logic, already suggested by the feeble *limpidness* of the text: "naturally," "of course," "it is apparent," etc. The problem this fact introduces is not merely linguistic but metaphysical. The world of other parts of the book, entangled and at times even impenetrable, is contrasted with a deciphered and depthless world, a flat world, expressed in a flat and obvious language. Look at the description of the cemetery attached to the asylum:

After living for some time, people die. There is no mystery in this fact. The cemetery is the enclosure in which the dead are buried. The city charges certain taxes for the time the burial lasts. Naturally we have our own cemetery next to the asylum, to which it belongs. The necropolis occupies a large area, divided into streets and lots. The widest street is the one by which funeral processions enter. In addition to the streets and lots there is also a morgue, where the dead who have not yet been buried are kept. In the asylum's cemetery there are many trees. The trees greatly contribute to the oxygenation of their surroundings which, as a result, become healthy and salubrious. Trees also serve as a shelter for birds, thus providing a place for them to build their nests, in which they lay their eggs. It is not surprising that birds are born of a mere egg. I am afraid of birds and everything in a tree is utilized, from the roots, plunged into the soil, to buds and sprouts, some of which become hearts of palm, on which man feeds; while others become fodder, of which the giraffe and the elephant make use.

The text impassively touches on the theme of death, insisting from the second sentence on the absence of mystery. This captious conviction is reinforced by topographic or administrative information, all banal: the size of the area, the levying of taxes, then passing on to a brief and anodyne dissertation on trees, no longer the ones she sees (those of the cemetery and of death) but trees in general, from which "everything is utilized." As if in passing and actually representing the counterpart of the absence of mystery in death, the idea that life is nothing to be surprised at either is insinuated in the apparently fortuitous allusion to birds and eggs. Can this parable (which, besides, is found in all the asylum sequences), latent in the two quotes given, even more in the last one, be denied?

FEBRUARY 7—"Why do I write? You ask me that? An intelligent man! Well . . . (*Laughs*). That's right, I don't know. I really don't know." (From the tape recorded by J.M.E.)

FEBRUARY 8—The language devoid of mystery that Maria de França uses when she's crazy implies the absence of mystery in the world. The reduction of world and word is akin to madness. Thrown into an impenetrable universe we attempt to name it, stubbornly, aware of our ineptitude. Naming, an intelligent act, is also—and because of this—a tormented act. Hence the adventures of language, expression—with its contortions,

pitfalls, obscurities—of this attempt, so desperate.
Yes.
How to name what eludes us, what denies and
conceals itself
—and how to glimpse, without naming,
what conceals, denies itself, eludes?
We name.
This means ceaselessly shattering our eyes on points
of steel.
But we insist:
we attempt naming, invent languages.
Trade? Task? Challenge?
It's difficult, we know that well, to name and see
—expressions of lucidity.

Is any light shed on life and death, though? You pass before them without surprise and calmly size up the extent of cemeteries, insensitive to the unlimited extent of death? You are the slavish repeater of a formalized language, convinced of its own effectiveness, since reality, you claim, is tangible and has no gray areas? In this case, between you and us, who see so little, and speak with teeth loose in our mouths, since we can hardly see, the images of the Earth obstructing (sheets of darkness?) our perplexed orbits, between us and you there are walls.

We know that we can't see because we see. You're certain you see everything and think you're naming everything? This is a trade for madmen.

What other, more suggestive way could Julia Marquezim Enone find to intimate to us her conception of language and of the relationship of language with the intricacy of things?

FEBRUARY 19—I go to Recife and see the Carnival. It's changed and become impoverished. But everything about some of the Carnival clubs I found in the streets reminded me of the "Morning Flower," where Maria de França and Dudu meet. I thought I recognized my friend's characters in more than one couple passing by holding each other, dancing the *frevo*. Making myself dizzy with the sound of the instruments, I followed a club and, at one point, I found myself in the middle of the romance, governed by the Sun.

I cross the Boa Vista Bridge, where Julia and I walked side by side for the first time (I had met her at an exhibition) and where, leaning on the iron rail while the night was rapidly falling over the river, I still didn't know that it wasn't going to be a fleeting encounter, that a still undefined—but irresistible—process had begun, bringing us together.

Under the pretext of trying once more to obtain the release of the novel, and, actually, with the purpose of seeing Julia's offspring and drawing my own conclusions, I go to the small town whose name I prefer not to reveal and where most of the Enone family now resides, including the girl. What's the reason for the distrust and even the hostility, tense and implacable, I find in this house? They seemed to wish that I would leave as soon as possible, pretended to ignore my suggestion that I talk to their ward and remained immovable about the book.

—Besides, you know, the decision does not depend on us only, there are other people involved. And why this insistence?

I ate in a shabby restaurant—I couldn't find anything else—its doors opened onto the street, in front of a primitive market, fruit and vegetables piled on the ground. Barefoot children leaning against the doorways with pieces of paper in their hands watched me, waiting for me to finish my meal and hand out the leftovers.

FEBRUARY 20—Continuing to deconstruct (and thus constructing) what is in itself inextricable, I will try to isolate and define the space of *The Queen*, in a way an extension, this prodigious space, of the birds casting a shadow on it, all huge, frightening Maria de França.

Who, psychologist or scholar of the novel, can identify the reasons why the reader in general only notices the action and the actors? At most, he also takes pleasure in the sentences expressing some kind of wisdom. Perhaps the old stories will give us a clue as to what nowadays seems a deficiency to us and might be the genuine way of reading or listening.

Let's open, with the reverence very ancient texts command, the collected writings of Marie de France, this Norman homonym of Julia M. Enone's character, about whom, after seven hundred years, not surprisingly we know little: she writes her lays[30] in England and dedicates them to Henry II Plantagenet, king of a court French in etiquette and language, like his wife Eleanor of Aquitaine. Marie de France's compositions keep to the plot, giving little information about the characters and even less about the ground on which they move: "There lived in Brittany an old and rich man." "Many years ago, two knights whose lands bordered one another lived in Brittany." "There was a baron who lived in Brittany." People wanted, first of all, the story; even the protagonists became interesting only to the extent in which they took part in frightening or sorrowful events. A path, a room or wood where the heroes meet emerge at intervals from this indefinite Brittany whose geography seems to be entirely contained in its name, but the action—direct and concise—dispenses with descriptive details.

The example of Marie de France is not unique and represents a tradition that would change only much later. The narrator will unfold a more precise scenery around the characters and the simple name of Brittany will no longer be enough. The descriptions of the setting—true arias at one time and detailed catalogs in Zola, for example—reach the modern novel and gain at times the hegemony, as in Part II ("Time Passes") of the delicate and elegiac *To the Lighthouse*, where the setting doesn't simply constitute the more or less thick background against which the characters are projected: brought to life by Virginia

---

[30]Archaic French: *lai*; Celtic: *loid*, song. The lay had lyrics and a melody, played with a sort of harp or viola. Two types of lays were cultivated in the Middle Ages: the long ones (among them Marie de France's) and the *Arthurian* ones, introduced in the romances of chivalry of the Breton cycle (Massaud Moisés, *Dicionário de Termos Literários e Ocultistas* [Dictionary of Literary and Occultist Terms] [São Paulo: Cultrix, 1974]).

Woolf's hand, the old seaside house in Scotland where before we saw the Ramsays, their servants, and guests, appears to us empty, closed and silent, visited only by the echoes and reverberations of the outside world, waiting for its old inhabitants (some of whom are already dead) to return. Curiously, the reader of our time doesn't seem to be following the novelist in his concern for space. He almost always appears scarcely informed—when not scarcely sensitive—in the face of the attention the modern novel devotes to the problem; and when he alludes to the setting of the book he's reading, like a courtesan of Henry's and Eleanor's in the twelfth century, he limits himself to saying that the story takes place *in Brittany*.

Yes, perhaps narrative, in its archetypal expression, doesn't expect anything more than a name from the setting—at most, an incantatory name. Would the narrator, then, abide by this law century after century? "Dance honored the gods; nowadays it glorifies the trained and vibrant body of the dancer himself"—declares Marquerol Quarez.[31] Julia Marquezim Enone, bearer of the restlessness and spirit of inquiry vital, today more than ever, to creativity, creates a setting not at all trivial which widens the significance of her book.

FEBRUARY 21—Divina Alves da Rosa, a pregnant woman from Ipatinga, Minas Gerais, was visiting her sister in Governador Valadares when she began to experience the first labor pains. Because she had left some papers at home, including her I.N.P.S. card, she went to four hospitals, a pharmacy, and the City's Service of Social Welfare Work, without receiving

---

[31] *Intodução às Artes do Gesto* [Introduction to the Arts of Gesture], trans. Jorge Prata (Coimbra: Edições do Rei, 1970), 12. Quarez, choreographer and faithful reader of the *Canzoniere*, draws in this work a very clear comparison between ordinary gestures and dance movements: "Between them there is the distance, surprising to many, between utilitarian and poetic language. Poetry and dance are performed in a degree of elevation whose intensity is rejected by the quotidian. But this height remains in the troubled community of men, like a memory. Let us remember Laura's stellar presence in Petrarch's life."

medical attention and as a consequence she died, together with the baby.

As to Expedito Esteves, he had the required papers, but his countless attempts to have his wife, Rita Correia de Araújo Esteves, thirty-three years old and seven months into her pregnancy, admitted to a hospital were useless. The Maternity Ward of Juiz de Fora turned her down, claiming that it was too early to take her in. Rita Correia de Araújo Esteves and her baby died without receiving any medical care. (*Jornal do Brasil*, 1/22/75 and 1/31/75.)

FEBRUARY 24—The characters move in a space both real and unreal, which Maria de França's mental state justifies or pretends to justify: *The Queen of the Prisons of Greece*, I insist, is a web of simulations.

Perhaps, as in a play of reflections (created, it's true, with obfuscated mirrors and in dark corridors), in my text I have passed by the ghost of this factory worker and maid, walking through doctors' offices and government offices, crossing the not imaginary streets of a real city, Recife, with its rivers and bridges, its port, its forts and the shanties forming a sort of black and putrid ring around the city. In this process of unveiling which is my commentary—and I will outline, I hope, the profile of the novel, in the same way I have already outlined some of its characters—it hasn't been possible yet to reveal the true setting of the story, in actuality a Recife that doesn't deny the real Recife and doesn't limit itself to its model either: it shrivels it up and casts a spell on it. It's as if the city were turning into its own map, so flexible that it can be folded up, without however losing its volume: as if it remained habitable.

FEBRUARY 25—In *The Queen of the Prisons of Greece* we have a space natural (there are the avenues and the neighborhoods of a city everybody can identify) and yet arbitrary. As always, the author is concealing her artistic choices. Those who know Recife will find it absurd for a character to come from Santa Isabel Wharf, turn right, pass the Central Station and cross the Santa Isabel Bridge; for Praça da República to be at the end of Rua da Concórdia; or even more for Maria de França, walking down Rua da Aurora, along the river, to take the Beco das Cortesias or to see the Seminary, both located in Olinda. As if turning Recife into a mobile structure, becoming disjointed and ceaselessly reordering itself, weren't enough, Julia M. Enone effaces the town of Olinda, eliminates the four miles that separate it from Recife and makes it invade and trespass the capital.

From this fusion a fantastic city is born, exclusive of the book, and whose impossibility escapes the observer who hasn't been alerted. Recife, a flat and nearly submerged city, is given Olinda's hills, it rises, and the bells of one, ringing, echo inside the houses of the other. In contrast to the mutable topography of the invaded city, with its parks fluctuating and becoming joined to others—separating later to form new impossible combinations—the Olinda of the novel is fixed and faithfully corresponds to the one you might visit. The inhabitants of the novel lose their way and, walking along a sidewalk in the port area, find themselves climbing the Amparo hill next. They may return to another point of Recife or the same place near the quays, with its heavy smells of crude oil and rotten fruit, but the plan of the novelistic Olinda, stable, perfectly reproduces that of the historical Olinda.

This hybrid space, in which a fixed space and a mobile space come together, is more suggestive and intriguing than the option favoring one alternative or the other. Nevertheless, how can we avoid the necessity of investigating what brings the author to integrate opposite conceptions in the same arena? Is she prompted by the law of variation? Does the author simply want to mix "truth and fiction," heedful of Horace's advice? Is she trying to compare liquids and solids, with their obscure occultist implications?

I don't know the answer.

February 26—I was discreet and even inaccurate when I mentioned the lunch in the town my friend's brothers and daughter live in a few days ago. I think I gave the impression that I was alone, but from a certain point on I had company. Maybe if I write about it the memory of what happened will stop bothering me. That's all. I don't think it sheds any light on

The Queen or even the act of writing.

The stew and the mineral water had just been placed on the stained plastic tablecloth when I saw the man on the sidewalk. He was wearing light-colored clothes and was pacing in front of the restaurant, as if he were hesitating to go in, his hands in his pants' pockets. Waiting for someone? From beneath the somewhat worn Panama hat, his right eye, blue and mocking, pierced me. I had the impression—but was it an impression or an absurd certainty?—that I had already seen that eye in a sewing basket. The cobblestones, the people—all poor—the merchandise on the ground, the walls, had a sacrificial air: offerings to some plundering and inclement god. He took his hat off with a quick and disquieting gesture (his yellow hair), shooed away the children near the doors and now here he was, at my table.

—Are you the teacher who . . .

That very moment, I knew. How? A thick wall had separated us—linked us, too?—for a long time. Now we were facing each other and it was my friend who presided over our encounter. I put the piece of meat I was eating back on the plate.

—Well . . . Julia. I don't know if she ever mentioned me. She must have. (The false movements of his arms, as if he were concealing a weapon.) She was my wife. I'm Heleno.

This meant nothing to me. Julia avoided saying his name and had never tried to describe him. How old could he be, now? His hook nose curved down over his slightly flaccid mouth, his forehead high and bony with wrinkles like seams, spasmodic contractions in his jaw. Forty-five? Despite everything there was a certain power about him, something flagrant, intense and nauseating. Like cheap perfume. *The Queen* is in his hands and perhaps the hands of a poor retarded girl in the care of uneducated people, who certainly view writing as defaming and even criminal.

—I'm going to spend a few days here, I want to have a look at this crap she wrote. It's my right. We were husband and wife.

Getting up or telling him to leave was getting harder by the second. Julia's life, which she told me about in bits and pieces—never an orderly account, nothing approaching a confession—takes on, in the presence of this body to which hers was no stranger and so close to me that I can hear, when it moves, the chafing of the coarse drill of his clothes, a bruising that penetrates my bones. Here, within my reach, in this stranger's worn body, is my friend in the bloom of youth, blind in many ways and frail in almost everything, except for her determination not to give in; here she is at a time before I had the privilege of knowing her, clearing her tortuous and undecipherable path, discovering the first secrets through this man she loves at eleven and marries before fifteen—already moving, meanwhile, towards me and her book.

—I'm not crazy enough to dig through that pile of paper. But I'm going to have someone read it, from beginning to end. I can burn the book if she doesn't tell the truth. The law is on my side. The little halfwit, the daughter of that bitch, doesn't have a right to anything.

He leaned over the table (still the inexplicable movements of his arms, with something incomplete about them) and I knew that he was going to insult me. I could almost foresee the insult sentence by sentence.

—After three months, I kicked her out. "Beat it!" Do you understand? Is that in the book? I doubt it. She was always a liar. I was the one who couldn't stand her and said: "Go fuck the devil." Do you hear me? I wasn't twenty-five yet, I've always been a man, the slut who complains about me hasn't been born yet, but she wanted to spend all day in bed.

The blue eyes try to read my face; I expose myself to his scrutiny. What is a body and what is the story of its passage through the world? Does the body inherit deceptions and pursuits? What was there left, in Julia's body—not a beautiful body, maybe, but soft and audible, yes, as if all of it breathed, with her flat chest, her thick waist and her slightly knobby knees—what was there left in her body of the remote collision with this stranger she had loved and who had wounded her? His memory, distorted, endured: the mirrors of memory. Are there mirrors of the body?

—Then she would show up, wanting to come back. I didn't have the strength to say *no*. She was very pretty back then.

Have you ever seen pictures of her as a girl?

—Yes. There's one on her grave.

Laughable assault. It hit him, but barely: he was a man with arbitrary values and death was probably worth nothing for him. Back then my friend loved him with a violence age would soon mitigate. But this ardor—she had told me—was still too immature to comprehend what Saint Bruno of Asti calls "the diabolical illusion of ecstasy." Her husband besieged her with pride and despair, tried to awaken her unknowing flesh: he battered the young body, from which he felt as distant as now. They separated four times, at irregular intervals; once, not all four times, she came back of her own will. One day, finally, the budding woman got a glimpse of pleasure, a reflection of what the male promised. But what she had glimpsed—she decided —she wasn't going to receive from him in all of its fullness *when the time came*. It was necessary to get ready immediately: she left him forever. Forever? No. There was that encounter, inexplicable, about which he tells me now.

—If she didn't scribble that book just to distort the facts, she must have confessed that six Januaries after the wedding I ran into her on the street—and you already know. (His jaw, knotting. Is he hesitating? Cigarette stains on his teeth.) I left a baby in there. For your information: we hadn't seen each other for over four years—got that?—and I was living with another woman. That's right! I can show you the place we went to. In Pina.

He's hardly interested in the book, it's just an excuse, an easy one, to talk about himself and offend me, but I know much more than he can imagine and what I know reveals to me the ignoble side of each of his words. The children near the door again, salt and mica in my sick eyes, the light reflecting on the stones. Julia and him on the beach, old Oton Enone washes his hands, it's no longer his business what she does or doesn't do, let her go whoring, rot in jail, be some gang's slut, go to hell, as long as he doesn't see, doesn't know anything. He puts the money in his daughter's purse: to buy a ticket and go to Bahia with some relatives who live in Salvador. There is still a disaster to come, a burden to receive and carry, a lesson to be learned, a degrading exercise (Julia and the man named Heleno, the two of them walking on the beach, the cheap hotel), she can't lie and tells her father what happened, she and that man, the footprints in the sand, the night in the room, the awakening, the empty purse, her father throws her out. Institutionalized for the second time, she has an abortion two months later in the Psychiatric Hospital and becomes sterile. The body is a story: that of its own course.

MARCH 11—Imitating Julia Marquezim Enone, who at times devoted entire mornings and afternoons to one paragraph, an assiduity aggravated in my case by the necessity to cultivate artificially, based on the example of a few masters, that kind of instinct by which the narrator chooses, from among the multiplicity of reality, fragments which, charged with meaning, lead us to perceive, or believe that we perceive, in their light, a thousand factors absent from the text (the implicit core of the text), I finished the entry dated February 26 on Saturday, after having spent close to ten days on it. Involved in the subject—note that the episode described was recent, and I can't say how much it disturbed me—it's also possible that my being involved interfered with my work as observer. Finally, there were, when I tried to describe the encounter with precision and a certain polish, some recoilings or distortions of the soul, preventing me from telling everything.

I didn't say that he whose name is Heleno—I saw it when he got up—had his left hand amputated at the wrist. My omission wasn't calculated and shouldn't be interpreted as a noble gesture: it wasn't meant to spare the man. I was reluctant to face the fact, unusual, of admitting to the existence of a rival in him. No, not in relation to Julia—in relation to the book. Unable to clarify whether she had married a maimed man or if the amputation had taken place later (I had no words to ask this inconceivable question), uncertainty ate at me, pertinacious as those fears, not always imaginary, that a mortal disease is discreetly making headway within us. The two options stood one against the other, full of consequences. Did my friend still feel both of her husband's hands on her young hips and was this the image that survived within them? The coincidence of the mutilated limb with the book's chiromantic background discredited this hypothesis, over which its opposite prevailed, as distressing as it was absurd: Julia M. Enone, as a child, meets and loves a disabled man, a cripple; years later, giving the impression of organizing her book as a play of allusions to the science of reading life and death in hands, she actually sets it up like an artificial limb, remaking, with such cunning alchemy, the hand the incongruous partner of her adolescence is lacking. A gift as ambiguous as the one she makes him of her body earlier, and a much more serious one.

Other suppositions arise and struggle with one another. But truth, in the end, is not very important. No matter what (would Julia have the answer?), my lamentable lack of strength stands out everywhere, I, whose summer is inevitably beginning to decline, a bachelor nourished on books and presuming to have acquired, in contemplation and meditation, a dusting of wisdom, anxious as if I were still in my ignorant youth and depending, to regain my peace of mind or whatever flaunts that name, on the relationship between a hand—smashed? chopped off with an ax? eaten by dogs?—and the structure of a text.

MARCH 12—"To protect even my *work*, not only from complaisance, but also from hatred. One day, deceived, I cried for many hours, and not exactly for myself: I was afraid that deception would poison my future work and, through my work, the hearts of others." (From J.M.E.'s papers.)

MARCH 13—In the previous pages I have described a process I was aware of, involving the abstruse entanglements of those who love, always exposed to base actions. Meanwhile, another movement, deeper and beyond my perception and control, was developing, was going to reach the book of the dead woman I love, my idea of the book, and in the early hours of the morning it manifested itself.

That's why, in the end, I'm including my last notes here. *The Queen of the Prisons of Greece* underwent an internal transformation without changing a single comma. The hand, not mine or anybody else's, the ideal, abstract, archetypal hand, which is definitely the framework of the novel, its structure, shriveled up, or, to be more precise, went away, leaving a vacuum in its place. The conception of the work, all it supplies with its ingenious (and secret) chiromantic allusions, the connection accepted by tradition—and incorporated into the book—between each person's hand and the stars, between each of us and the Creation, everything now seems a mistake. Through me a denial coming from the outside, from our changeable and ephemeral universe, wormed its way into the walls of the work and there it lies, beyond my reach, sad.

MARCH 17—I'm going to rectify what I said a few days ago. I would keep in my book the last four or five pages, with all that is confessional about them, even if the shattering episode they deal with had not had any repercussions on my understanding of the novel.

I decided from the beginning to make the present commentary permeable to the ever ignored moment of its elaboration. But nowadays art—a phenomenon, with the intensity we see, typical of our time—is many times the inflexible, closed demonstration of theoretical principles. Thus it takes on the character, to which our contemporaries remain inexplicably oblivious, of a work with a thesis, not an ideological, but a formal one. And only a desire to avoid programmatic vice—assimilated perhaps from the book itself that I'm studying—that, and also the sense of propriety, almost always exacerbated in shy people, has kept me from mentioning here the unbearable sound of machinery—mechanical saws, bulldozers, concrete mixers—the habitual and exasperating background noise of this book of mine.

I should do it without any fear, though. This would add to the text, which might appear to be woven in silence, a sort of background and a sense of resistance: in the heart of clamor and harshness, it attempts to become a melody.

MARCH 18—The geographic dislocation approximating the solid town of Olinda to a disarticulated—or subject to inconstant articulations—Recife is not a closed invention in the book. It's associated with another, even more suggestive, which stresses the singularity of space in the book itself.

The Queen of the Prisons of Greece revolves around an anomalous perception. Even when she is lucid, Maria de França, the apparent source of the discourse, emerges as the bearer of a vision both truthful and oneiric—which is repeated in the duality of the setting, firm and fluid, precise and uncertain. Like a checkers player, who sacrifices a checker in order to get ahead in the game, Julia Enone makes a concession to verisimilitude and thus frees herself for the experiences she shrewdly wanted to put into practice in the area of the novel. Maria de França's madness, a "natural," convincing reason, implanted in the social background of the book, is first of all a screen to conceal the real, essential game played in the area of fiction writing. It eludes a precise diagnosis and is always leading us to problems of composition, involving concrete reality and language. Essential clue in the deceitful structure of the book, mask of the author, it makes any attempt at delving deeper into the subject look like distortion and anything that is calculated, arbitrary, like the well-armed troops which, in wartime, make the ground of amphibious Recife/Olinda shake from one end of the novel to the other.

MARCH 19—It's in the papers: Attorney General Oscar Xavier de Freitas decided to close the inquiry on "Operation Camanducaia" because in his opinion no crime was committed.

MARCH 20—Who are the soldiers who garrison the novel? After reading it, the first time and perhaps others as well, what's left of their silhouettes and weapons? Maria de França goes from one place to another and keeps running into them. In the beginning one has the impression that the action of the book, still not very explicit in relation to time, runs parallel to some armed uprising, historical or imaginary. Vague military operations reinforce this supposition and we begin to wonder how these men, whose aspect and countenance the text says nothing about—they're always "the battalion," "a squadron," "the patrol," "the armed band"—will enter the story that is taking shape. Suddenly, an isolated word rings—what's so strange in its timbre?—it sounds strange and alerts us to the fact that these warriors may not be using the clothes and other accoutrements we had attributed to them:

Can you hear, firm footstep, nobody moving and even so the marching cadence resounds in the air, the thump-thump-thump, thundering like the blow of a rifle butt on a door, so different from the step of a civilian, the sun sparkles from musket to musket, from buckle to buckle. . . .

Musket? It could still be an inaccuracy on the part of someone who sees a king in the state governor. Three lines later, all doubts dissolve. The defense of the port, stone fortifications, trenches on the beach are mentioned, and then we realize that certain anachronistic elements in the architecture and the furnishings—such as windows with no glass and thick curtains—are being introduced, even though sparingly, and that, *in the same way Olinda penetrates Recife*, another more distant time, still undisclosed, is invading the time of the story and will remain in it, concrete and in the margin, inaccessible: an ancient war, between sea and land (a repetition of the antitheses fluid/solid, Recife/Olinda?), takes place, incongruously, in the setting of a story that's ignorant of it and on whose course it will have no influence whatsoever.

MARCH 21—The interpretation I offer—which, strictly speaking, denies the status of character to those shadowy forms removed from time, preferring to agglutinate them to the idea of space—is arguable, even if we consider that they never move, although they are almost always seen in action, forming, all together, a sort of album, a gallery of battle paintings, superimposed on a scenery that resentment and those bullets no longer have anything to do with. I don't want to impose, or even propose, a thesis. My position is cautious, not at all arrogant, and as flexible as possible. Of course I don't choose this perspective at random or by whim. Those armed soldiers don't alter the story in any way; but they do alter the space significantly. Without them, the imaginary operation with which Julia M. Enone makes the space of her book become surreal would ignore time, it would be limited to one category only; with them, refugees from a past time, a ubiquitous temporality is born with which the entire space will be saturated. The *today* and the *yesterday*, simultaneous, become superimposed on the reconciliations of mobile/fixed, liquid/solid. The smooth façades of recent buildings coexist with the geometric inter-lacing of the *mudéjar* ones; the painted walls with the red adobe walls; the asphalted streets of the present, with the cobblestone lanes of the past, winding and without sidewalks, shaded by large balconies.

MARCH 22—*Yesterday*. This term, in the sense I used it, has no limits. Such abysmal expressions were created, like a large part of the language, by frivolous people, lacking the pride of effi-ciency. They float in the air, these nebulous words.

MARCH 23—No. I'm being unfair, and obtuse, which is more serious: the reason for what I've been writing these last days escapes me. Now that I think about it, the imprecision of *yesterday*, where it occurred, was not undesirable. It certainly suggests the progressive fashion in which the reader identifies in the novel those military figures which he initially imagines inconsistent, signs of the heroine's mental confusion. Unable to situate them, when the sun reflects off their muskets for the first time, the reader throws them into a vague period of three centuries or more, the most remote limits of this past time coinciding with the presence of the discoverers. The fortuitous participation of Indian soldiers makes establishing dates more difficult. Do these warriors belong to different times? They finally manifest themselves completely and once again we notice Julia Marquezim Enone's tendency to hide her game: the time of the strange armies is delimited with precision and there is nothing accidental in their subsequent appearances—which, with slight distortions, some changes in the chronology and in a more or less veiled manner reproduce one of the capi-tal events of the history of Brazil. Which? We shall see shortly. To reveal abruptly what in the novel is unveiled little by little would be uncouth.

MARCH 25—My life-style and my modest ambition make me a man not worth wasting one's time with, something like a dipsomaniac or a drug addict, in short a hopeless case, which assures me little transit among more or less educated people. I wouldn't say that this saddens me. I agree with Saint Teresa of

Jesus, who, because she didn't have confessors "as learned as I would like," preferred to the "half-learned" those with no learning at all, because these neither "trust themselves without asking somebody who is learned, nor would I trust them."[32] But don't think that I live isolated or that my colleagues don't seek me out either. Mainly some professors of Speech and Communications who, when they're not too preoccupied, come and get out of me what they can, curious, as they would do with De Quincey, the opium eater. This is what happened yesterday, and, in a moment of abandon I found myself talking about these journals. I didn't regret it, because someone suggested, after hearing me, that the texts of madness might be inspired by the *Manual of Composition*, by one Carlos Góes.

I bought two copies of the book: one from 1961 (11th edition) and another (14th edition) from 1968. The older one has an introduction by the author—member of the Academy and therefore immortal, though I don't know whether he's still living—dated March 1930; the one from 1968 still has the introduction, but—as some ladies past their prime do with hotel registries—the date was omitted. The 1961 title page reads, a little like old tonics against baldness: "NEW AND PREVIOUSLY UNPUBLISHED METHOD, SAVES THE TEACHER THE WORK OF HAVING TO GRADE TEST BY TEST." In 1968 this lengthy bait undergoes a cut: the method is no longer "new," but continues to be "previously unpublished" in spite of its thirty-eight years of age.

These clues are indicative of the spirit of this successful manual and of each edition, but what concerns us here, I verified as soon as I saw the pamphlet, is that it really is the model for the formulas proposed by Julia Marquezim Enone to represent, beginning with the theme of madness, important divisions, all leading up to a certain idea (as I see it) of language and our understanding of the world. There one can find entire passages of *The Queen*, with few or no modifications at all; these pages now give me the impression that the cynical author plagiarized the novelist. It's understandable. Carlos Góes's fraudulent descriptions and dissertations (passed on

---

[32]*Obras Completas* [Complete Works] (Madrid: Aguilar, 1951), 42.

over almost half a century, like counterfeit money, to defenseless pupils), transposed to a dense context, become charged with significations and undergo a sort of unmasking, with some of what they unwittingly represent coming to the surface. Examining, half amused and half angry, the models which my friend really takes as such—in another sense, though—I note: to highlight the effect she was looking for, she chose, in the ample repertoire of the *Manual of Composition*, by now among the books I call celestial for lack of a better term, next to the *Modern Course in Oratory*, by Admir Ramos[33] and the *Lovers' Secretary*, she chose with irreprehensible consistency the texts in which the apparent solidarity with reality is faultless, flowers of the most obtuse sensibility, rejecting those in which the inevitable occurs, that is, those in which alienation and confusion, concealed behind a highly suspicious objectivity, half consciousness and half reality, gradually reveal themselves, as in the following "model," in which the resemblances with the passages of the novel previously discussed are apparent:

We call "domestic animals" those which man has tamed and domesticated, turning them from brutish and wild beasts into instruments of his richness and prosperity.

They are: the dog, the ox, the horse, the donkey, the camel, the dromedary, the cat, the elephant, the sheep, the goat, the domestic birds, the pig, etc.

The dog was the first to be domesticated. It guarded the primitive man's cave against the assaults of the wolf, the tiger and the lion.

There's a point in the perception of things in which one no longer grasps the difference between a dog and a dragon. Let's return to the world of crazy Maria de França, less extravagant.

MARCH 27—

> *Morta Laura, il passato, il presente*
> *e il futuro, tutto gli é tormento e pena*
>
> La vita fugge e non s'arresta una ora,
> e la morte vien dentro a gran giornate,

---

[33]São Paulo: Companhia Brasil Editora, no date, of course.

e le cose presenti e le passate
mi danno guerra, e le presenti ancora;
e'l rimembrare e l'aspettar m'accora
or quinci or . . .

No, Petrarch, your sonnet is not hard enough to celebrate the anniversary, the second, of Julia's unfair death, crushed, five months after having finished her book, by a green GM truck, 35-inch chassis, I-beam type front axle (8,300 lbs. capacity), fluctuating-double reduction rear axle (20,500 lbs. capacity), 23-gallon fuel tank, diesel, air brakes, 12- and 14-ply tires, loaded, total gross weight 49,600 lbs.

APRIL 4—It will be necessary to transcribe four parts of the novel in which the enigmatic presence of the soldiers recurs, selecting significant fragments in order to avoid very long quotations. There's something artificial and even disfiguring about my expedient. It confers a clarity upon something that presents itself as an instrumental solo, cut by the din of tymbals in the book. But isn't this also the way in which novelists proceed when they're developing a character? Don't they select artificially, among the infinite number of possibilities (or of what they have observed), the few elements which, even in contradiction, give consistency and meaning to the characters?

What's this? Sword firm in hand and feasting? Sentries along the coast, high and low, steel barrels aimed at the fishes and midnight darkness in the noon sky, the flash of the firecrackers next to the balloon, that ship in the plaza, on dry ground, full of sailors, and the drums, and the fiddles, and the flutes, and the guitars, forty armed recruits (of the Fatherland children?) and a bugle, the ox with green ribbons in its horns, cheer up, everybody, we mustn't see or think about the sixty sea towers, the sixty traveling towers, loaded with lead, with *brote* crackers, with spears, with words of command, the People of Recife delighted and deceived. . . . (pp. 36-37 of the manuscript)

—Don't always be so glum, Mister Antônio Áureo.
—Maria, I l-l-liv . . . I lived sadly and s-s-s . . . sadly I laid down my arms. I know all the passwords of the world. Even eternity is a t-t-t . . . time b-b-b . . . bomb.

A time bomb? Really? What do you all think? Mister Antônio Áureo, an olive sprig in his lapel, his s-s-s . . . his straw hand on my shoulder, stepping very lightly on the cobblestones in his high lace shoes with soles thinner than tissue paper, soul shoes, f-f-f . . . follows me on this forced march and never gets tired, looks suspiciously at the man in the helmet who stands in the Alto da Sé checking to see if the sea is green, splits with the drumbeat, grumbling, can you hear what he says? I can't. He gnashes his teeth and gets mad spitting down below, one spit after the other, fusillade around the port and the hoists, he puts his hand between his legs, takes out his culverin, a tiny little package, folks, and he cries oh-oh-oh . . . over here, look, turning a complete handspring in the direction of the bells striking noon, the tall and short buildings, the flags on the poles, the clouds, the warehouses, the wharf, I'm feeling kind of dizzy and look away, he points to the reefs:

—Look! Didn't I say? Unholy phalanxes.[34] Look at the waste. The damage.

There was no need to point it out. Eight or ten ships, dear listeners, amidst the smoke, all listing to one side, some sunk and some still visible, the mast of one tearing the sail of the other, the disastrous, the fearful, the unbearable, sunshine on the hulls, mortal light, a naval squadron caught in the trap. (pp. 79-80)

I leave the Benefits office, the sun very hot and borne by the heat a late afternoon feeling. Come see the vessels in the north branch of the river and all the people drowning, children, grown-ups. What waters are these? Four grey doves and a white one looking for food on the Santa Rita Wharf. TheSupreme Medical Committee is going to examine my request. The Franciscan Convent with its doors smashed in, smoking, about to crash on top of the Court House. That's right. Instead of the certificate, an official letter. Ah, yes. Men wearing helmets, some with little birds or gewgaws on their headgear, about to invade that house, as big as ten, up above. The king leaves his palace, blinking, one arm shielding his wee little eyes, how hot the sun is! He throws his hands on top of his head and runs inside, ooh, help me, don't let one of those soldiers piss all over me. We know our duty.

---

[34]This locution, a little unusual, is found in the Hymn of Independence: "Do not fear unholy phalanxes/Presenting a hostile face." Various syntagmas taken from the civic hymn book punctuate the war scenes, repeating, without the same breadth, the process of incrustation of the popular song repertoire in the text.

Come back next week. Five hundred muskets, five hundred throat-pieces, five hundred drums, five hundred trumpets, five hundred baldrics land somewhere. (p. 188)

This is the second time I've ever seen a real fire, run and see it too, if you can, the ships are loading and unloading, ten in the morning, the hoists, the oily water, the sailors, nice galley, the stevedores, the reflections of the hulls, and in the middle of this calm, inside the machinery of the day and the works of the day, the clouds of smoke, billowing, blowing the top off the warehouses, and the flames raising the masts higher, how many ships? twenty? thirty? lots, filled with treasures, the smell of tobacco makes the vultures drunk and the molten sugar burns the skin of the catfish. Come! (p. 264)

APRIL 8—Nightmarish images? Images of war, parallel to the ones we have been seeing in all the newspapers and TV screens these last days. Driven by the Liberation Front's advance, before which any resistence seems futile, and with Saigon's surrender imminent, hordes of stranded deserters and civilians are pouring into the still unoccupied areas. Disbanded soldiers disown their flag; rape the women of their country; shoot their own mother, if she crosses their path; some try to escape by clinging to the landing gear of jets and are cast off in the sky, fall, go drink the China Sea. And if, in the novel's phantom war as well as the one ravaging Southeast Asia, many among the defeated expose themselves to danger when they try to escape by swimming, some facts—identical in substance—change appearance. In South Vietnam a nuclear reactor is blown sky-high with dynamite rather than let it fall into the hands of the communists; in *The Queen of the Prisons of Greece*, the burning of warehouses and ships prevents the destroyed merchandise—tobacco, cotton, Brazil wood and sugar—from being of any use to the invaders.

APRIL 9—From being of any use to Holland. Since that is what this is all about, as it becomes clearer and clearer. All the war iconography superimposed upon the setting of the novel, reconstructs point by point, with few changes in the sequence and in the facts sanctioned by historians, the conquest of Olinda and the port of Recife by Lonck's and Waerdenburch's men in 1630. Following, it seems, Homer's example, who avoids recounting the entire Trojan war, a subject, according to the well-known formula by Aristotle, "too vast and difficult to encompass at a glance," as we read in the *Poetics*, Julia Marquezim Enone didn't presume to inflate her book with the twenty-four years of the occupation, including Nassau's times and the battles that shattered the invaders. She limits herself to the stage prior to the arrival of the naval squadron and the two weeks of the siege—begun on the 15th of the month of February—culminating with our surrender.

APRIL 10—I return to some points of the four passages I recently quoted. We will observe the parallelism between the war scenes casting a shadow on the novel and the arrival of the Dutch forces in Pernambuco; and you will follow the novelist in her efforts to conceal the nature of these allusions, in a sort of conflict between history and poetry.

The whole first passage, for example, develops the opposition contained in the opening sentence—"Sword firm in hand and feasting?"—one of the elements, *war*, being expressed in a symbolic fashion ("sword firm in hand") and the other, *feasting*, named without reticence. I will point out, in passing, the absolute coherence of the formal solution here: the contrast between symbol and pure designation mirrors a psychological reality. Put in charge by the Court of Madrid of coordinating the captaincy's defense, Matias de Albuquerque organizes outdoor celebrations aimed at dispelling "omens and fears" as he readies fortifications and soldiers.[35] It was therefore the *war* (concealed, in the sentence, by a symbolic figure) that required a disguise, and not the *feasting*. Hence, the exhortation: "cheer up, everybody! we mustn't see or think."

This play is projected into the paragraph only in part, all of it variegated with frontal designations and enigmatic images, without the former always being associated with *feasting* and the enigmas with *war*. There are, as can be seen, the "sentries,"

---

[35]Rocha Pombo, *História do Brasil* [History of Brazil], vol. 1 (São Paulo: W. M. Jackson, Inc., 1935), 310.

the "steel barrels," the "armed recruits" and the "bugle," the "spears," the "words of command," unequivocal images of war. The "sea towers," the "traveling towers"—inventions, I believe, prompted by Vieira[36]—call, on the other hand, for another level of comprehension. In this case, the sibylline quality of the metaphor is balanced by the number, in a way not accidental in the least. In fact, the expeditionary squadron consisted of 63 units, consisting of "35 large warships, 15 yachts, 13 sloops and two seized enemy vessels, with a crew of 3,780 sailors, 3,500 soldiers and an armament of 1,170 cannons of all calibers," as Johannes de Laet, who based his work on ships' logs and military leaders' testimonies, assures us.[37] The small numerical difference shouldn't surprise us and is justified by the existence of values that transcend the trivial truth, elevating it, a phenomenon developed with refinement by the writer Thomas Mann, in at least two points ("Seven or Five" and "In the Number Seventy") of *Joseph the Provider*. Narrators and historians obey different laws.

Full of seamen, the ship, associated with the apparent images of war, casts anchor "in the square, on dry ground"—an anomalous space—and with this maneuver enters unreality. This, if the fact that the author doesn't refer to the *war*, here, but to the *feasting*, escapes the reader: she's alluding to the Ship Catarineta, a popular revelry of northeast Brazil which the Englishman Henry Koster apparently describes for the first time (*Travels in Brazil*, 1816), but which can already be seen, in

---

[36]"That confused multitude of naval towers, made up of eighty-seven ships, many of extraordinary largeness, filled those seas with awe . . ."—Antônio Vieira, *Sermões* (Sermons), 6th ed., vol. 9 (Porto: 1909), 359.

[37]*Historie ofte Jaerlijck Verhael van de Verrichtingen der Geoctroyeerde West Indische Compagnie. Zedert haer Begin, tot het eynde van't jaer sesthien hondert ses-en-dertich* (Leyden: 1644), 174. In addition to the conquest of Pernambuco, de Laet recounts the Dutch piracy off the coasts of the West Indies and the struggles with Spanish galleons. We also see Holland in the Hudson and in the Gold Coast. But don't believe even for a minute that the narration of so many maritime adventures would make this Antwerpian's report, detailed to the point of noting the ships' origin and date of departure, entertaining.

the background, in a sketch by Franz Post. Based on the wreck of the ship that was sailing to Lisbon from Recife in 1565,[38] it represents, with dancers and singers, the crew struggling against the Devil, Hunger and Going Astray, finally reaching terra firma. I don't know of any source explicitly mentioning the Ship Catarineta among the celebrations with which Matias de Albuquerque "delights and deceives" Olinda and Recife. Is there, however, a more accessible prefiguration of the Dutch threat, which the ship in danger survives, led by the illustrious and loyal captain?

Another enigmatic image of the *feasting* is that of the "ox with green ribbons in its horns," surely a detail from *The Sea Horse*, a northeastern pastoral play which the intolerant chronicler of social customs of the past century Father Lopes Gama calls "a heap of nonsense." The many characters of the play—people, animals and fantastic beings—sing, drink, dance and run, for eight hours nonstop. Finally the Ox dies, "for no reason at all," says Lopes Gama, and is resurrected thanks to an enema. I will refrain from pointing out the equivalency, in this short passage of the novel, between the musical instruments and the words of command or between the fireworks and the spears, elements whose identity is apparent in their names and obviously associated with the opposition feasting/war.

My attempt at deciphering still lacks a discussion of the device by which Julia M. Enone reveals the nationality of the offending army in her text. There's hardly anything left of Holland's legacy in Brazil. Even our toponyms ignore it; no city name recalls the provenance of those adventurers. As for the language, it appears to have retained only one word: *brote*, one of the goods on the ships—along with lead and weapons— which was "the military cracker, paid during sea voyages and distributed to soldiers on duty."[39] It has also been spelled *broth*,

---

[38]This is Pereira da Costa's thesis, in *Folk-lore Pernambucano* [Folklore of Pernambuco], first separate edition (Recife: Arquivo Público Estadual, 1974), 254 and ff.

[39]Tarcísio L. Pereira, *Clavinas e Rendas* [Rifles and Pay] (São Paulo: Melhoramentos, 1956), 73. I am indebted to this author for the remaining information in this paragraph.

and one scholar suggests that the word might come from the Dutch *brood* (English *bread*), written *broot* in the seventeenth century. *Brote*, having undergone, I believe, a number of transformations, was incorporated—hard and round—in the dietary tradition of the Northeast. In the passage transcribed it's equivalent—in the author's discreet and, in a manner of speaking, mischievous way—to Holland's flag.

APRIL 13—I reread the pages in which I describe the encounter with that poor Heleno, tied to Julia M. Enone's life—who never used her married name—and cornerstone in the troubled formation of her destiny, and I see that it's necessary to fill in a blank. There I talk about a second internment in the Psychiatric Hospital, while nothing is explained about the first.

About three years after her precocious marriage, Julia separates definitively and moves in with her parents. One of her sisters becomes engaged; her fiancé has a brother who is also to marry soon. Was the young woman trying to repeat, in a less clear way and without the same impetus, her mother's maneuver when she snatched the widower Oton Enone from her sister? She had gone back to the Normal School and certainly there was a troubling ambiguity in the seventeen-year-old schoolgirl, married for three years but actually without a husband, a sort of mix of maturity and greenness. The brother of her sister's fiancé gets involved with her and she becomes pregnant. Her father and brothers demand that she have an abortion, she resists. The child is born; old Oton Enone, by his own determination, gives it to its father, now married, with his wife one month into her pregnancy. Julia's reaction is violent: she smashes the glass window with her fist, attacks the nurses, and heads for the nursery with a piece of glass in her hand, but she's stopped at the door. Forced into an ambulance, she's taken to the asylum, where she spends almost thirty days, as an indigent. Her husband denounces the little girl as illegitimate and disappears, but without breaking up the marriage.

Julia, discharged, helps out in the hospital's office without pay, until her father comes to get her. At one point, an unusual occurrence, a multitude of workers stops the bus. Only then did she discover that it was May 1st and that six hundred backwoodsmen of the Planters' Society, nucleus of the Peasant Leagues, dark, gaunt, ragged, dirty (like the debris pushed forward by the flood, fouling the Capibaribe), had arrived in Recife for the Workers' Day parade. The year: 1956.

She starts reading everything she can lay her hands on, at times spending the entire day in the backyard with a book. She finishes her studies at the Normal School and seems completely purposeless. Suddenly, she begins to go out a lot, her absences grow longer, some nights she doesn't come back at all and refuses to explain where she has been, her father heaps insults upon her, some man? he asks around and finds out: many of the letters received at that time by administrators and plantation owners, urging them to report to the rural unions, or else they will have to come "by force and by violence," are written by her. Taciturn, barefoot, with a scythe in her hand, she takes part, to swell the numbers, in workers' demonstrations in Cabo, Aliança and Vitória, even at the Galiléia Plantation, this before the government of Pernambuco expropriated it in order to divide it among rebelling sharecroppers. It's at this point that her father, struggling for an authority he perhaps no longer believes in, decides to send her out of state, and the final encounter with Heleno takes place. Was she really going to buy the ticket, or use the money to support an uprising in the sugar region, which was then making the Northeast tremble? I never asked her. I avoided forcing her defenses as much as possible. It's difficult to ask someone we love and who at eighteen, inconceivable among the middle class, which she did not belong to anyway (did she belong to any class?), but normal among lower-class women, already carries a biography of half a century or more.

APRIL 15—Our first epic poet, in the *Prosopopoeia*, mentions "a girdle of stone unkempt and alive." He's referring to the sandstone formations the city of Recife owes its name and origin to: the natural girdle, visible or submerged according to the tides, made a port of the peninsula. At one point, the wall ended—it was the passage for the ships. Thus the future city was born, destined to overseas commerce and protected from ill-intentioned visitors. If necessary the gap between the reefs, secret door, could be closed against the enemy.

Matias de Albuquerque realizes what he has in hand to defend himself against the imminent aggression; he restores the fortresses nowadays known as Buraco and Brum, creates militias, orders trenches dug; and completes the half-submerged wall, "unkempt and alive," by stretching an iron chain across the passage. In order to thwart the assailants further, he sinks a ship in that same place.

The chronicles tell us that the confidence created by the street dances and popular representations vanished at the first sight of the enemy masts, entire families fleeing with what they could carry before the first shot shook the trees. Such a premature reaction, countered by the courage shown by many soldiers, foreshadowed the frailty of the armor with which our captain tried to oppose Holland. Thus, even though the rough sea allies itself with the land, hindering the precision of the Flemish artillery, the impact of the attack is so great that, to those sustaining it, it seems capable of breaking the iron chain in two and reducing the ship sunk in the passage to foam. Matias de Albuquerque blocks this passage with the sacrifice of eight more ships.

This is the prodigious shipwreck Maria de França and Antônio Áureo witness; and in which the "spirit of light," angry, sees so much waste. Impossible to tell whether his judgment reflects the writer's position in the face of this historical fact or whether it expresses in a general way the reaction of the poor.

APRIL 17—When I transcribed in its entirety the action snapshot in which the ex-barber and his friend climb the Alto da Sé—from which, with his obscene gesture, he insults the cities of Olinda and Recife, once more fused together—I apparently went too far. Extracting the allusions to the sentry and the tactical shipwreck with which the port is closed up would have been enough for the intended demonstration. But I wanted to underscore, there, a discreet and fortunate occurrence of infiltration, in the semantic area, of the dominant theme. Mirroring the introduction of the battle scenes, the text begins to bristle with expressions linked to war, some with access to the civilian mode of speech: "passwords," "forced march," "drumbeat," "fusillade" (which is a discharge of many shots one after the other without a perceptible pause), "culverin" (ancient artillery piece, long and of long range) and other terms the reader will see.

So many military allusions are contrasted with the olive sprig in Áureo's lapel, a peaceful motif, introduced with the discretion peculiar to my friend's art. Deep down the ex-barber, in constant and declared opposition to the world, of which *he knows the passwords*, aspires to an impossible armistice.

APRIL 19—"The case of backlands specialists Orlando and Claudio Villas Boas' retirement, requested four years ago, is apparently nearing a resolution after a lifetime spent with our Indians in a pacification effort held in high regard by everybody. Everything will depend on the pension granted them, which, according to estimates based on the salaries of both, would be inferior to their current needs and, futhermore, would not measure up to the importance and danger of the mission they carried out in the forest." (*Jornal da Tarde* [São Paulo], 4/18/75.)

APRIL 23—The Dutch attack, by land, is carried out by way of Olinda, with 3,000 men advancing along the beach, followed at a short distance by a small formation of launches, all spitting hot lead. Is this what is deafening so many? The captains order them to resist and they, turning a deaf ear, hide out in the backcountry or try to save their families. Soon over 500 Dutch marksmen invade the southern part of Olinda. The Jesuit convent yields, the news that the seat of the captaincy is in the heretics' hands runs through the citadels like fire and many quench their thirst forever, trying to escape by swimming. Matias de Albuquerque, aware of the defeat but still undaunted, moves with only twenty followers to the Village (or Settlement) of Recife, sets fire to twenty-four ships laden with sugar, cotton, tobacco and Brazil wood, besides burning the warehouses, "all of the houses in which there was sugar," as we read in the letter in which he recounts his decision.

I take for granted the presence of all these events in the third and fourth quotations. But it might be wise to call to mind the mutual penetration, in the novel, of the uneven Olinda with the hardly uneven city of Recife, almost an extension of the sea, a coincidence that clarifies some images of a surrealist tone in the third example. One, the Franciscan Convent (Olinda) "about to crash on top of the Court House" (Recife); another, "that house, as big as ten, up above" (the Jesuit Convent, to be sure), which the frightened governor (the King, in the text) sees in the air, above the palace. The simultaneity of episodes— troops disembarking, conquest of the convents, death of fugitives—occurs in other parts of the novel and has already been discussed.

The description of the burning ships and warehouses clearly takes as its reference the one slavishly copied from the *Manual of Composition* and contrasts the model's illusory balance with a deceitful and highly expressive disorder, a peculiarity—not exclusive, to be sure—of its poetics and in which the syntactic turmoil reflects an immersion in reality, in its turbulence, a union, a harmony, an accord disrupted by the acute phases of madness, the bristling syntax being the expression of this disruption.

APRIL 24—Having clarified the absolute parallelism between the war scenes scattered throughout the novel and the invasion of Pernambuco—a connection possibly misrepresented by the choice of examples, which make it seem apparent, but are actually disseminated throughout the entangled text and thus misleading for the observer—a hypothesis regarding the motif of the intermittent fusion Recife/Olinda begins to surface. It wouldn't be difficult for Julia Marquezim Enone, so bold in her invention of the scenery and not at all conventional in setting up the mediation, to represent, via Maria de França, scenes from the invasion of Olinda without bringing the mountain to Mohammed. But who knows if it didn't seem too much to her to gamble with the perception of space and time in these terms, infusing the narrator's vision with a city far from where she's ordering her discourse and, simultaneously, the three-centuries-old ghosts of a war?

That would indeed be a rare and exemplary case in which the effectiveness of results comes from the excess of resources. The fragmentary images of 1630, dispersed among two separate cities, command the reader's attention precisely because of the impossibility of their resurgence, of their renovation, of their transgression of the laws of *time*, is added the impossibility of a transgression of the laws of *space*. With winged machines, Julia Marquezim Enone moves the hills and buildings of Olinda (some of which are reborn of dust, with their arks, their armoires, their canopied beds, in this magical event), mixes today's capital with yesterday's, joining—and in this manner establishing them without any possibility of rejection—visions removed from one another and, from a natural point of view, doubly inaccessible to the "I" that sees and speaks.

I insist: my position before literary works is reverent and not too fond of certainties. I'm not the kind of person who asks questions and then turns them into convictions. The hypothesis above coexists in me with another, opposite to it: that the concern for space and the subsequent removal of Olinda could have led to the Dutch War motif. In any case, there reigns, undeniable, removed from intention and origin, the phenomenon of an uncommon problem of fiction, situated, by science and the author's intuition, in the tenuous frontier where reason, fascinated, surrenders to the absurd.

APRIL 26—Of course some will reject the fact that Julia M. Enone, being able to choose from the long history of Dutch rule in Brazil episodes favorable to us and, more than anything else, those culminating with the final expulsion of the conquerors, preferred precisely the invasion and the fall of the captaincy.

It must be noted, however, that *The Queen of the Prisons of Greece* excludes triumph from its themes. Here is, in the lineage of *Jude the Obscure*, of *Hunger*, of *Manhattan Transfer*, a book of failures. The heroine, member of an oppressed class, struggles for years with bureaucracy, which misleads her and whose language she attempts to learn, always in vain. What would a series of "positive" pictures evoking the country's victory and the expulsion of the invaders do in a book constructed in this manner? These pictures would be an expression of that rhetoric, devoid of substance and as if suspended in air, she takes aim at so often in her book. Friar Manuel Calado writes *The Valiant Lucideno* in prose and verse to sing

> Olinda freed
> From the tyrannic furor of the Dutch,

as he solemnly promises in the dedicatory epistle to His Serene Highness Lord Teodósio, Prince of the Kingdom and Monarchy of Portugal. But tell me whether Holland's debacle was of any advantage to Maria de França and the rest of her class.

On the other hand, who is not aware of the greed with which one part of the planet exploits the other?

It is more truthful and significant for Julia M. Enone to have mined her book with scenes of the occupation and not of the expulsion of the invaders: they better reflect our reality and the reality of all countries occupied nowadays—by arms, by gold and by less tangible means. The fact that only Maria de França and, once, Antônio Áureo, see the war scenes, while everybody else is indifferently going about their business, seems to me to simply reinforce this meaning. Matias de Albuquerque put sentries on the hills of Olinda, to watch for the enemy's masts. But who can see the forces invading us today?

APRIL 28—Hypothesis: Julia Marquezim Enone introduces the *invasion* motif to explore that of *resistance*.[40]

Matias de Albuquerque, defeated, doesn't give in, organizing—between the Capibaribe and the Beberibe, the two big rivers of Recife, on a hill inland, equidistant from Olinda and the port where he set fire to the ships—what was to be called

---

[40]It can even be added that this coded message has a specific target—the existing political system. The future writer's militance in the riots that shook up the sugarcane region of the Northeast in her youth would reinforce that interpretation. But wouldn't this be limiting the scope of the motif? The resistance of the destitute is a powerful theme. The representation of destitution hits harder than the representation of resistance.

Arraial do Bom Jesus, a nucleus of resistance for eight years. White people, Indians, mestizos, African slaves and, later, even Henrique Dias's black troops, free, would represent in a symbolic manner the people of Brazil in this famous redoubt. Without there being any description of the Arraial in the novel (and there could not be, since its appearance and size changed according to the circumstances, today pasture with scores of oxen and tomorrow an inconceivable citadel, surrounded by snakes), Maria de França makes occasional references to this nucleus.

MAY 6—The true weight of victory—always bright—and of its darker counterpart in novels calls for some reflection. There are snares, deceits, misunderstandings. I don't want to see the end of heroes who triumph in love or battle. No enemies stay dead forever—their death, in any case, is never the death of Evil—and what passionate love is immune to senility and to the end? Even so, it's important, in life and in stories, that those extraordinary moments in which the beloved surrenders to the vehemence of the one who loves, or the antagonist is crushed, shine. What reader of novels, wise and experienced, did not catch himself wishing for Amelia Sedley to finally accept William Dobbin's patient love in *Vanity Fair*? Can I deny having wished with all my heart that David Copperfield could unmask Uriah Heep the crook? Can I deny my joy when I saw him fall? Yes, those moments in novels exalt us just as similar moments exalt us in life, raw as our vision of things might be. Transitory, they correspond to a happy conjunction of circumstances and vibrate with harmony: there's an accord between man's desire and the variable universe, we penetrate the fog enveloping us, we experience something to which we give many names and which has none. Exaltation? Bliss? Ecstasy? We are on the other side, with no memory, and if we still have any remembrance it is that of the desire now fulfilled. We know nothing, anymore, of old age, of the ephemeral, of death. Many times the writer tries to represent these unnameable happy injunctions. What for? To magnify, by the arts of the imaginary, such occurrences; to oppose a kind of eternity to what escapes us so quickly.

But the narrator who insists on the representation of harmonious moments, giving ordinary treatment and a certain invulnerable air to what we know is rare and fragile is not true to life and, therefore, to the readers. It's unacceptable for him to reject the negative aspects in his work, for the very reason that this is the stuff of life, and hence comes much of the strength and transcendence which, from Oedipus to K., ennobles so many narrations, so sympathetic to the uncertainty of our condition that any happy graft would destroy them. What is the meaning of an Ivan Ilyich saved from death? Nothing doing with a triumphant and surviving Lord Jim. Such works want to represent, in the glare of an intense light, some poignant aspects of the human condition—and those deaths, in them, are the generating forces of the texts that recount them.

MAY 9—I see her on the TV Globo News. She married at thirteen and worked in the fields almost all her life, without knowing until today what it's like to wear shoes. Four children died in her arms: she would put a candle in the dying child's hand and let him die. As far as she can remember, she never cried. She saw her husband die; and her mother, poisoned by a rattlesnake.

—Snakes don't bite me: they coil around my arms and I hold their head like this.

Now she makes rag dolls and misses working with a shovel.

Her name is Gertrudes Maria da Conceição, she was born in Guatinguetá, Minas Gerais, on January 19, 1842, and only now, at 133, is she applying for retirement benefits at I.N.P.S.

MAY 11—The birds Maria de França sees everywhere are the same ones the children of the Northeast are familiar with: black-throated cardinals, guans, parakeets, tinamous, sandpipers, tanagers, a varied list that rarely repeats itself. Could they function as a compensatory element, softening a scenery we know to be threatening, transfixed by images of a dead war—without our knowing with any certainty, in the end, where unreality lies, whether in Maria de França's vision or in the length of time we objectively interpose between what she witnesses and the endless war dates of textbooks?

No. They are detached from their natural function, seeming full of power: the character sees them as huge. This anomaly, eventually, becomes desirable, as in the scene in which some hummingbirds, with a thirty-inch wingspan, break into the Capela Dourada, one summer afternoon, with the gold of the carvings reflecting in their many-colored and rapidly changing plumage, amidst a fantastic silence. But in general—with their sharp little beaks resembling the teeth of a pair of pliers, their finely clawed little feet grasping with the firmness of pincers, their hard little eyes, cassiterite coins, their round and unrelenting stare, their bristling plumage, their frightful song—they fill with menace the already problematic space the protagonist moves in. Once again Julia Marquezim Enone is attributing to Maria de França's madness her own inventions and using this pretext to present to us—without ostentation, as if she were just quoting, transcribing—her own vision of reality, almost always disquieting.

MAY 12—When I was a child, entering a dimly lit and, most likely, empty room, I sensed a presence, an inaudible yet real breathing. The same thing happens to me in *The Queen of the Prisons of Greece* with the birds' gigantism, something identical, as if some secret ear or eye of mine sensed, there, an invisible being, below the level of certainty but within the limits of conviction. Not, perhaps, a metaphysical or calamitous entity: in any case something veiled, inaccessible, with all the seduction and menace pulsating in secrets.

It's not difficult for me, putting aside the instruments bequeathed to us by those who attempt to decipher the soul—or, simply, to establish a terminology for its most flagrant movements—to see in these frail and gigantic animals the epitome of the world. Maria de França fears them and voices her fear many times, during the acute phases of imbalance as well as those of apparent sanity. Incomprehensibility compounds this fear. How can the birds be kept in cages smaller than themselves? Why do they shrink after they die? They: the fugitive, volatile universe, illusory and terrible.

Yes, everything seems clear and in keeping with the central theme of the book: man unarmed in a hostile environment. But the mysterious breathing persists within the logic of the overall picture. Something I don't grasp is secretly watching me from in there.

May 15—What I wrote above will sicken the respectable critic, who takes a solemn attitude toward literary works, as the most prestigious circles implicitly legislate. I'm not, however, a respectable critic, I don't even aspire to being a critic and, as far as respectability goes—so often an industrial virtue, like endurance in engines or color fastness in fabrics—who ever said I possessed it? I'm a sensitive man and, from this point of view, out of step with my times, a sensitive and grieving man, simultaneously the bearer of his fascination for a text and of his love for the one who created it. I have, therefore, plenty of freedom to develop my book, intellectual adventure and also, in its own way, act of love, and nothing obliges me to exclude from this essay what I can't explain.

Did I talk about my uneasiness in the presence of the huge birds and the uneasiness Maria de França's fear causes me? The scene in which she secures protection against them makes an even deeper impression on me and causes me the same vague discomfort (the occult and inexplicable breathing!). The episode occurs only in the last third of the book, after the breaking off of the engagement by the center forward, but it's being prepared for since chapter 2. However, we don't get any sense of what the heroine is saying when she talks about putting away—in her ears, in her breast, in her eyes, in her hand—the attributes of one or another character. Or when she focuses on one of these traits in an exaggerated manner:

what an ear, what an ear, full of little twists and turns, and she listens carefully, she listens well, a courteous ear, hurt by rough voices, by honey-tongued lies (covered with flies), what are you doing there, ear, on this man who doesn't deserve you?, listen to me, little ear: papoose, lollipop, silver bells, tic-tac-toe, gewgaw, chow-chow.

May 16—Dudu, wounded by the "vile betrayal," withdraws. The prospects this commitment offered were fragile, maybe there was no prospect at all, he loses ground on the soccer field and off, but the pluck with which he ignores his failure and keeps struggling (the Tower's inferiority never keeps him from trying, with his reverse kicks, to lessen the disadvantage or even win), his dedication and maybe even his hurried air, of someone who almost kicked the ball out of bounds and is running back to the middle of the field, transform Maria de França's life for a while. When he breaks up with her, she spends a sleepless night, and this restlessness is conveyed in a long passage, furious and incoherent:

. . . also, black and blacker still, I tear, he bit, the blow, we rend, coal more trash, lizards still, are you leaving? clogs but cuts who wants a lid loaded shoo. Hello, out there in Radioland! Are you sleeping?

The morning, comforting for the sleepless, hits her, even worse than her nocturnal journey, with

the birds' belches, their garglings, do they gargle stones? shards of glass? vengeful whistles.

Then, so as not to continue without a protector, exposed to these numerous creatures, nimble (their anatomy seems to her designed solely to shoot their beaks, to fire their beaks), she falls ill and, in a kind of lethargy or ecstasy, in eight days and nine nights, creates the scarecrow.

Only then is the purpose of the acquisitions, or kidnappings, or mutilations revealed, the feet, the skinny arms, the ear "full of little twists and turns," those eyes "to see floods and blusters with," fragments scattered in twenty-seven characters of the book that will be combined in Maria de França's scarecrow, fantastic protector, successively called by its creator the Breeze, the Big Wind, the Sumetume or Escape Hole, the Tower, the Big Rain, the Creature, the Súpeto or Sudden, the Bright Shield, the Their Scare, the There, the Man, the Báçira.

MAY 17—The analysis of these epithets, whose connection is not easy to discover, gradually reveals a link between them. They all converge in the notions of gentleness, strength, protection, fecundity and largeness, attributes of an uncommon being, linked to God and the only one capable of protecting her from the birds. What makes the consistency of this series less clear—and not by accident, I believe—are some terms of enigmatic or rather uncommon meaning, like *sumetume*, both the escape hole where the paca hides when pursued by dogs and the exit of a tunnel; or *súpeto*, ancient spelling of *súbito*, sudden, surviving in the expression *de supetão*, all of a sudden.[41]

As for the *Báçira*, the last name given to the scarecrow and in this manner highlighted, made prominent, no dictionary records it. Ancient cartographers had a mythical vision of space: the familiar boundaries dissolved in dreams. Their maps weren't a mere projection of known oceans and lands; they enlarged the world, they didn't limit themselves to what travelers might encounter; in addition to guiding, they led astray; while informing, they were also a record of fears. I have in front of me the map of the Turk Piri Reis, who was neither an amateur nor an occasional traveler, but a connoisseur of the sea and of the science of maritime navigation, a true admiral. The 1513 map, which is indebted to the Mohammedan cartography of its time and makes use of Carolingian models, incorporates the tale of a Spanish seaman, imprisoned in Turkey after having served under Christopher Columbus. This colorful gazelle hide is teeming not only with intersecting lines, but fantastic images as well. A monkey dances with some lascivious monster, here's the man with his head below his shoulders to whom Othello refers before the senators, a couple in the middle of the sea is sailing on a fish and feeding on it. They're all signs of the unknown, apparent in the absence of an end or a limit for this map of the Earth. Beyond, beyond what? Such an interrogative, in Marcgrave's Brazilian map, is naturally less abysmal and has a name: the Báçira, now the Pacira Range, previously Monte Trovão, Mount Thunder, or Serra do Abalo, Earthquake Range. Not too far from the port of Recife, fifty or fifty-five miles, the Báçira, however, awed and curbed the passage of adventurers more than the entire width of the ocean: "isolated, placed in the middle of the wilderness, it was the

---

[41]This epithet, actually, seems a little out of place in the sequence. Could it be a false clue, to hinder deciphering? I don't know whether I incur a biased interpretation when I associate the term with the idea of *susto*, scare, of unexpected arrival, of an abrupt and gruff gesture.

frontier, the absolute limit of everything known."[42] Doesn't ending the construction and naming of the scarecrow with a word so heavy with connotations on the part of Maria de França seem to suggest that, in this creature of hers, the idea of spiritual vastness and mystery rises above that of mere protection?

MAY 22—Expressly and admittedly conceived to neutralize a component of space in *The Queen of the Prisons of Greece*—or what this component represents as a real or imaginary threat— Maria de França's scarecrow is also linked to the setting through his speech, in which, in a curious piece of rhetoric composed of meaningless sentences, anonymous songs, popular sayings, parables, quatrains, palaver, enigmas, prophecies and metaphysical inquiries mixed together, he digresses about his own identity, relating it to the topography in which he's a perplexed stranger.

His function, therefore, doesn't merely consist of chasing away the huge birds. Who knows, even, whether, in such an artful book, infested with false passages, this task isn't too explicit to be true? Who can assure me that the scarecrow—the Shelter, the Báçira—wasn't created above all to launch his speech, in some ways the climax of the work, vertex of many themes scattered throughout it, and that in which language, managing to, incidentally, break with meanings, reaches a diapason of rare intensity? Speech, public oration and not dialogue: there is, between the Súpeto and Maria de França, an obscure identification, as if the two bodies had the same mouth, as if they had shared the same bed, inhabited the same dream.

---

[42]Luís da Câmara Cascudo, *Geografia do Brasil Holandés* [Geography of Dutch Brazil] (São Paulo: José Olympio, 1956), 195-96. I'm rearranging above some of the words of this scholar, the only one in whose work I found—by accident—information on the Báçira, one more vestige of the Dutch presence in J.M.E.'s novel. Besides, as we shall see later, Marcgrave's map helps us to understand certain obscurities in the speech of the There.

MAY 25—Inadequate light, paper too dark or light, small print, crowded page—and even, I believe, an excessive interest in the text—anything can lead me to periods of blindness or forced rest in dim rooms. Deep inside, I'm grateful to my ailment: it's as if reading were a secret love for me, always in danger and subject to reparations. Even early this morning—I had read a lot, last night—I woke up with a sharp pain in the back of my eyes. I wandered around the dark rooms for a while and finally I opened a window. It was after two, the street was deserted, I distractedly looked up and what I saw made me shudder: the moon was black, no, the color of blood, and seemed to be melting in a second, catastrophic death.

What kind of irrational man continues to exist in me, in spite of everything? Upset as I was, it was hard for me to relate the lunar disintegration to the idea of an eclipse. Even later, when I remembered having read in the papers the announcement of this phenomenon (this is the shadow of the Earth, man!), even then I still felt a weight inside. More: I could swear that the spatial relationships between the buildings were changing, that earth and sky were coming unhinged. Perhaps my retinas, still afflicted, were subverting things.

MAY 27—Frailty of the soul! Faced with a speech like the scarecrow's, so bristling with meanings and enigmas, here I am, as if nothing else mattered, heedful of a brief allusion loose in the text, only because I fancy I know its origin. We were in the living room and she was embroidering, with her head bent. What inadmissible acuity allowed her to feel my gaze and, hence, guess what I was thinking? I look at her face, the somewhat chastened skin of her pure and delicate face, forever altered by livid spots or sudden blushes. I see her, in her reverie, her facial muscles relaxed: tiny vertical lines are beginning to show above her upper lip, thirty-three and a premature sign of age is already beginning to appear. I silently envelop her in my compassion, she, whom I love, is aging, her youth is slipping between my fingers. Julia raises her head, large placid eyes, the shiny lenses and round wire rims, smiles as if she didn't know anything and says:

—Be quiet!

As if she didn't know. But she knows, she saw without seeing me, she read me. Words of the Súpeto:

"Woman! So young still and your lips already pinched? Youth passes, it's gone, it used to be, to be is to perish, la-de-da, your head bowed and old age a swarm of wasps building their nest, there, in the hollow of your mouth, tsk. I scare birds, but not time, I scare birds, not decay, birds I scare and nothing else."

MAY 30—Having delivered this speech, the scarecrow becomes silent and is not mentioned again. A deceptive omission, actually: from this moment on any word about birds and the fear they cause in the book ceases, in a long—metonymic?—process in which the cause is referred to by its effect; or, better still, by the lack of allusions to the latter. At the same time, the silence established around an element elaborated with such precision as the scarecrow, who seemed to be destined to govern the last fourth of the book, introduces once more and with greater amplitude an obsessive theme in Julia Marquezim Enone, that of forgetfulness.

The scarecrow speaks, and his speech, echoing the author's concerns, is truncated by lapses. More than once forgetting what he said, he repeats or interrogates himself; he hesitates in the middle of a sentence, while what he was going to say escapes him.

I don't know if I said it and if I already said it I'm going to say it again. What was it now?

Shoo, then, because there they come and the surf is rising? when, with my feet on the ground . . . on the ground. . . . On the ground? Feet?

Meanwhile, the absence of memory, which up to a point seems connected with his speech, turns out to be of a more profound nature. The scarecrow believes he has lived a past he knows nothing about: what he does know about himself is the present; then he inverts the situation, wondering whether what has just arisen is not exactly space, whether the absence of a propitious space—now created—was not keeping him from establishing references and learning his own identity. Such speculation, however, is a game and a pretense—he will remain a mysterious figure, impenetrable as his monologue:

> Birds and
> children may
> see me and I shan't say
> who I am.

JUNE 8—I'm familiar, to a lesser degree, with the depressions that at times assailed my friend and made her hate her book. I've sat in front of my notebooks and annotations for the past eight days, numb, watching the hours slip by. I pore over the scarecrow's speech and each time I feel more lost in this veritable room of mirrors, in which objects become confused with their reflections.

No, it's not that. I can distinguish the real objects from those that are secretly watching me, untouchable, from deep inside the mirrors: but I distrust everything, the tumultous speech of the scarecrow sounds familiar to me and full of cunning. Those who think that I shouldn't talk about this understand nothing. Imagine: you recognize, speaking in some part of the house, your own voice, and what it says, even though it seems innocent, is an accusation and it stings. Not that the Tower's speech is my enemy. I am referring to the duplicity, to another face, a false bottom, a mask. Where is the real face of such ambiguous words?

Where am I coming from, what was there? The memory of things diverges in this L, in this tilted L, an L upside down, the wind peopled with birds comes and blows the dust of experience far away. Another memory is born, Maria, full of whistles, many-sided. The cutting knife severs without any pain. I smash the horses' teeth. Grass blades in the cows' mouths. Everything is going to die, wind and venture little endure, endure little and maybe don't endure at all, you, walls and roofs, listen closely to what I'm saying, volcanoes die, peacocks cease their cry, everything is going to die and only they are left, thanks to them you are, I am, we are, here they are: floating, a flock of squares, winged, above the checkerboard of death, without bottom or edge, the zero of the end, where cries can't be heard.

It's night and it's day, it's here and it's there, I am and I am not my-self, the change, the passage, the trans, I'm going and I'm already there, I go out the window yet I'm not moving an inch, me in the middle of the tree, my arms open (two or four?), my hands open (four or two?), my heart open, What did I just say? let's go, every-body, I protect Maria de França, I love Maria de França, I set Maria de França on fire, I save Maria de França, I make the birds smaller: Maria de Franca's frightened heart beats trustingly within my lucid shadow.

Whoever reads this, consider my confusion at the scare-crow's thorny speech. I will stress here an advantage over narrators: they're dealing with characters and I'm dealing with a text. They want to illustrate the hero's character? Here they go, mustering a whole expressive arsenal to win our trust (a trust a good part of contemporary fiction attacks, calling for a new, more complex, kind of support). But if *I* want to demonstrate aspects of the book whose depths I've been sounding for so many months, a character of my own in some ways, since all it would need is to be an imaginary book and not a real one, I entrust the reader with the text itself, evidence trustworthy above all others. It's as if a novelist, by some miracle, took us to see his character in flesh and blood, in action—the character, not the mortal being it was molded on.

So it is with the two passages of the speech I have tran-scribed above, in which the mysterious tone that disconcerts me can be clearly perceived. Some unintelligible expressions in it have their origin in cartography and—one more link with the Dutch presence in the Northeast—transpose into words some of the conventions of Marcgrave's map. The letter L, for example, inverted and in a diagonal line, "tilted L, an L up-side down," stands for an uninhabited place, *domicilia deserta*. The squares represent fountains; the checkers, salt marshes. Having pointed this out, the obscure allusion to the "flock of squares" floating above the "checkerboard of death" be-comes clearer: we're simply dealing with the contrast between life and barrenness, with the hegemony of life. Still in Marcgrave, the tree symbol stands for an open field and when the scarecrow says that he's "in the middle of the tree" we are to read it as "in the middle of the field."[43]

But we have to admit that these decipherings reveal little and perhaps don't uncover what's essential. On the whole, the speech remains hermetic. Even the confession of love, intense and proud—"I protect Maria de França, I love Maria de França"—has an ambiguous side to it. Why is the shadow enveloping her frightened heart "lucid?" Who is the Bright Shield talking about when he refers to "they," in the feminine, who hold us "above the checker (or salt marshes) of death, with no bottom or edge?" Filled with riddles, the scarecrow's speech baffles me, a lengthy enigma planted in the novel, stone in my path, mysterious deck of cards.

JUNE 10—In the middle of the night, half awake, I spy on myself, I, a man fast asleep. The infernal speech is still going on inside me, unfolding in countless ramifications.

JULY 8—My eye problem strikes once again and interrupts the normal course of my life for almost a month. I didn't read or write anything during this time. It won't matter, then, if I prolong the interruption a little longer and talk, tomorrow or later, about the last weeks before I return to *The Queen*. Now that I think about it, the experience I went through and, if such a name fits them, the reflections that assailed me are not entirely extraneous to the book I'm trying to analyze and to my own analysis. They complement both texts, and simply going back to my essay as if nothing had happened would seem contrived.

JULY 10—I'm not going to describe how the attack manifested itself. I will simply say that it was the strongest yet and that I was under the effect of painkillers most of the time. When I emerged from my lethargy my niece, Alcmena, arrived from

---

[43]Other conventions of Marcgrave's: a circle with a point in the center and a cross on top: water mill with a chapel; without the cross: without a chapel; without the central point: the mill is turned by oxen; circle with four cardinal lines: corral. (Cf. Luís da Câmara Cascudo, *op. cit.*, 188-89.)

Espíritu Santo to assist me for a few days (she had to leave before I recovered my vision, so I had to resign myself to listening to her), was reading, in that slightly husky and ever so soft voice of hers, writings that insinuated in my soul images both luxurious and terrible: *Journal of the Plague Year* by Defoe, and, in a French translation, scattered writings by Dürer, including the journal of his travels to the Lowlands, in 1520, in which the artist is constantly talking about paintings, civil and religious buildings, food, wines and various foreign currencies.

Tainted by the texts I listened to, I, floating in a verbal space, a foreign city someone described and which because of this existed, believed myself a victim of the plague who had forgotten his own name. Day after day, I offered pieces of brocade and delicacies (echoes, still, of the merry Christmas in Serra Negra?) to anyone who would bring me my identification papers; nobody understood me and still I thought I would survive, would triumph over the plague and that the gates of the city would open, freeing me, if I could only remember my name. But I couldn't, even though—contradictions of the fever—I knew who I was; the scarecrow's speech, deafening and with a life of its own, thundered in the darkness and there was, just imagine, there was a moment in which, losing all sense of my previous life, I recognized myself in the middle of the doomed city, my arms open, beaks of birds (or of the speech?) plucking my eyes out, tumors all over my body, and these tumors were the speech again, painful and, even though pounded into my body, untouchable, beyond any comprehension. At one point, I realized: the key was there, near, within my grasp, here. Saddened and awestruck, I exclaimed: "I'll find out?!" But the revelation slipped away and this filled me with great joy.

JULY 11—Don't think that yesterday's notes sum up my long month of immobility. For example, I didn't mention a valuable detail. Dürer writes: "art is lost very easily, and it takes countless prayers and a very long time to find it again." In the desolation of the plague, I inquired about my identity and, in the course of this search, I was trying to find some lost art again, moved by Dürer's sentence. Identity and art were becoming confused.

More than once I heard voices I identified as belonging to the novel's characters. I can still hear Maria de França's: lilting, coarse, a little frightened, but turning fright into sarcasm and defiance.

JULY 12—I seriously doubt that the spiritual blindness of so many characters, from King Oedipus to Riobaldo, is accidental. The fact that the truth they never—or only very late—see is within the grasp of these beclouded characters makes this phenomenon more intriguing. The hero lives with the revelation without recognizing it. What is the frightening recurrence of this motif due to? To the fact that it evokes our own blindness in the presence of the hieroglyphs that surround us.

To fight against the pride that at times assails me, to deny the mystery of the text; the way so many times we reject, in other fields, the mystery of things.

JULY 14—Convalescing, doing everything with parsimony, my senses are getting sharper. Last night, reading the *Metamorphoses* aloud, I discovered some passionate inflections I had never discerned in myself before and which didn't agree with Ovid's text. If I look at the mass of buildings from the window, I also make discoveries, like those two steeples on the right—I don't know of what church—and some ancient roofs. Yesterday a crane which today has disappeared was moving behind those roofs. Normally I wouldn't notice the difference: I would have forgotten about the crane and the large yellow bird that alighted on one of the steeples. I regret not being able to explore this temporary sharpness. All surfaces shine as if they were enameled and even faint colors blind me.

Note: just like old and very sick people, lately I've been watching myself more than usual. As if I distrusted myself, as if I feared that something was happening inside me. I'm invading my book and my friend's with this more than I had wanted. Back off, if possible.

JULY 15—The mobility, the uncertainty, the fusion—the cities of Recife and Olinda crossing over into one another—the iconography of the Dutch invasion somehow projecting the urban landscape through Time and, also, the element of threat, contained in the gigantism of the birds, all this transfigures the setting in *The Queen of the Prisons of Greece*, making it unique, original, specific to this work and entirely renewed by the imagination.

But perhaps there would be the risk of too big a gap between the space of the novel and ordinary space, in spite of the numerous allusions to the two real cities, to traditional buildings—such as the monastery of São Bento in Olinda or the Court House in Recife—and to real street names: Amparo, Concórdia, Príncipe, Sol. There was also the danger of a truncation or, at least, an attenuation of the connection between this magical space and the theme of destitution, whose importance in the book is undeniable. Julia M. Enone skillfully eliminates both possibilities by a new singularity: the central character's appraisal of the urban debris.

JULY 16—The way in which this appraisal is made exudes irony. Maria de França, living on the edge of starvation and lacking the means to adequately provide for herself, repre - sents the majority of the Brazilian population, or, in wider terms, two thirds of the world. Limited by her condition, she's insensitive to the silverware and china displayed in the shops, to cars, luxury homes, good fabrics, restaurants and everything that denotes abundance: she only grasps paucity. Perhaps this trait contradicts a general phenomenon, the hypnotic power of the superfluous dazzling the poor nowadays. The echoes of this novelistic find, however, seem more important to me than the simple record of a proven distortion and, as far as I can tell, typical of epochs like ours. For Maria de França, totally limited by a frugal existence, richness and luxury, in-accessible in every way, escape even her perception.

JULY 17—But is it really true that the needy's indifference to wealth lacks psychological value? The aboriginal African people B. L. Magyar lived with for eight years was indifferent to phenomena like eclipses of the sun because they didn't grasp their importance.[44] For Jean-Paul Sartre, the work exists only on the level of the reader's capability;[45] beyond this, an education would be required to shed any further light on it. As far as wealth goes, the understanding of wealth, one could ask if such an education is not being provided by advertising. If it were, this instrument of capitalism, generating, at first, an erroneous notion of possessions and necessities—as it tends to happen, in the beginning, with any apprenticeship—will have a subversive role in the long run.

JULY 18—Okay. Let's go back to Maria de França, for whom there is so much abundance in Recife that it runneth over. If you have any doubts, check the garbage cans before the Sanitation Department trucks go through the downtown streets and, in the outskirts—since class differences manifest themselves in the most unexpected ways—the horse-drawn wagons. Unfortunately all this richness, she realizes, is going to waste for lack of care and method. If the things put out in the cans for pickup were properly sorted out, how many notions shops the discarded buttons could supply, and how many broths would the chicken legs make! Such sorting, she observes, doesn't occur to those who put out the garbage; thus, every treasure included in the trash, clean in itself, dirties the other; even a piece of soap or a metal scouring pad, things meant for cleaning and therefore hygienic, will ruin the leftovers of a soup.

She realizes that many people don't know the distinction between pure and mixed—between sterile and dirty—and twice she describes the joy of the poor contending with flocks of vultures and stray dogs—in the garbage dumps that the Sanitation Department, poorly served by incinerators, erects in some points of the city—for the goods there offered.

Seeing a pig grunting in the muddy alleys of the periphery, hens scratching in the garbage dump, or some wretched horse roaming through the brush, she gets, discreet at first and then barely held in check, this notion of prodigality. But, even more

---

[44] Quoted by Ernest Grassi, *Arte e Mito* [Art and Myth], trans. Manuela Pinto dos Santos (Lisbon: Livros do Brasil, n.d.), 41.
[45] *Situations II* (Paris: Gallimard, 1948), 96.

significant, she doesn't take into account the birds in the air (possible prey), or the trees on the public streets (free firewood), which confirms the intention, ironic, of representing the producers of garbage as dispensers of goods.

Oblivious to birds and trees, the scarce flowers in the parks, and rain water, she gratefully inventories the goods scattered over the street and sidewalks, cigarette butts or pencil stubs, loose screws, string, pieces of ribbon, rubber heels, broken combs, empty popcorn bags, chocolate wrappers, soda and medicine bottle caps, fabric samples, twisted paper clips, bent pins, plastic flowers without stems, empty match boxes, burnt-out light bulbs, dull razor blades, dead batteries, all these trifles we are usually so indifferent to, and which her eye, turned to roving out of necessity, appraises as if they were sterling.

JULY 19—Russian and North American astronauts are linking up 656,000 feet above the Earth. Once more the waters sacrifice entire towns of the Northeast, some practically erased from the map, the Capibaribe floods 80 percent of Recife and 700,000 people are stricken, leaving 35,000 homeless, without mentioning the destroyed houses, the 620 miles of railroads washed away by the the flood, the 100 known casualties and the threat of epidemics.

This is not the only mournful news spilling out of the newspapers into my book, invading it. The obsolete equipment of Rio de Janeiro's Central do Brasil train station causes a disaster of huge proportions, with derailment, 11 dead and 372 injured; the cold sweeping over the south-central part of the country kills homeless in the cities and causes the most devastating freeze ever suffered by Brazilian agriculture, bringing about unemployment and a disastrous drop in the production of wheat and coffee (immediate speculation, with an increase of several points, on the stock markets of London and New York).

JULY 20—I'm going to counterbalance yesterday's entry: the President of the Republic has signed the law creating IMBEL, a company destined to manufacture war material, an event that was greeted enthusiastically by the private sector. The sales director of Rossi, traditional supplier of the army, exemplifies the euphoria of this branch of industry when he declares: "This week in Brasília I told three generals they can even ask for a bomb. We'll make it right away."

She will turn thirty in two weeks, on August 6. She measured exactly 13 feet, 9 inches; five feet in diameter. Five thousand men, over a period of two years, were enslaved to this machine, complex, demanding and even delicate in all her 10,000 pounds. Although there was nothing superfluous in her (she was a creature of our times, fond of pure lines and averse to frills), her heart or soul, the living part—the one capable of killing—weighed perhaps not even 45 pounds. When she exploded, raising an incandescent column, as fiery, irate and dazzling a being as could ever have been imagined or feared, higher than the highest mountain, earth and sky yielded, water was no more, the flames poured down the course of rivers, 70,000 buildings came crashing down and, among the 240,000 dead, if this really deserves the old name of death, all that was left of some was a shadow on the barren ground. On August 6 it will be 30 years since it happened. Only 470 to go for the effects of the explosion to wear off. The plane that carried the thing (who remembers anymore?) was called *Enola Gay*. The name of the city is also beginning to pale in the world's conscience and so it must be written: Hiroshima.

JULY 21—Looking at the map of Recife one is aware of the presence of water. But it's only flying over it that one can see how flat and wet the city is. Besides the sea which seems to dominate it and the large mangrove swamps—with their sickly dwellings balanced on stilts and upon which the brightest sun, when it is reflected, loses its luster—a livid and dirty hole, there are the rivers, several of them. Before becoming what it is now, the plain, submerged or nearly submerged, was crossed by rivers nearing the end of their journey, connected by channels. The smaller rivers originated in the plain and the larger ones came from afar, from the Mata or the Agreste regions, like the Beberibe and the Capibaribe. Visitors can go to Recife and not see the other rivers; impossible, however, to ignore the Capibaribe, native of the Borborema plateau, which flows through the heart of the city, winding through hills of clay and sand.

Well then, the motif of squandered wealth—real or imaginary, apprehensible or not—always linked to the junk thrown out in the streets, allows the author, via Maria de França, amazing variations on this river, recording not only the animals and things

(is this a mattress? a mattress sailing along, a treasure, who knows if it doesn't contain, along with the bedbugs, money stashed in its straw?)

but also the waste that industry poisons the river's waters with, and it climaxes with the apparently exalted—actually, sarcastic—inventory of goods born by the Capibaribe, transformed, through the anomalous appraisal of someone who has nothing of value, into treasures up for grabs.

Those who live by its banks get used to seeing dead animals and debris floating down the stream: heavy rains at the headwaters or anywhere along its course. In addition, everybody is aware—and the latest news only confirms it—of the threat this river, scenic and tranquil, represents for Recife. In the flash floods—whose proportions have grown to such an extent over the last decade that the safe areas are decreasing and the damages are increasing, and an inundation which will turn the capital into a heap of mud is in the forecasts (which shouldn't be viewed as a pure coincidence or a natural disaster)—the Capibaribe carries along, disjointed, the worlds it crosses. Plantations, small and large livestock, of hide and feather, dwellings—the timberwork and the household goods —people, what don't you see in this deluge? and even an anonymous weir loosened from its moorings can thicken the water of the flood with its water lilies and fish.

July 24—Yes, along with the flotsam and jetsam from the streets, the debris rolling into the Capibaribe and the sea's invasion of Recife, live and dead fish entering through the windows, snakes coiling in the cornices, overturned cars in the trees, things torn out of place and drifting in this muddy stream smelling of putrid rats, everything exactly like the images in the papers and on TV these last few days, at one point in Julia Marquezim Enone's book a huge and misshapen creature flies past, a weir. Amidst the chaos of the flood Maria de França tries to make out the blurred outline of this lost reservoir. This motif, launched as if by accident, more than once taken up again and never developed systematically, as if the immensity of the image precluded further amplifications, transcends the theme of squandered wealth and also prompts an observation.

In spite of the links persisting between them and their common origin, there are contrasts that don't escape the novelist between the debris carried by the river and the little things thrown in the street, bestowed, in the sense that garbage, in Maria de França's conception, is bestowed upon people in general. The owners give up what, in principle, is no longer of use to them (hence the gratefulness of our factory worker and maid); the terrestrial animals, the furniture, the pieces of fence or roofing reach the mouth of the river against their owners' will. The irony here doesn't come from the intentional mistake of seeing a gift in the distracted gesture of discarding something that has already been used; it's born of an obliteration, still intentional, of discernment: what comes tumbling down the putrid waters of the flood is exalted as a sign of abundance and not of ruin.

Suggestions of another order and, in a manner of speaking, inexhaustible, are contained in the image of the weir submerged in the river, its boundaries invading the river and being obliterated by it. Here we echoed the same play of mutual penetrations previously noted in the space of the novel and clearly expressed in the fusion Recife/Olinda.[46] Two images stand out, in my opinion, in the voluminous mass, liquid, amorphous, without borders, to which the character-narrator wants to attribute a form: one is that of the novel itself, a world immersed in the world, penetrated by it and penetrating it, while an active consciousness maintains the

---

[46]These invasions, involving different areas of reality and taking place, at times, halfway between reality and imagination, represent in *The Queen of the Prisons of Greece* a constant among the most expressive, a veiled and engrossing theme running through the novel.

limits of the work conceptually; the other is that of the consciousness, lost in the immensity surrounding it and trying to remain whole. This consciousness, in this case, belongs to all of us and, at the same time, it has a name of its own: the weir that has come with the flood, from somewhere in the Mata or Agreste region, is called Maria de França.

JULY 29—If the brief allusions to the insignificant objects abandoned in the street and the junk seen in the Capibaribe follow the heroine's wanderings, this is not the case when she mentions the flood and the weir. It's as if, in the privileged time of the novel, the external, real time, ours, were evoked by means of catastrophe and this huge image; or as if in the imaginary Recife, invulnerable to wear and tear, flickered the memory of the mortal city, of which it—the Recife of the book—is the reflection. But this impossible weir transmigrated from the novel becomes part, in its turn, of the real city.

AUGUST 1—I was waiting for a bus in front of the Municipal Library when I saw a tall man in a white suit cross the street and head slowly toward the Mappin shopping mall, elbowed by the crowd. The way he was dressed, contrary to custom in this humid and sooty city, was the first thing that caught my eye about the man, besides his height. I followed him from a distance, drawn by an irresistible curiosity that seemed natural to me. He crossed the first floor of Mappin without paying attention to the merchandise on display, went on to Barão de Itapetininga, crossed over to the other side of the street. In spite of his height, the crowd was such that I lost sight of him. He turned at the curb, slightly stooped, his long arms almost reaching his knees: he was the very picture of the black man Rônfilo Rivaldo. The same pockmarked skin, the slicked-back hair, the expression half benevolent and half sly, the rotten teeth. He looked at me, then turned and walked away, moving his long legs more briskly, as if he urgently needed to reach Praça da República. Only then, and even then only fleetingly, since several vehicles came between us, did I see that a slight woman, whose face I couldn't make out and who was doing her best to keep up with him, was by his side.

AUGUST 5—The natural, so to speak, sequence of these notes was meant to lead us, through the examination of the remarkable space invented by Julia M. Enone, to the problem of time interwoven with it, so much so that, at times, I avoided discussing—straying from the plan I had conceived—its nature in *The Queen of the Prisons of Greece* only by dint of artifice, as at the points in which the war scenes arise anachronistically. But literary composition, as we know, has its whims and it can happen that a different notion of logic—more discreet and, in some circumstances, more relevant—will subvert the plan for the structure.

Here, this notion is a kind of play between the concrete and incursions into the abstract, an oscillation, my friends, like the one presiding so many times over travel books, in which snapshots of the landscape and meditations on the people, when not on the traveler himself, alternate. Wouldn't hinting at the space of the novel and, without any break, its time, be carrying too far the oscillatory movement in the direction of the abstract, and thus cause a certain arrhythmia, contradicting what I had established?

This principle, a little vague, doesn't presume in my case to establish the parameters for a debatable ability in the execution of the work. Like the "inhabitant of another world," Bioy Casares's "catfish," who couldn't stand dry air and survived only as long as a fountain was kept in his hiding place, I breathe abstractions with difficulty and try to return, without very long intervals, to a more humid atmosphere.[47]

Let's put off the ruminations on time in *The Queen*, then. I will return, with the reader's indulgence and perhaps to his relief, to the people of the novel.

AUGUST 6—Mr. Reinhold Stephanes admits that the service provided by I.N.P.S., currently under his direction, "in São Paulo is inferior, overall, to that of all the states of the south-central regions," but he announced "serious and urgent measures."

---

[47]"El calamar opta por su tinta," in *Historias Fantásticas* (Buenos Aires: Emecé Editores, 1972).

The commotion, here, in several branch offices, which open at seven in the morning, begins the day before, at dusk, when the first patients start forming a line, where they spend the night. In Tatuapé, when the window opens, there are usually five or six thousand people, coming from several peripheral neighborhoods on the east side. Eighteen hundred of these receive assistance and the rest go back home, to other offices or else, enraged, respond with shouts and at times even throw rocks at the employees.

In spite of the "many things that have already been done in this area," as the Minister of Social Welfare Nascimento e Silva said last May, "there is still much to be done."

AUGUST 7—At the beginning we outlined the profiles of Antônio Áureo, Belo Papagaio, Dudu and Rônfilo, showing their connection with the chiromantic scheme of the book. Later other figures crossed our pages, with greater or lesser prominence, according to the degree with which I reacted to them, but always incidentally. If he was paying attention, the reader will have gathered that in Julia Marquezim Enone's book, whose central character endlessly wanders through streets, courtrooms, doctor's offices, government bureaus, jobs and the Mental Hospital on top of that, there lives a small crowd (twenty-seven characters contribute to the creation of the Súpeto), and that in it happens what's inevitable in densely populated novels, where the construction of the characters is urgent and summary and only four or five are developed—if this many. The deduction is correct, but the case at hand presents a less schematic picture.

What we have said about the relationships between the structure of the novel and chiromancy suggests a tendency to allusions, notably allusions to clusters, more than to isolated people or things. Where is the author going to draft her characters? Where are her models? Many of the people she hated or loved (did she ever hate anybody?), she was acquainted with, or simply saw one day, inhabited my friend's soul: more than once she told me how she remembered the traits of strangers she had run into on the street many years before. But the discipline with which she organizes *The Queen* doesn't allow the book to be turned into a mere gallery of the memory. We've seen, for example, the literary origins of Belo Papagaio, largely molded on an obscure and remote adventurer of the seas; and those of the protegé of Albert Magnus, inquisitor and martyr, the illiterate Rônfilo, developed with fairly complex intentions.

AUGUST 8—Rônfilo Rivaldo, who once again provokes my speculations, illustrates how diverse the convergent lines of a literary work are and how such diversity always corresponds to the ambition of the plan. Pedagogue and clairvoyant, he turns, abruptly and without this change influencing the course of events, into a quack odontologist. What's the meaning of this development?

Superstition and science, it's true, didn't always exclude one another. I am reminded of the founder of the Academy of Secrets in Naples, Giovanni Battista della Porta, who died in 1615; an alchemist, he also left works on optics, the elasticity of air, pneumatics and atmospheric pressure. Rônfilo Rivaldo's "scientific" metamorphosis, should it have in view this concili-ation of mental tendencies, brings us to origins and purposes which can't be integrated in the coherent framework I've been uncovering. This supposition is fertile for the study of the novelistic process. "Those who believe that all fragments of a narration are born of the same intention and converge, in perfect harmony, in whatever direction, are wrong. The work alone receives and justifies what is associated with it, nothing else. One object, yet capricious, apt to assimilate foreign bod-ies, it is molded by the writer's multiple interests in everything that—of importance or without a clear value—left a lasting mark in his soul."[48]

Even more fertile, in this light, is the presupposition that Rônfilo Rivaldo's new profession, illegal, has no meaning. The introduction of a motif may be a gesture of love, cyphered, decodable only by its true recipient; it may remain in the work like the seashell picked up during a morning stroll which we

---

[48]From J.M.E.'s papers. I don't know whether this observation is hers or if she copied the fragment quoted above from some book.

keep, trying—to no avail, as you know—to preserve the sound of the sea and the shadow of the morning; it may be chosen for its rarity or, on the contrary, its exemplary banality; it may be destined to break up a series, disrupting its harmony and thus disorienting us.

AUGUST 10—Very different reasons from those leading to the creation of Rônfilo Rivaldo—and, also, more superficial in their schematicism—govern the selection, manufacture and conveyance of the specimens representing the bureaucratic world in the book. In *Ulysses*, Joyce brings the heroes of the *Odyssey* to the Dublin of 1904, reducing them to a farcical and deplorable level. Chaste Penelope? Her name is Marion Tweedy: a veritable slut. Fearsome Ulysses? Who but Bloom the cuckold. Nausicaa: the crippled Gertie McDowell. Circe: Bella Cohen, procuress. Julia Marquezim Enone brings to Recife heroes (who knows how real?) of the history of Brazil, condemning them to an obscure and completely anonymous life.

The Iron Marshal comes to life again, with no power, uniform or rank, in Flor, the errand boy,

an asthmatic wheeze, the look of a dead man and a vengeful heart, but who is he going to take revenge on if he can't remember who he's after?

Rio Branco punches in and the revolving chair squeaks under his weight. Arrogant and perfumed, busy with the way the desks are arranged, he's constantly looking outside—a not so subtle allusion to his ardent desire to be admired in Europe —oblivious to the files sleeping in the drawers and his duties as department head. Rachitic, enervated, vain, smelling of camphor, convinced he knows "by heart" all the case numbers he keeps "in his pumpkin head" and always wrong, Rui Barbosa—Barbosa Neto—with no chance of rising to the presidency of the Republic from his wretched archives, has forgotten all about the Civilian Campaign and become a fanatic supporter of militarism:

I'm ashamed of being honest. The Fatherland is an extended family, and therefore it's only run by the sword and the gun.

Of the model consecrated by tradition, the proliferating rhetoric, pompously displayed even at the teller window, has survived:

Take this paper, convey this letter, be the bearer of this document, and, yesterday as today, now as always, always as ever, insist on laying claim to your rights, in demanding what's yours, in fighting for your prerogatives, in vindicating your claims.

Even Dom Pedro II, a myth of benevolence and love of learning, appears now and then, coming from the warehouse, white beard, a cap—abridgement of the crown?—side by side with the republican leaders, always admiring the telephone, already old and still working as a substitute and trying to inflict upon his associates a small collection of sonnets. Even more touching, but drawn with no less caustic a stroke, is the transparent figure of Santos, the accountant: the desk and the chair he occupies, placed on a platform, are, in addition to this, higher than the others. Staring into space, oblivious to the petitioners filing by the counters, he's constantly reworking his plans for a hot-air balloon, without realizing that the era of balloons has passed and that, having arrived too late, his only prize in the world will be anonymity. But perhaps he sees things clearly in the end: like his model, he commits suicide.

AUGUST 13—It is said that if Homer's poem is resurrected in Joyce in a degraded form it is because our world is incapable of creating another *Odyssey*. Would Julia Marquezim Enone likewise suggest, with mordancy and disenchantment, that nowadays we're not capable of creating heroes like yesterday's? A reasonable hypothesis that the examination of our present reality seems to sanction. The last national heroes arose half a century ago and have since sunk into oblivion, routine or disrepute. When they died the news passed us by—the way a breeze passes—and it's possible that some died without the country knowing it. One of them, survivor of a small group of eighteen who took to the streets in 1924, weapons in hand, willing to die and perhaps even wishing for an enemy's bullet, in the heart if possible, so that the flow of life wouldn't deny the splendor of that unique moment, would cross the country twenty years later, enveloped in his still living legend, which he himself would begin to forget before everybody else. Heroes wouldn't even be born from the smoke of World War II. Many were killed and lie in Pistoia, buried with their names, nobody knows where the survivors have gone, and the names of those who led them mean nothing to us. Political activity has led many to exile, death and the business world—and the truth is that, among all of these, only the latter still preserve a certain mythical splendor. This shouldn't be surprising. National heroes, nowadays, all confined to television and professional sports, earn in one day more than anybody eats in a year. To make things worse, these myths of ours, without a single exception, profess an absolute indifference toward all the problems afflicting humanity. None, unlike heavyweight Cassius Clay, would risk his career and title for anything in the world —for a cause, or a principle, or an idea, or out of obstinacy. Neutrality, an equivocal luxury, is their norm and this doesn't diminish in the least the opinion the general public has of them.

AUGUST 14—Yes, this rather sad phenomenon may well have contributed to the degraded resurgence of some myths of our national history in *The Queen*, my friend's solution thus showing some similarity to Joyce's, on a smaller scale. I'm always afraid to risk hypotheses and interpretations. We are interpreting a literary work and, a circumstance to be taken into account, a work still unpublished. Thus the risk of limiting the range of its meanings is amplified, as little as my authority (nonexistent, anyway) might be.

AUGUST 15—The commentators established an allegorical interpretation for the Sacred Scriptures, which was soon sanctioned and has continued throughout the centuries. Even Homer was allegorically interpreted, in the debatable effort to legitimize his poems as the fruit of wisdom. According to Melanchthon, Luther's friend, he founded astronomy and philosophy when he described Achilles' shield. The same process would involve the author of the *Aeneid*, "replete with learning," as Servius, whom I read years ago, says. A complex trajectory, traceable only by means of lengthy studies, has the pagan and biblical allegorism converge in the Middle Ages, where its authority is undisputed. Those who are interested in this topic know that this conciliatory effort, not limited to the two great epic poets of antiquity, had already set in by the third century. Clement of Alexandria sees in Solon and Empedocles intimations of God. Hercules, Samson and David, in some ways, would become confused. The conciliatory effort would be disputed and finally repudiated. But the notion of literary work as allegory would endure, untouchable—and, later, a whole doctrine would be created to justify the need for allegory:

a) reason, incapable of comprehending divine matters, could only grasp them by means of allegorical mediation;

b) allegory, depending on a master or decipherer, remained veiled to those unworthy of the truth.

AUGUST 16—Rejecting the second postulate (b) and deliberately illustrating the first (a), an anonymous text of the time, the *Quest for the Holy Grail*, attests to the resonances of this phenomenon. The characters, incapable of interpreting the events they come face to face with, always receive the corresponding explanation from others, depositaries of knowledge. "This lady we understand to be the Holy Church, which keeps Christianity in the true faith and is Jesus Christ's wealth. The other lady, who had been disinherited and had declared war against her, is the Ancient Law, the enemy always warring against the Holy Church and its supporters."

A tale from the *Disciplina Clericalis*, that of the converted Jew Pedro Alfonso, tells of a man who went on a journey and his wife, who during his absence received a lover in the house. When the man returns unexpectedly, his mother-in-law stalls him by showing him an embroidered blanket, from behind which the intruder escapes. Preachers explained the story in this way: the husband, traveling abroad, represented the Christian, eternal pilgrim on earth; the adulteress, lust and vice; the husband's return, repentance, prayer and fasting; the evil mother-in-law, the sinful world, which blinds the man with the blanket of vanities and pleasures.

The *Quest for the Holy Grail* harbors this kind of interpretation and, in the words of an essayist, "contains its own gloss."

But, in spite of this rendition—who knows how truthful?—the story sets its snares and, quoting the same scholar, who has some interesting thoughts on the matter,[49] "within one system of interpretation, several meanings are offered." That is, even appearing to accept the authority of the anagogic interpretation, to the point of incorporating it, the anonymous narrator, within the clear-cut symbology adopted, leaves open alternatives that are at times in conflict with it.

AUGUST 17—Such alternatives are linked, deliberately or not, to a fundamental artistic problem, that of the meaning of the work (or of given parts). What does the reduction of so many Brazilian myths to the gray bureaucratic life mean? What does Ulysses' transformation into an insignificant Dubliner mean? A few answers tempt the observer. Correct ones? No. There are no absolute answers, in this case, but rather possible answers. Not even the author is a reliable witness: he doesn't control his creation entirely, in which obscure elements subsist. This doesn't keep us from venturing hypotheses impossible to confirm. What matters is that they're recognized as a testimony of the work's effect on the mind of the observer and not as a deciphering that reduces it to a coded—and therefore limited—message that goes against the nature of the artistic object, which is never a depository of meaning but rather a detonator of meanings.

---

[49]*De amore et dilectione Dei et proximi*, by the Dominican Lazarus of Padua (1313-1370), facsimile edition in the journal *Drum* 2.4 (Spring 1972): 80. It is said that Lazarus had become so impregnated with the *Quest for the Holy Grail* that he *emanated* the text: those who knew him ended up by knowing the story as well, even though they didn't hear one single word about it from him. In addition, he had incorporated the book into his daily life, and he saw symbols he couldn't resist explaining in everything: "If there are four of you receiving me and you welcome me with two windows of this room closed and the one in the center wide open, this means . . ." The most curious thing is that, according to the tradition, Lazarus of Padua attracted cryptic phenomena: a lion which had escaped from a group of mountebanks entered the refectory where he was eating, his wine, when knocked over, spilled in the shape of a scimitar, etc.

This even if it takes on a precise meaning in the creator's mind.

AUGUST 19—Thus, it is shielded by my freedom as reader, and without closing myself off to other interpretations, that I suppose there is a caustic intent or even a provocation in the motif discussed. A personal quirk, and therefore without any critical validity, inclines me toward this hypothesis: Julia M. Enone, despite all her reading, was, without forcing or flaunting it, a woman of the people, with a talent for speaking in its name, to see from its side, which writers never achieve. Inversely, Brazil's national idols, those consecrated with monuments and their names on public streets (what Brazilian town doesn't have a Rua Barão do Rio Branco and a Praça Marechal Deodoro?), if they accomplished memorable feats, always kept their distance from the people, and their indifference toward the humble resembles that of today's heroes—athletes and TV stars. Immersed in aristocratic dreams, abstract ideals moved them; or ideals of power; or none. It's the official apparatus, recognizing them, for different reasons, as their servants, that would bring them to what Talleyrand calls "lay canonization."

Julia Marquezim Enone pulls them down from their pedestals, deprives them of titles, wealth and vestments—if military, of epaulettes and weapons—changes or corrupts their names and throws them into the limbo of public service, more or less in the same way Dante puts his enemies in Hell. All are physically and morally identifiable by an attentive reader.[50] But, eliminating the circumstances that favored them (where would the Duke of Caxias earn his fame if there were never a Paraguayan War and, consequently, a battle of Humaitá or Lomas Valentinas?), there they are, at counters and filing cabinets, anonymous, out of step with the world and anxious, as if they were aware of their divestiture, these legendary men, now ousted from the legend and only slightly bigger than Maria de França.

---

[50]This allows us to appraise, once more, the reach of the literary work, off-limits, in some of its aspects, to the reader of other latitudes.

AUGUST 20—Should I add that these disfigured figures are nothing but extras and that, in the final analysis, taken all together they form a larger entity, the bureaucratic mass, incarnation—out of touch, anachronistic, confused—of the out-of-touch, anachronistic, confused social welfare system? Alone, none has the life nor the strength radiated by Belo Papagaio or even Antônio Áureo, the ghost. Even so, in the subordinate position the book's plan allows them, they breathe: tangible and impalpable both, they play on our credulity, they win us over. Why? What hoax overcomes our certainty of their nonexistence and disarms us?

Some writers, who Julia Enone found irritating, talk about characters who walked in through the door and demanded a place in the book being written. "What are they trying to say? That they're clairvoyants?" Her reaction was justifiable: the only door through which a character, be it main or secondary, enters is the craft, "repertory of solutions, common or surprising, by which the novelist attains certain results," according to Norman's pragmatic definition.[51]

As for me, for a long time now I've been finding an additional pleasure, heightened by our life together, in following our author in the task of creating a character. Those who have read *Tristram Shandy* will remember how Sterne leaves a blank page in the book for the readers to draw the gorgeous widow Wadman, thus making them collaborators in the work. An illusory collaboration, skillfully directed by Sterne: we never saw, he says, an object that excites the senses so; the portrait must be as close to our mistress as possible; and in no way at all resemble our wife. In the wake of Lessing, his contemporary, for whom the detailed description of feminine beauty is useless and always inferior to ideal beauty, he doesn't want to tell us what the widow's lips or knees were like. All he wants—and gets, by this artifice—is to excite our imagination and evoke a sensual atmosphere around this desirable woman. He doesn't neglect to add:

---

[51]C. D. Norman, *The Novel and Its Problems* (Manchester: Typhom, 1971), 121.

Was ever anything in Nature so sweet!—so exquisite!
—Then, dear Sir, how could my uncle Toby resist it?

Cunning Sterne! Your clever maneuver diverges so much from the laborious process set in motion by Dostoyevsky to describe Raskolnikov! I tried (I needed to efface this imaginary creature whose manner bewildered me, could there be something of me in him?) to follow the tangle of knots that causes him to exist. I saw how the author begins the novel, putting Raskolnikov in motion—"a slow, irresolute step"—a man of action, then proceeding to sketch out the sordid place where he lives and his uneasiness when he runs into the landlady, an inexplicable fact for the future murderer: he's planning "such a terrible act!" Knowing what the character thinks, what he feels, his secret decisions, doesn't oblige the narrator to understand the "indistinct words" he mutters. I see, Fyodor Mikhailovich: your purpose, more than introducing the character, is to instill a feeling of incompatibility; and the path you choose, you old trickster, is to insist on physical discomfort, the heat, the hunger, the heavy air, the people crowding between scaffoldings, the piles of lime, the stench, the dark halls, and you don't even spare us this low blow—to allege that the picture was "mournfully repellent." I saw this and more, I followed the tracks of this composition rich in details and, after all this, having reconstituted the master's clear-sighted and solid operation as much as possible, I find again, as disturbing as before, with the same dubious energy, the murderer of Lizaveta and Alyona Ivanovna.

AUGUST 26—But the equivocal blank page on which some naive reader, taking the invitation seriously, will draw Sterne's beautiful widow, and the invisible observer shamelessly following the student's steps in Petersburg, knowing everything of what he must know and speaking for both, are just two instances—the first inimitable—of a complex art, practiced by craftsmen. Everything in the novel, complicated, cunning machine (the novel doesn't surrender itself in a day, doesn't reveal itself through idleness and is not born of woman), everything in it is fabricated and requires artifice. Creating a character doesn't simply mean being able to see it but also choosing an attitude and a modus operandi in relation to it, urging the potential reader toward a calculated vantage point, an emotional as well as spatial position: the density and the tone of the information governing the way the figures are arranged in the whole, here the main characters and in the background of the painting, anonymous, at times, the extras.

J. M. Enone, as if she were certain of her untimely death and avidly struggling to mature, manifests an awareness of this problem, an aptitude and a diversity of methods above the current standards. Could she have written and destroyed other novels she never spoke of? In order to give consistency to the multitude in her book she makes use of significant names, brief emblematic traits, leisurely descriptions or, inversely, epitomes, accumulates or disperses, feigns objectivity or allows herself to get involved, everything with a keen sense of gradation and a skilled hand. Each figure receives a treatment that situates it, clear-cut or diffused, in the whole.

I'm not going to enumerate these methods. What for? Masterly and diversified as they might be, I have already seen them and will see them again in other works.

AUGUST 27—"All I want: to write a book. Just that. Will I be worthy of it?" (From J.M.E.'s papers.)

AUGUST 28—Maria de França's anomalous consciousness, capable of invading other people's souls, transcends the ordinary constraints of space and time, a foreseeable phenomenon in this novel of permutations, *where everything invades everything*, it being inevitable for the internal laws of the work to lead to invasions of a cultural order. But if Maria de França's diction to some extent reveals her personality, as tradition prescribes, it undergoes constant modulations (remember the syntax of the *Manual of Composition* employed during periods of hospitalization). As a consequence, one notes a curious inversion, so daring that I venture to wonder whether the author had gauged its effect. Maria de França, narrator and character, is characterized, indeed, by means of her speech. At other times, however, through the structure of her discourse itself, made up of perverted allusions to the lexicon, tone and phraseology cultivated in the field in which other characters hold sway, *she characterizes them*. Constant targets of this game, as we have shown, are medicine and law.

The figures born of such an inadequate—yet fascinating, in its daring and slyness—method certainly tend to uniformity and never to singularity. There, too, Julia M. Enone extends the craft, superimposing upon individuals, with the stratagem of an allusive enunciation, leveling and captious, the class mask in which they obliterate themselves. But who will agree to be obliterated? To set oneself apart, then, by means of group codes, becomes the way of denying this obliteration and of simulating some sort of identity. Caustic, Julia M. Enone makes a novelistic practice strong again by displacing such debatable codes, distorted, into Maria de Franca's mouth at the same time that she chastises:

the obliteration of the individual;

the arrogance of the group;

the vacuity of the code disguising all this.

SEPTEMBER 2—He died today. His name was Orlando da Costa Ferreira and I hadn't seen this attentive and demanding reader, to whom I was linked by books, for a long time. His interest, however, more far-reaching than mine and more scholarly, went beyond texts: he was intrigued by the book and its metamorphoses. The book? Typographic characters, types of paper, engravings, archaic or modern methods of reproduction, page layout, bindings. This knowledge, which increased throughout his life, never turned into an act of possession or pride; knowing was his way of loving. He didn't collect rare books and I doubt that he coveted them, given the little sway avarice held over him, even in its nobler forms. So as not to hoard what he knew, he'd been devoting nights and Sundays for almost twenty years—twenty or more?—to a study in which he condenses everything he learned and thought about books. Now he was trying to publish it when he dies (the hell with it, Orlando!) manuscript in hand. Despite everything, his death doesn't move me as it should. I see it from a distance, you know what I mean? and all I wish, I admit, is to draw the shades, sleep a whole day and night, deaf, without being shaken awake, as has been happening, by those brutal noises whose origin I can't discover, cries, isolated shots, metal clangs, horses' hooves on the damp ground. I feel like I'm running away from myself and when I wake, the sharpest blade, the question that's been throwing me out of balance lately, surfaces: "Who am I?" Are these restless nights weakening me? What is the soul, after all, if it depends on the body so much? Your death, then, doesn't trouble me, Orlando. Good-bye. Is that all? Undo your pants, piss one last time on this country that never repaid you in any way for all you gave it and then turn your back, go on, scram. Your book is written, and well written. The end.

SEPTEMBER 5—In the same way in which the bureaucratic world is filled with our historical myths, J. M. Enone, rejecting once more the confessional line and always conceiving of her book in an allusive manner, as removed from memory as possible, peoples the asylum with figures taken from the literary world, not with the lunatics she had the opportunity to observe the two times she was hospitalized. Similarly, she doesn't transpose into the novel characters of Brazilian fiction, disguised or not, by recreating them. The cells, courtyards and infirmaries of the asylum are crowded with writers. Dead and living. From Father Anchieta to Clarice Lispector.

Some I couldn't identify. Or has she placed them there, as she always does and as happens so much in other books, to break up the series? I don't recognize the courteous and well dressed lunatic constantly talking about slaughters; or the mediocre and fat fellow with the white turban, covered with charms, who's always waving rue branches and alligator teeth in the air, with a leaf cigar in his mouth, to drive the Ancient Serpent away, or busy with black hens, I'm going to work a charm, greetings, spirits. But the dark-skinned one with his face painted with white lead, in top hat and gloves, mischievously winking, is certainly Machado de Assis; the one who thinks himself the master of a black nurse, who adorns himself with macaw feathers and dissimulates everything behind pompous sentences, is the author of *Iracema*. Who doesn't recognize the gruff and unsociable madman, parricide and uxoricide, morose, constantly growling at the sick and the sane alike, as if everybody there were a formless dog about to bite? or the unstable imaginary landowner, inspecting, counting, and appraising in the air his pastures, plantations, oxen, land grants? or the nearsighted one, with the leather cap, bow tie, rosary around his neck, silk socks and patent leather shoes, brandishing an invisible rifle with medals on its strap night and day and shouting:

"Howdy, old timer, I'm coming and I came, fear? worry? I'll fill 'em full of lead!"

who doesn't recognize him? One of the inmates, his skin blackened with coal dust, bound up in his straitjacket one and a half times, protests against everything, shouts loud enough to be heard in the street, and is obsessed with climbing walls. Look at the restless old man, haughty, with beady cynical eyes, the nose of someone sniffing out the world, his mouth a twisted and caustic gash: he wields a tin guitar and with a sharp tongue ceaselessly lashes out at the Treasurer, the Supreme Judge, the Pope, the Superintendent and the King: Gregório de Matos.

SEPTEMBER 6—The I.N.P.S. dentist in Teresina, Antônio Martins, had another employee of that institution, Antônio Ferreira da Silva, shot. A man of modest means, he paid for the murder by installments, 5,000 *cruzeiros* as the down payment, and the balance to be paid in 20 installments of 500 *cruzeiros* each. The killer, from the Military Police of Piauí, assisted by two other corps members, was reported to the authorities and apprehended hours later, without even having received the first installment. The dentist, in his deposition, admitted everything, adding that if he earned more and could find some gunmen with guts, he'd have them kill six more I.N.P.S. employees "who don't deserve to be alive."

SEPTEMBER 9—Madness and the asylum, in the *Queen of the Prisons of Greece*, go beyond the merely episodic, and their value as social commentary is irrelevant. The idea of isolation, expressed with supreme irony in the grotesquely precise syntax sterilizing Maria de França's speech when she's an inmate, goes beyond these correlated motifs, proliferating in capricious variations. The decision to fill the asylum with writers, recognizable although stripped of their names, becomes part of this motif. Out of the question, in my opinion, is the hypothesis (here's a presumptuous writer, if we accept it) that she would have thrown them into a nuthouse to suggest an inadequate perception of reality on their part. The dissociation between consciousness and reality, there, manifests itself—on the individual level, not as a general phenomenon—in the artificial and idealizing language of the romantics, especially José de Alencar's. That is: the author, as is characteristic of caricatures, expresses her attitude toward the model with the distortion of certain traits and the combination of transparent symbols. Solitary, sarcastic or ambiguous. Common to all, only solitude, segregation.

Isolation, in this case, suggests and almost demands the kind of reading Witt calls *secular*, contrasting it to *oracular* reading.[52]

SEPTEMBER 10—A writer's work prompts him to seek solitude. All forms of society are familiar to him, but there comes a day when he shuts the door and it's then, when he seems to be cutting all ties with everybody and, on top of that, practicing a language that isn't commonly used, that he joins the rest of

---

[52]"Secular: the reading that presumes to see clearly. Oracular: the reading that sees enigmas in the texts. Secular: interpretive reading. Oracular: magical reading. The Translation and the Wonder. The mask covering an uncoverable face; the mask covering a thousand possible faces" (John Williams Witt, *Positions & Suppositions* [London: Sagittarius, 1960], 13). The author's patronymic sounds familiar, reminds us of *Witt's Pills*. In fact, the quoted Witt is a direct descendant of the famous physician and, as it happens, he would marry Evelyn Bruce Ross, niece of the equally famous Doctor Ross, of the *Life Pills*. Could this explain his style, so synthetic, identical, at times, to our Oswald de Andrade's? Cf., e.g., the *Anthropophagic Manifesto*: "Anthropophagy. Absorption of the sacred enemy. To transform him into a totem. The human adventure. The wordly finality." Etc.

the world. Of course this is not a magical act, and writers can err: in the difficult solitude of their work, only a few manage to intensify and deepen the ties with everything that is, materially, far away. Unamuno, reflecting on the poetic act and social life, speaks somewhere of the "thick crust of reserve that separates us from one another" which the poet, in the solitude where lies come undone, dissolves. Maria de Franca's companions may symbolically represent the condition of voluntary recluse, peculiar to the writer in the creative act.

However, if, by dint of familiarity, we grasp the character of this novel, if the course of events manifests itself through our protracted examination, it doesn't seem to us that the writer's paradoxical maneuver—withdrawing to better delve into his relationships with his fellow men—is preponderant in the motif which is troubling me now. Julia Marquezim Enone doesn't seem to be inclined to this kind of mentality and always leaves the writer's intimate dilemmas aside in her book, since she's scarcely interested in this rather elaborate vision of the relationships between the person who's writing and everybody else, which she believed masked a vague sense of guilt. Besides, all psychology rang false to her, an attempt at self-justification and, if possible, absolution. Those who have followed us throughout this book will have gathered that her tendency with phenomena is rather toward challenge, offensive, aggression—an intriguing tendency. (At the circus she preferred the equestrian numbers to the magicians, the tightrope walkers and even the acrobats performing on the high trapeze. The horses galloping in a circle, egged on by the guy cracking his whip in the air in the middle of the ring.) Thus another view— plainer—of the writer's isolation fits better the general lines of the novel, a view turned not toward him but the society that rejects him. Such a perspective, of course, doesn't rule out the other one; it becomes superimposed upon it.

SEPTEMBER 12—No. From the velveteen to the hypotenuse, to brighten, insolent syntagma behold the ophidian, suture and knot. It's I who thus command, desire and order, I dare to. Why these twists and turns, these catlike movements? Let's attack head on, aim for the bull's eye, put our cards on the table. Julia

Marquezim Enone is her book and a few revealing sentences. And even they may not reveal, but trick, conceal. She died and I loved her, which doesn't mean I knew her. Besides being a commentary and, to some degree, a substitute for a work still inaccessible to the public, maybe this book is, who knows?, not the *testimony of someone who knew the writer* (a way of resuming our life together in an illusory way) but, on the contrary, an *attempt to know her*, yes, to unveil, by delving more deeply into her text, the person I loved and still love—the way you can love a shadow. It's also possible that this inquiry won't lead to any truth—and that I'm just constructing, on top of my friend's novel, another novel, another friend, in the image of models unknown to me and which nevertheless control me. Or maybe that which I'm trying to throw light on is my own face, like old Montaigne ("it is me I am portraying"), my face, yes, but from a different angle and with a different intent, because for a long time now (forever?) I've felt like I was running away from myself while asking without answer: "Who am I?"

SEPTEMBER 13—Whoever I am, I want to see—and, by seeing in this way, I see and make the others see the author in a certain fashion—I want to see in the lunatics of the novel, in the lunatics' confinement, mainly, the dark and raw side of the business of writing, the condition of the writer in some country where his essential act is tolerated only when emptied of meaning and where, if admitted into the society of the sane, it's under surveillance and on a provisional basis, like those retarded people who are allowed to go home for Christmas.

We'd have a variation of what happens when Maria de França's discourse stops being the expression of the one who's speaking, reflecting instead in its organization, in its tone, the group (more than the individuals) it refers to: the preoccupation with characterizing the real inmates of the "Tamarineira" is absent (or irrelevant), and they're not there to evoke a certain somber image of the setting. Even though in the writers whose work shows an effort to ally themselves with the people (I said effort, since what literary work manages to cross the barrier and become, truly, an expression of the people?), even though in them the grotesque strokes are attenuated, what

Julia Marquezim Enone shows and judges, by showing them, can't be seen and isn't even named: it's that which encloses, the outside, the other side, that land.

SEPTEMBER 14—The other side? Yesterday I thought about this expression. No: I fought against it. A man lives his monotonous life, brightened by only one important event, already passed. Someone approaching fifty, a lover of texts, dealing with the most beloved text of all because he knows it was constructed while living with him, during the most meaningful years he's ever known. Day after day he writes down as well as he can his intimate journey through this text, obeying voices he initially believes he knows, certain that nothing will surprise him, alter the course of his life; he carries on like this until suddenly an adjective, *other*, uncovers an unknown ambition. Something new and serious has happened to him: he's a writer, and along with this condition he's accepted the confinement, the seclusion. But I won't allow myself to be seduced. No, I'm not a writer, rather someone cautiously venturing into the engulfing universe of writing. Somebody who intrudes upon a foreign culture and assimilates its values. The world he explores may (the equatorial forest enters through the openings and even the walls of the buildings that defy it, it breaks in through the wooden floor, invades them, upsets the plumb and the level, turns stones and the memory of stones to dust), it may, the world he explores, prevail upon him. His intention is to return.

SEPTEMBER 15—Indigence and magic of metaphors! How can the written work and the virgin forest be alike? What a chasm between a man in my situation, even though sounding with a sort of fervor—but without having taken his vows—the depths of the intense use of language and the isolated building in the midst of the jungle! Despite everything a mysterious process impregnates reality with its dubious likeness: and the likeness, stronger than reality, clothes it for a moment.

SEPTEMBER 16—When will I consider these notes finished? I have a plan (which is being followed in the same way the unruly branches of a tree follow their pattern as it's printed in a manual), but the fear of eventually losing this familiarity with *The Queen of the Prisons of Greece*, which is not, as we know, familiarity with the novel alone, brings up new questions. I push them away and, in spite of the fact that I dread the end of the book, when I don't know what will happen to me or what I'll do with my solitary days, it dominates me, the simulacrum of a conclusion is clamoring (whence?) and imposes its urgency upon me.

Because of this, against my wishes and alleging, too embarassed to tell the truth, a worsening of the eye problem, I've given up almost half of my classes. How many days ago? Two? Four? I can't remember exactly, an unforgivable fault in a diary or imitation of the genre. It's as if the time of the novel, as fluctuating as its space, influenced me. I surrender, now more resolutely, to my book—of which I have become a servant.

SEPTEMBER 17—I've given in, here and there, to the temptation of allowing Julia's delicate profile to appear in my study. With this choice I've broken laws which, strictly speaking, don't affect me, bent as I am upon an adventure and not the disciplined execution of movements extraneous to me, although, I believe, much more correct and effective. I'm not writing this to excuse myself, but rather because it occurred to me that some important touches are still missing from the portrait.

I'm mainly talking about the two occupations she pursued after she came out of the Mental Hospital for the second time: for a year and a few months, between 1961 and 1962, she was a teacher at an elementary school in Alto José do Pinho, where ten-year-old students showed up with knives; she was an employee, selected by competitive examination, of the National Institute of Social Welfare, and fired after five years of service, halfway through 1967, for dereliction of duty, after an erratic career, with increasing absences. Her two occupations explain in part the subject of her book; but it's not impossible that she took these jobs to acquire information about the subject she had chosen. At the I.N.P.S. she meets Gilvan Lemos, who already had one book in print and who was always lending her books, besides entrusting her with his new manuscripts, hardly knowing that she, despite her apparent lack of direction, was unswervingly moving toward the determination to write, fixed in her mind long before.

In the period between her dismissal and our first encounter, at the first collective exhibit of José Cláudio and Montez Magno, two rare artists with something angelic in their manner, both of modest means and who, even so, took her in so many times, she went back and forth between humble jobs and periods of inactivity in the current meaning of the word, when she found her way into libraries, or in the *Livro 7*—whose owner lent her foreign editions, which she returned immaculate—or in the house of intellectuals, such as Hermilo Borba Filho, Paulo Cavalcanti, Jefferson Ferreira Lima and Gastão de Holanda, where she spent days reading or talking. It was also common to see her in Recife and Olinda, with the air of a pilgrim, in her Franciscan sandals and secondhand clothes, wrinkled, but always very clean, a bag with a bar of soap and vague manuscripts she didn't show to anyone slung over her shoulder, her silent silhouette gliding along the walls of art galleries, wandering through bookshops and record stores without any money, when she wasn't walking the streets, soaking up the topography of the cities that her book was to join together, preferring the places where people with menial jobs, or temporary occupations, or without any resources at all in their life swarmed, oppressed—dock workers, peddlers, beggars, prostitutes, gypsies, street singers—fixing in her memory the hungry faces and the singing voices of her people.

I read in the *Estado de São Paulo*, almost a year later, that a Weimaraner had eleven puppies and, as the article went on to say, that the undeniable merit of having introduced this breed of dogs in Latin America belongs to Mr. and Mrs. Blinstrup. "Keeping in mind that the Germans wanted an animal with the characteristics of their own race, the Weimaraner had to have blue or amber eyes. To that end certain cross-breedings were carefully studied and selected."

Between the ages of twenty-seven and twenty-nine—when, even in the marginal state she exists in, she earns in Recife, among small circles, some kind of consternated prestige, since nobody believes that she'll still make good on her intention, apparent, at that point, of writing—the only occupation my friend returns to with some regularity, through unforeseeable gratifications, is her work at the medical office of the Northeastern Legion of Assistance, where, like the penniless nuns of some religious orders, she used to perform all kinds of chores, from mopping the floor to soliciting donations.

Uncommitted as she was, it's not surprising that she'd accept the invitation to come and live with me, having barely met me. Here, during an increasingly closer relationship, she began her book without delay and, in these rooms visited only by the arid sounds of the city, a melodious sound arose, that of the text that was growing.

You will forgive me, then, if at times I'm tempted to see in our encounter some kind of design that would allow us—in a mutual play of influences—to exist. Without this conjunction, more intricate than you can imagine, what would I be, and where would I be? Roosters, covetous of their own glory, will peck the feathers from their own body and hide away, undone.

SEPTEMBER 18—No real essayist, dealing with a literary work, would dare make the confession I'm about to write. It would mean admitting to inexcusable flaws in his capacity for analysis and even a possible clouding of his judgment. Who cares? I'm a created being, imperfect, bearing witness to an imperfect creation. Imperfect, and why not, as alive as I am and capable of mischief.

During the night of March 27, second anniversary of Julia Marquezim Enone's death, I saw a cat spattered with mud jump from a garbage can downtown and slink away, its tail thin and low, along the curb, vanishing between the bars of the sewer grate. As if this tainted animal were coming from the streets and inscribing itself, with infinite dissimulations, in the novel I'm confronting, enlarging it, here I find it again. How long I have been carefully studying the heart of this book! Maria de França's cat had been hiding between the lines as if they were furniture or leaves, escaping me—and only a short while ago did I discover her and followed her deterioration, puzzled.

One can see in *The Queen of the Prisons of Greece*, in the fact that it conceals, beneath an appearance of simplicity, a complex and—the word leaps out at me—abysmal structure, an attempt at imitating the appearance of the world and, concealed beneath appearances, its truth, slow and unlikely to reveal itself even to a trained observer.

Now my own mistake, not seeing what I was seeing, contributes in its own way to underscoring and magnifying this aspect, if indeed the text never performed any sleight of hand on itself and if it does not casually magnify itself, in its then specious innocence. Maria de França's sterile cat, on the contrary, undergoes a pitiable series of losses.

SEPTEMBER 19—What place does Mimosina or Memosina (the name is spelled both ways), Maria de França's sterile cat, have in the book? Purely accidental, in such a highly constructed work? Is she born only to hide from birds—*topos* of the "topsy-turvy world"—and emphasize their gigantism, suggesting that it's real, and not the result of madness? Maybe. But what's the reason for sterility or, rather, for her growing indifference to males? In the beginning there's nothing abnormal about Mimosina. But there comes a day when she no longer seems to recognize her kind, as if she had lost the sense of smell and gone blind:

What's wrong Mima, Memosina dear, you're not even looking at the young man, the graceful one, with his little tail sticking up, just the tail? Eh?

Cats, when they have intestinal problems, eat certain leaves, they take care of themselves. Mimosina, sick, forgets medicinal grasses. Later she wanders from house to house, forgetting where her own is, no longer answers to her name, stops meowing, tries to eat bran and corn, fights with the tomcat, kills him, tries to devour him and, finally, her "sunflower color" turning to a shade of grey, she begins to scurry in an increasingly strange way aiong the baseboard; then one day she starts to squeak (did you turn into a rat, Mimosina? afraid of what cat?),

sticks her head in a hole and dies like that. The cat spattered with mud and resembling an otter slinks away in the gutter.

SEPTEMBER 23—Mimosina or Memosina. This name evokes some term of endearment, there's a naive and familiar ring to it. No, not to make her degradation more poignant. Look closely! Behind this process there may be the exhaustion and end of all things, but it's reminiscent of a phenomenon of our times, the collective dissolution of memory, which the book we are immersed in recalls (not to forget?) at every moment. The bureaucrats of the welfare system are always getting their instructions confused, Belo Papagaio and Maria de França meet again as if nothing had ever happened between them, Dudu's death doesn't affect his fiancée, nothing stirs up memories, here is the constant trait, common to the characters, all of them, running through the narration. Even the scarecrow's speech mends itself here and there, in a sort of struggle for remembrance. In actuality, all this alerts us to a deeper and perhaps irreparable forgetfulness.

Hesiod says that in the beginning was Chaos, dark and boundless. But Gaea, the Earth, arises, and from her the firmament, Uranus, will be born, her equal in extension, to envelop her entirely. Gaea also creates the high peaks and the thalassic abysses. She takes her own son, Uranus, the starry space, inside her and, among the fabulous beings they beget, Mnemosyne, Memory, is born. Memosina or Mimosina are distortions of this name, bookish and lacking emotional charge.

Remembering, then, would be an essential act, closely linked to the Earth and the stars enveloping it. Creation, Understanding, and Direction, Bearing, are rooted in it.

Memosina, wretched little animal, epitomizes the phenomenon the novel and the world are steeped in, the general obliteration of memory, a metaphysical disease (where is it born and how to make it regress?) which plunges mankind and its works into insanity, senselessness.

Rainy afternoon, cut by gusts of cold wind. I open the study window, breathe a tepid breeze, saturated with sea smells, as if some spectral beach were emerging out of this solid city.

Who or what saves us from forgetfulness? Before, even the most ignorant among us knew "why." When we didn't know, no need to justify, to construct explanations to take the place of knowledge in us or, in its stead, of certainty. Not that we knew everything. Who ever did? Not knowing, though, was a kind of joy, we'd say to ourselves that we didn't know and we'd go hunting, to try to catch, to try to know—and at times we brought back, in our hunters' nets, prey we invented (they snorted in the trap) which lived for a hundred years. What did it matter if they were real or not? We believed in them and this belief gradually formed a geometric order in our formless souls, a system was born, a harmony between us—and what? Between us and Something. A complex and infinitely dangerous game. And yet we didn't rest: to insist was an act that implied its own continuity. Absolute, in those times, the clarity of incomprehensible things.

Thus, it was possible not to succumb and, glory to our boldness, we enlarged the infinite world even more. Everything, however, jubilantly moved from one extreme to the other and this flight, and this trap, and this dance step, had a name: nexus. If we invented the pitcher, we had the water, the hand, the glass, the mouth in mind. The spear? Look how long it is, how branched and tortuous. There is my hunger, beyond my caution, beyond my arm, beyond my eye, beyond my skill, beyond the animal's hot machine, vulnerable: this is the spear. Who would waste his time with spears that were ignorant of the act of hunting and the necessity to wound, locking inside themselves this aggressive device, thus lifeless? The animal fell, wounded, and this didn't maim the world: its death was an event rich in memory.

Now we wander, proud and sad, from futile act to futile act, molding sealed vases and cutting circular spears that no longer bear points. A frightful beast, with a twisted nature, was born of the universal weariness and rules among us: it voraciously eats its tail and swallows its own gullet. Creations and acts perish: its internal respiration, deadly.

Nobody suspected that the memory that's lost today is this, personal, with which we fix our lives—leather stretched between sticks. I can and I do live while the features and, even more ephemeral, the words of my dead ones and the weight, on my skin, of their hands die in me. But if I don't recognize my own kind? If I don't know what for? If I forgot the reason? If I lose the secret? I know, I know that one doesn't live by determination alone and that death is prowling, prowling, I know that I'm powerless against it. Perhaps a man thinks, like those who have just lost an arm, that he's still moving his amputated hand.

What would lead J.M.E. to follow so methodically Memosina the cat's going astray, from the time she chases mice, until she changes skin and dies of suffocation, the hole she puts her head in serving as her gallows? Conflicting preoccupations were brewing in my friend, fertile receptacle of things and names. But will there ever exist for the creator, if creator and precisely because creator, other problems besides his own craft? Sympathetic and vulnerable, he almost always meddles in other areas, outside this incandescent orbit. Out of desperation, reverence or rage, however, he only understands, as a way of life, fabricating his objects, and because of this vows a desperate love for his work, like someone who, having lost all of his children, still has one left and showered upon this sole survivor his love for the dead ones as well.

It's raining incessantly and I'm feeling sick. I keep asking, dazed: "Who am I?" Even without a clear answer, I'm preparing to face the still obscure event taking shape. I've begun to exist in a state of expectation and uncertainty. Come what may, I'm ready.

There's an apparent contradiction in the way the book develops the theme of lost memory. Things, when they forget their own nature, lose direction, although it's not correct to say that they degrade themselves, because they don't really come down in rank, but rather they are displaced, they cease to be what they were once, they become innocuous. The vase, an impenetrable sphere; a closed hoop the spear. Memosina or Mimosina, bearer and focal point of this theme, goes astray and, having lost her wind (did she also lose her claws and teeth?), she turns into a rat and dies. Throughout the rest of the book, however, the theme manifests itself in a less drastic way, without the coherence with which it's organized in Memosina—and dispersed, fragmentary, inapprehensible, so to speak. There, once again, I learn about the art of the novel and art in general. Not only do the extras that Maria de França's lot depends on have a short memory: she, too, is prone to forgetting. Among this group forgetting doesn't seem a monstrous fact, an aberration, but instead a sign of the erosion of the world, of its wear. Hence something normal, inevitable. To operate in a more coherent manner, repeating throughout the text, in the other appearances of the theme, the parable expressed through Memosina, wouldn't be what we expect from Julia M. Enone, from her misleading poetics, with its propensity for masks. The solution noted above *unravels*, in a manner of speaking, the theme, preventing it from pointing in any one direction and, at the same time, insinuating, by means of a precise thematic unity, calculated down to the minutest details—the bankruptcy of instincts in a domestic animal—the main direction.

Bewildering discovery. As long as I don't get involved with a text through which I hopelessly reveal myself (since, no matter how much I try to hide, if I say "I" it's this I that makes me, and in this case, what could making mean but forming, giving, revealing?), as long as I come and go in the world, self-assured, a man with his hammock anchored in many concrete points, proclaiming with a firm voice an "I" that's the image of my face, not even death threatens my identity.

But if I take a piece of paper or, even more serious and frightening, if someone takes a piece of paper and writes "I," and, behind this pronoun, puts me in his place, who can guarantee me anything anymore? Here I am, then, being born of a grammatical expression the way sound is born of the mouth, here I am at the mercy of this articulation, exposed to it, defenseless. No, I mustn't say "mercy": if it can lie to me, then I myself, making good use of it, can impose any presence whatsoever on some distant recipient. My molder will be the text; and the recipient will never be able to revolt against it, to deny it. I can make myself another person in writing, I can make myself everybody, except one—the one that, really and infinitely, I am in Time.

And that's not all. The identity of the written word is problematic and it's linked to the way the nature of the person— true or fictitious—responsible for the enunciation reflects upon its inflection. You read, noticing the unsteadiness of the handwriting, different from the way it was ten years ago, a letter from your father. This man's thick "I" anchors the piece of writing in reality and you will probably keep it forever, as you will keep his old pocket Omega. But . . . what if the letter, printed in a volume by Turgenev, is written by a certain Rúdin to a certain Sergei Pavlovich? Eh? There that word, printed, removed from the manuscript and the hand we knew, simulates everything: it simulates the addresser, it simulates the addressee, it simulates the letter and, above all, it simulates a piece of writing different from what it is. The fiction is not only in Rúdin's letter; it's also in the typographical impression.

However, there's still a simile, a parallel between the imaginary letter of the imaginary Rúdin and its graphic expression. Place the text you're reading, like a mold, over the text it seems to repeat and which, think about it! is engendered by its equivocal "reproduction." How can I not get upset at this versatility—which only now seems to reveal itself to me—of writing? And there's more, how can we still give the same name to the rather purple prose in your father's letter (the paper permeated with the smell of tobacco), which you can almost touch as you could touch his face, and that other piece of writing, ghostly, attributed not to a being who writes it but one who utters it or, a more involved case, to a being who acts, or, to be exact, is acted out, in our mind, by its unviable discourse, centered on an "I" whose nature eludes me?

This sudden bewilderment at the mutable nature of writing drives me crazy. I am a spider spinning my web. But I, the source of the web, have become ambiguous (the "I" of the text is an empty shell) and nothing forbids me to write—which may be false or not—that I'm weaving the web and weaving myself simultaneously. Woven into my own discourse, I have entered a sort of placental cloud from which I might emerge as creator as much as created, a servant of creation. Especially since whoever will be reached by this murmur, mine, will have no other expert's report, no other clue, no other witness, no other evidence. We are incontestable, I and my other reality, deeply rooted in me, dissociated from me, the speech. Nocturnal packs of hounds quench their thirst in the river and cloud the water with a barking that fills the fishes' bellies. I can or they can (who knows anymore? who's sure of anything anymore, here?), by means of one of those chemical reactions a long and restless use exposed the writing to, rescuing it from a strict and utilitarian servitude and opening up risky possibilities, I can or they can, it's only a matter of lightly touching some delicate instrument, changing the identity of this monologue I've been living with, or, instead, confirming the latent suspicion that it's showing you a false façade; I can or they can free it from all real ties with my hand: then, having struck upon the essence of the monologue, here I am equally stricken in my "I," here I am stricken in my essence and in the same instant I turn out to be another, no longer a writing entity but one that's being written. The author's ghost giving rise to an imaginary being, with a different makeup, immersed in a singular version—which could even be called magic—of space and time.

Lieutenant Pavel Nikolai Neverov could barely feel the pistol's handle in his freezing hand. It had stopped snowing, the woods were completely still, and he heard, behind him, his adversary's breathing, smelled the faint scent of sandarac resin. In two months it would be spring and not even Anna Andreievna would remember this duel any longer. They began to walk in opposite directions, their boots creaking on the snow-covered ground. At the third step, before anyone realized what was happening, Neverov turned, aimed and blew out his rival's brains with a single shot from behind.

The awareness of the alternatives—so seductive!—this monologue centered on the "I" (whose "I," friends, mine?) stirs in me an exaltation filled with jubilation and terror, as if I had been disguising myself until now, as if I had been playing a role, as if I were hiding my true nature or didn't really have one. Behind the words I set free (which, note the difference, I **write** or **utter**), or, still, which somebody attributes to me, my existence becomes more problematic. *Alternative #1*: confirm the central image of the science teacher, anonymous admirer of the literary word, restless and curious observer of the novel, surviving lover of somebody who finished, right before dying, some mysterious book: everything will be seen in the same light. *Alternative #2*: insinuate that the book is indeed real, not the figure of its commentator, invented to protect the true friend—also anonymous—of the deceased, thus avoiding complete exposure: here is the doubt being instilled, here is the subtle doubt arising, lightest of oils. The entire lighting changes and each word spoken resounds with a new timbre.

I'm afraid, though, that many may already be suspiciously rejecting my identity and therefore my nature. I'm not going to try to persuade them of the contrary.

Maria de França is receptive to reading. Mechanically, so to speak, she responds to the printed word, wherever she finds it. Nothing, therefore, even remotely related to any idea of cultural development. On the contrary, in transit in a world she doesn't understand, having access to the infinity of writings in which she's submerged—medicine and canned food packaging, instructions, fliers, almanacs, popular poetry, commercial signs, billboards, loose newspaper pages—only contributes to her confusion. Primarily the access to scraps of newspapers and illustrated magazines.

Strictly speaking, she doesn't differ in a substantial way, save in degree, from the modern newspaper reader. One thing is certain, not once does she buy the day's paper at the newsstand, and it doesn't seem to occur to her that it might be possible. But who nowadays is sufficiently informed to learn all of the vocabulary and establish all the indispensable connections between facts when going through the papers? It's enough to stop reading them for one week—or less—and it's as if we had missed the final chapters of some absurd and labyrinthine feuilleton. New names have appeared, including those of countries unimaginable until the day before; we don't know the outcome of episodes that engrossed us; others, nebulous for us, are making headlines. Even those who read them every day come across facts that, even when they stretch over months or years, they can't understand, as if it were some unfathomable metaphysical problem, which may have prompted Cardinal Cicognani to declare in an interview with *L'Osservatore Romano*, upon his nomination as Dean of the Sacred College of Cardinals in March '72: "Yes, God knows everything. But not everything that gets printed in the papers."

What do these printed pages whose global content defies divine omniscience mean for Maria de França, then? Precisely what they are, for everybody, to a greater or lesser degree: the unfathomable jungle of the world, this mystery made even more impenetrable by the way in which Maria de França receives them, in bits and pieces and almost always late.

In the same way that, as far as wealth is concerned, Maria de França is only sensitive to insignificant things, in the papers, even though she reads names and facts, she only perceives as true those that inscribe themselves in her life's orbit: destitution and hunger, fires, assaults and vendettas, weddings, floods, military parades, processions, car accidents, and, emerging like a familiar refrain from among sounds as unfathomable as they are harsh, some truly human figure, which she transforms into a temporary ideal or, at least in one case, permanent ideal, inaccessible model, like Ana the thief, from some place called Greece.

In this place called Greece, which, in Maria de França's mind, floats like an island on a huge sandy cloud, the invincible Ana wanders until her death, obstinately rejecting any productive occupation, compelled by or dedicated on principle to all kinds of hoaxes, from swindle to theft, with the only restriction, which she imposes upon herself, that she operate unarmed. Constantly changing her last name, but keeping her first, to honor what she considers her *trademark*, she works her way up from Crete to the continent, in a ship painted red, like Ulysses' winged vessels, operates in the ancient Cythera and then in Sparta, crosses the Peloponnesus, is arrested and convicted in Marathon, in Athens, in Samos, in Corinth, in small towns on the Ionian and Aegean Sea, inscribing upon all of these names, magnified by historical and mythic events (where are you fighting now, noble Achilles, and you, who subjugated Persia?), inscribing new feats, individual and lackluster.

This juxtaposition escapes Maria de França, who's simply attracted to the cunning with which Ana, persistent but ill-starred in her heists, having been arrested and convicted so many times, moves within courts and between prison bars, inaccessible entities for Maria de França but without secrets for the modern-day fellow-citizen of Minos, judge of the infernal court, since, while in jail, she managed to obtain a review of the trial and a pardon, when she wasn't vanishing through the walls like a shadow eluding the wardens' vigilance, only to show up and be caught again in the least predictable places, coming, with the passing of years, punishments, convictions, pardons, and escapes, to embody a legend, that of the woman who knows all the loopholes in the network of power and administration—be they written within the laws or set in stone—to the point that she's welcomed with honors in the cells she's confined to and receives, without the slightest irony, the title, undisputed in the continental part of the country or in the islands, of Queen of the Prisons of Greece.

When she was already approaching her end, a magistrate, in court, tried to show to those present the iniquity concealed in her eyes. The answer, the only one that remains of everything the prisons and courts of Greece heard from her mouth over half a century, has become famous:

—You're mistaken. What I conceal in my eyes is fear. Fear of knowing how time passes.

Let's stress the importance of the Queen of Prisons in relation to Maria de França—and her value in the novel as well. With a penchant for breaking with the work world, Maria de França, however, doesn't rebel—deliberately or impulsively—against property and the means of protecting it. Thus, it's not as a counterfeiter, con woman, two-bit whore, or pickpocket that the Greek woman grows in her imagination, achieving the stature of idol or myth. Her prestige, rather, is born of a skill that Maria de França considers superior and Dudu the center forward practices in modest proportions—the understanding of something impenetrable, bureaucracy, possibly just a metaphor for the world. Ana, for Maria de França, represents something she herself will never become—the lucid heroine, the clairvoyant, nimbly weaving her way through mysteries and obstacles.

Understandable and clear (to the degree that anything is clear in subtly constructed works) Maria de França's attitude with respect to the Queen of Prisons; not so the impression the statement about fear and time, obviously beyond her comprehension, makes on her. Can I myself say that I understand it? I limit myself to conjectures. We can't expect the text, attributed to Maria de França, to help us either, as much as it distances itself from realistic works, which are fond of everything natural and sensible. The problem is a curious one. Julia M. Enone, indifferent to a flat coherence which clings to the episodic and ordinary vision of reality, opts for another kind of coherence, directed above all toward the work, to its structure. It doesn't matter—here's the essence of the solution, of the snare—if the concept admired by Maria de França is beyond her understanding. What does matter is that this admiration valorizes it: that Ana's words, thus highlighted, gain prominence in the whole and establish themselves, without possible doubt, as a piece of work deserving of notice.

Time accumulates changes in space. In order not to be aware of its passing, Ana, terrified, travels all across Greece, from city to city, from prison to prison: she flees the transformation of things and, thus, from learning one of the ways in which time flows.

Any work or construction—embroidery, house, family, poem—teaches us a little about the way time passes. For this reason Ana rejects any regular commitment, always running from circumstances that might allow something to grow in her hands. Perhaps the things she appropriates and whose production she didn't contribute to in any way don't seem to bear the mark of time to her.

Impossible flight. Inglorious struggle. Ana of Greece flees knowledge of the inexorable course of time and is thrown in prison, to experience in that immobility the passage of time and thus despair: this is her punishment. But doesn't she love the interiors of jails in a way precisely because the immutable nakedness reigning there simulates eternity and turns its back on time? In this case, why is she fleeing? Did she always flee the moment she surmised, in some olive tree luxuriantly growing in the prison yard or in the way the wind began to blow against the walls, the danger of understanding?

She preferred cities. Not so much because riches and ambitions accumulate there, favoring plunder. No. Rather because in cities she feels the unfolding of seasons less. She only sees the countryside when she's traveling—between one city and the other—and hates farm tools.

Did she have the illusion that time, emigrating from Crete, was slavishly following her same itinerary? It's known that she saw herself in mirrors only by chance and that she barely knew what her own face looked like. Mostly, she retained nothing of the faces she had lost. Thus, she could always suppose that this young woman standing in the square or this one passing in the train, her eyes wide open behind the window, was herself and time returning. Which, therefore, justified this doubt: "Was time passing?"

Her name itself, Ana, suggested the idea of opposition, of contrary movement.

Some fish in the Middle East, unresigned to the passing of waters and their subordination to this liquid element, come up to the surface, use the rudimentary claws adorning their ventral and pectoral fins, climb—pitiful mute birds—the trees flanking the river and, gasping for air, try to escape the current for a short time, without knowing that between the branches an equally incessant river is tearing away their scales. Poor Ana!

Faced with newspapers she doesn't understand, with instructions she doesn't understand, with esoteric approvals and denials, with mysterious delays, Maria de França, miserable, realizes that everything is escaping her and fervently longs for the supreme metamorphosis: to turn into Ana, the Queen of Prisons, to understand the impossible, to decipher the mystery.
Then they'd see.

How does time pass? She was afraid of other things, but not of uncovering this secret. A handicap she's not even aware of helps her: she confuses time references. *Tomorrow*, in her mind, is an impenetrable notion and never turns into *today*, into *yesterday*.

"Before it's too early." "When was nonce once?" "Never put it off until yesterday if today is gone and already coming back." "Dudu, my angel, is today tomorrow?" "Too late for later and even more so for never, do you know, did you know?"

Early and *late* obliterate each other in the same vague conception, as well as *after*, which is also, simultaneously, always *before*. This anomaly prevents any of the useful notions according to which we and time feign a sort of mobility from crystallizing in her mind: there I'm running toward some moment in the future, which approaches, turns into the past, and moves away. Maria de França doesn't name these changes of perspective between the self and certain configurations of time—and it's as if she were floating in a boundless expanse, inclined to immobility, yes, contrary to any fluvial image, an expanse, yes.

" 'It's no use speaking to it,' Alice thought, 'till his ears have come, or at least one of them.' In another minute the whole head appeared."

Sharp and wary eye! Do Ana's words carry the weight they seem to or am I deceived? Look out! Maria de França's disturbed mind, unsuited (a deficiency manifest on several levels) to the ordinary understanding of time, finds a perfect match in the fragmentary way in which she receives and reads newspapers. She confuses *before* and *after*? The loose pages of the *Jornal do Comércio* or of the *Diário de Pernambuco* that pass through her hands, wrapped around merchandise, pulled out of the garbage, carried by the wind, repeat this abstract phenomenon on the concrete level. If Maria de França's disease (here not so much mental as verbal), making words like *before* and *after* impenetrable, tends to dilute the book in time, the occurrence of real historical events—not in the sequence in which they would have taken place but disconnected, loose, contingent upon random encounters with outdated snatches of news, sometimes years after the fact, whose date we can only guess—the anachronistic succession of these events, placed in the backdrop of the heroine's undeterminable bureaucratic peregrinations, makes the process worse. At first sight there seems to be an impropriety or whim in it: there's something superficial about the solution, a solution turned toward the structure and indifferent to the thematic nuclei of the book, perhaps in contrast to them. What is the point of this distortion of historical time, this dismemberment, in a story deriving its strength, to a large extent, from deferrals, from the slow grinding down of desire, in a word, from the accumulation of time? This objection is not as pertinent as it purports to be at first sight. On the one hand, what happens there with time imitates point by point the disarticulation of space: the permutations or shrivelling of the real topography. On the other, I don't think the obfuscation of time mitigates the most despairing aspect of Maria de França's struggle with the bureaucratic world. On the contrary, all this long involvement, tainted by the imprecision the confused mind of the factory worker gives rise to, dilates even more the years over which the action unfolds, immersed in this way in a less trivial category of time, exalted by a certain transcendence and filled with echoes of eternity. The wordly fate, without detriment to the biting and caustic side, aimed at an anomalous society, is reflected and simultaneously appears like a peregrination and torture outside time, in the always-never, in hell.

Here I insinuate my suspicion. From newspapers which, in the diverse universe of typography, better convey history and the succession of days and which, ironically, appear in the novel to contribute to the apparent disintegration of time, Maria de França learns of events that seduce her or cause her anguish, among them Ana of Greece's adventures. However Ana, a figure associated with space, always in motion, seems a bit marginal to the whole time scheme in which she appears. Wouldn't her confession, of what propels her from one end of Greece to the other, from one end of life to the other, the fear of knowing how time passes, also be a dodge, a trick (Julia M. Enone learning with her character), illusorily nailing her to a cluster of themes from which she really stands apart?

Beyond doubt: if the author places at the center of her work a disorderly consciousness, it's to give order to the whole by means of certain laws. Among them, that of concealing as much as possible her experimental ambition. Not interested in the slavish reproduction of things and, along with this, supposing that some connection with ordinary reality is indispensable to the genre, she creates an eccentric language, radio broadcast and world, while indirectly justifying them with the heroine's mental disorder, as if everything derived from this and not from her own restlessness. Thus, pretending to be compelled by her character, whose madness is supposed to be tinged with denunciation (it manifests itself as a consequence of professional failures), she deals with and solves in her own way some of the most stimulating problems of contemporary fiction, culminating with that of time and its transgressions, to which even scarcely adventurous narrators are sensitive nowadays.

Fanny Brown, the cripple, with her two useless arms or, to be precise, without them—and those who lack arms lack breadth, of course—never having known the excitement of running down a hill or the pleasure of an afternoon stroll in a rose garden (she was born without legs), was carried from one part of the house to the other like an object that did not fit anywhere. As if touching her body were each time more distasteful, they began to move her with the help of a shovel. They became so proficient in this kind of exercise that they would move her even when it was unnecessary. For the ill-starred Fanny Brown the shovel was what the winds of passion are for others: what use was her will against this tool made of wood and metal?

The jumble of news Maria de França plows through makes establishing a chronology for *The Queen* almost impossible. The heroine's long itinerary in government offices and her private life follow one another in rigorous order, everything recorded with precision, in a clear time structure, imitating the stack of papers which supposedly document her case. These events, however, albeit ordered and presented in rigorous sequence, are projected against a chaotic background—and this background ends up by having repercussions on the events in the foreground, drifting in a time as torn up as the newspapers which, while seeming to inform about it, provide false clues.

Does Julia Marquezim Enone disseminate these clues as a puzzle for the readers to piece together? I don't see why. The imprecision deriving from her method doesn't diminish at all the severity of the struggle between Maria de França and the welfare labyrinth, just as it doesn't mitigate—but rather worsens—the feeling of absolute futility the successive decisions of the various offices cause us (never the final decision).

What happens if we try to fix the limits of the long peregrination before the fallen heroes of the history of Brazil? A census of the historical references indicates that the most recent is King Constantine's deposition, a fact by which our character is moved because it happened in the very same Greece as Ana's, and sets the conclusion around 1967. But not all the scraps of newspaper whose contents the book reveals fit in the phase between our character's employment in that textile factory—when she learns how to read—and her ordeal in the government offices. Two allusions to World War II, for example, are clearly anachronistic. News regarding nuclear power plants ("Bomb's Explosion Leaves Crater") is always turning up in the papers, as we know. On the other hand, only a patient and possibly fruitless investigation could situate the news that "father, physician and jurist condemn abortion even to prevent the birth of monsters"; that Melminno Ratto, sailor, stole parts from the ship on which he served, offering them to his lovers on shore; or tell us on what date that white bird that had gotten stranded, if indeed there was a bird, arrived in Cabo Frio from the Bahamas or, according to some, from Terra Nova.

One can then situate, without a great margin of error, the end—but not the beginning, no—of the hellish years in which Maria de França pursues the impossible, querying an adverse entity, whose secrets she never penetrates, unlike the eminent crook from Crete.

What photograph is this? Men and women, a little girl, standing or sitting, dressed as if they were going out for a stroll, dressed for the picture illuminated by a light that unifies their faces even more (what undefinable trait gives a familiar air to all these smiling people?), gathered in a yard in the suburbs or the interior, the rose bush in the back and a piece of wall, an old Sunday afternoon, hot and clear. Who are they? Certainty of knowing them, like those faces we encounter and can't place, but here it's a whole group that defies me, in this yard and at this time where perhaps my youthful voice was heard. What if one of these faces was mine? I insist on trying to identify the ones I can make out, in tearing away the membrane that keeps me from walking up to the group and hearing their voices, the creaking of their shoes. All I get out of it: to pretend I remember the yard and the wall that even back then are secreting the insidious smell of old cardboard, peculiar to photographs forgotten inside drawers and closets for a long time.

I think she's hiding from me. Otherwise, how could I go so many hours and, at times, entire days without seeing her? In this she's like certain aspects of works of art and of life, which flicker in our mind, revealed—so clear!—only to vanish again in the shade. It's not that we forget the deciphering and now become distressed at the charade once again impenetrable. No.

Deciphering and charade fade, in the work and in life: we forget that once, we saw clearly, that there was a loophole there through which we had entered. No mark gives the experience away, those concessions leave no scars.

Don't we all have dreams in which we know and after which, awake, we're just as blind as ever, barely able to remember what we dreamed, before forgetting it all? It's the same with her, who always manages to hide and conceal even her feces, even though the apartment offers few hiding places —few rooms and little furniture. When I least expect it, I see her in the middle of the living room or at the foot of the bed, sitting on her haunches, her streaked feline eyes each time smaller, her face more pointed and more miserable her appearance, her short hair a little oily. I take her into my arms, she opens her mouth and tries to meow, a gurgling sound comes out of her numbed throat. On the floor again, she reaches the door, quick as a half-stumbling rat, looking back with such an intense expression of fear that I have to struggle not to cry out. She will disappear for a long time and I will forget about her. There she is, wretched, looking at me from behind the legs of the chair, thinking she can't be seen and smiling with a slight sardonic rictus, as if she knew things I don't know. Her pupils shine vacuously.

Your book, Julia, is slowly beginning to close for me. I know and you knew that works of art are as unlimited as our grasp is limited. For this reason art seeks more lasting and, in some ways, indestructible incarnations than men: so that many minds, successively prodded by the work's never-ending secrets, may accumulate decipherings. It's for this reason too, as you knew, that we preserve them: because we know that they try to speak to us, they try to speak to us, they try. Among your papers there were some clippings about archaeological excavations, the plan of the Treasury of Atreus, Thompson dredging the Sacred Well of Chichén-Itzá, the Mayan star found over a century ago by Stephens in Honduras. Why? The man who removes the dirt that has accumulated over a civilization and seeks answers in its ruins is like those who, rejecting the inexhaustible world, pore over a work of art, trying to penetrate it. The difference between one and the other is that the exhumed civilization might exhaust itself one day.

But how to accept, silent friend, that the craftsman's limited mind is capable of conceiving and finishing a product whose greatness supplants us? It's the work and not him, as limited as we are, that knows more than everyone else. The creator simply becomes open to the world and its mysteries, without understanding them and without naming them. The artist: urn of air. Hard task, this he forces himself to, with tools whose keen edge has almost always been dulled by good and bad use, to represent something he doesn't know himself and whose meaning is revealed not even to him! Swords ringing.

It was a 16 by 23 foot room, pleasant, with a shiny wood floor and flower vases. The old man hammered the wall full of holes and suddenly realized that behind the wall there was another one, made of steel. He pulled open the sheer white curtains and looked out of the window: it opened onto an abyss whose bottom he couldn't see. He made a hole in the floor, heard the river solemnly flowing below and plunged into its mighty waters forever.

It was late at night and the house was quiet. Seated in my unforgettable friend's favorite armchair, I held in my hands Saussure's *Course in General Linguistics*, glancing with apprehension at the door now and then, as if I were waiting for someone, even though only the police are in the habit of coming so late. The lamp shone brightly on the book, my white shirt, the wine-colored armchair, leaving the rest of the living room in darkness. One time I looked up from the book and I saw a rickety, dirty animal on the rug, a male or female cat, in profile, its forepaws stretched out in front of it. "Like the Sphinx!" What kind of animal was this and how had it managed to get in here? This question seemed to become consumed in the flames of what I saw, the intruder was real and, without ceasing to be real, *it was her own invention*, death and eternity met in it, the limits of imagination were expanding and moving toward me—not only that, the whole world was rotting in this animal where forgetfulness reigned, at the same time that another memory was being born out of it. Slowly, its darkness invades me, I get up and, without knowing why, my hands like gloves never worn, I throw open my arms, stifling a cry, I don't know whether of joy or horror.

The 7th Cavalry Regiment, with their red tunics and their sabers unsheathed, slowly marched down the hill. Only the muffled beat of a drum could be heard. At last, they stopped at the entrance of the town, the flags fluttering in the morning breeze. On top of the mountain, the huge head of a horse, made of all horses, rose, growing even larger as it rushed down and crushed the town beneath its hooves before the soldiers' furious gaze.

Certain that the time has come and without knowing what transformation is about to take place within the boundaries of the night, I wander, bareheaded, the night drizzle burning in my eyes and wondering at the sudden gusts of hot air, as if a train of fire, silent and invisible, were passing through me, fast, from time to time. Hardly anybody in the streets, it must be very late, an occasional car drives by at high speed, the night watchmen blow their whistles, my new shoes still creak a little and each of my steps echoes, as the dogs' barking echoes in the dark yards. Several feet above ground in my living room, a dubious cat is slowly magnetizing the world with its essence, irradiating everything, and perhaps that's what I'm trying to run from, I, this anxious man, bespectacled, his hands in his jacket pockets. He walks up Rua Pamplona and stops at the Avenida Paulista: the traffic lights blink on and off, reflecting in his hair, almost completely white. The impossible sound of a wave crashing on the rocks comes toward him and he's assailed by a strident smell of seaweed. Narrower and more pleasant, this avenue, when the truck crushed your slight body here, Julia. Was there a September afternoon when we strolled down this sidewalk, holding each other, stepping on the purple flowers of the ipê trees, since replaced by asphalt? I cross the avenue and, further on, I get lost on Rua Sílvia or Doutor

Seng. The suspicion I've always had, that Julia Enone was trying to say, in a terrible way, something so serious that only the act of dying could possibly express it, becomes a certainty. I mustn't be far from Morro dos Ingleses now, but how to know for sure, among all these demolished buildings? The lights go out, my investigations seem more difficult and the night infected by Memosina or Mimosina, who governs it from up above or slinks down some gutter, ambiguously. I can see nothing beneath the overcast sky and the searing morning dew feels sharper, luckily I'm wearing a hat. What could that green and gold light flickering behind the buildings be, moving, as if a fantastic ship with all its lights on, or a great flaming whale, rising from the earth, were sailing in complete darkness—only its halo visible—the deserted streets of São Paulo, describing a curve? Your life, Julia, was an extended vigil and everything was preparing for your book, end of the journey. It was the gold of your existence, what's left of what time consumes, nothing in you was worth what it could be worth—and how else could you have expressed such a serious conviction if not by your own sacrifice? Moving closer, as if it were coming my way, sinuous, the green and gold halo, full of sea and a chorus of voices singing very far away, I don't know where I am anymore and I'm afraid of going on. The fact that you loved and inspired passion, that you were in the bloom of life and love (of the one who loved you and your own) had reached its plenitude, was to be your rhetoric, enhancing even more what—in a more covert manner, as you preferred—you had decided to say with your death. Difficult decision, in which detachment and cruelty are fused together. But doesn't saying what's essential for us always have something mutilating about it? You died because dying was hard. The rhythmic sound of footsteps is coming from some street covered with darkness, how do they manage to see in the dark? they're getting closer and they aren't speaking, I slink along the wall, step in a puddle, the water gets in my shoe through a hole in the sole, a bugle seems to resound from within the earth, muffled, the patrol crosses the street, not from one curb to the other, they cross it as they were coming out of the houses on one side and entering the houses on the other, I can't see the militiamen, I can hear them marching and the creaking of their boots, the discreet ringing of metal, the breeze they make when they pass, it blows through the tails of my loose old coat, as thin as a sheet. Then I discern a faint light on the left, not the great moving halo, but a small fixed nebula, and I go looking for it (this is what wayward travelers do in stories when they discern a lantern), the place where I am is higher than I had imagined, suddenly I see lights in the distance, a ship, the lights' reflection, it's the sea. Didn't that used to be terra firma and clusters of buildings with red lights on the lightning rods? The waning moon floats almost on the line of the horizon and the ocean wind blows through the holes in my clothes, I would pull off my big brimmed hat if not for the string fastening it under my chin. Did the lights come on again or—these, shining bright—did they never go out? I run my formless hands over the rough surface of the bulwark taking shape before my eyes (cloth hands?), I see a sentry box on the left, a bell begins to ring, I turn my back to the sea and the ship, I walk without feet, like a drunk, over the cobblestones of this steep city, full of old churches, I walk down an alley (Beco das Cortesias), Rua do Sol, Amparo, São Francisco, a beacon is revolving overhead, la-de-da, what am I doing here, what street is this, there are the old two-story sobrado houses and the wharf on the other side, its trees bent over the water, where did I see those bridges before, and who can tell me the name of this river, stinking of fish and mud? Who are you, empress or whore, courtesan, your face half concealed among the veils of dawn, approaching me beneath the trees along the wharf? La-de-da! Hello out there in Radioland! That's too hot to handle, sister! Everything getting screwed up, the saw teeth, the pincer grips, the pistol triggers, the hammer handles, the nail tips, the knife edges, the dignity of you know who. But let's go, let's go on with it! What pinches, secures; what hurts, cures. It's night and it's day. Once upon a time? Here I am: undone and redone. Where am I and who was I, who am I? In the world I find, in the world I leave. Hello out there in Radioland! I kindle, I blaze, I burn, I parch. I am the straw fire, the fire-eater, the Greek fire, the fireant, I'm no denier of fire. Once upon a time we will be. Who did my ridiculous hat belong to? To a poor leprous and deaf-mute man. What's this coming out of my mouth? Puff of wind or windstorm, dust blowing, flies, clouds, paper kites, fifes, explode, globe? Once upon a time there was a man. He left with a wish, came back with two fish; he left with two fathers, came back with three sisters; he left with three cousins of mine, came back with four rhymes; he left with four verses, came back with five cradles rocked by old nurses; he left with five songs to lull babies, came back with six matronly ladies; and when he tried to stop all this gibberish, he took everything he had and came back with just the wish. La-de-da! Where am I coming to and where are we going from? Where am I and who was I, eh, who am I, scattered and unified game, created with cards from twenty-seven decks, with dominoes from twenty-seven sets? Sign and tip. If my hands are made with strands of rattan, can I have a fate, a mission, a grand plan? Tweedledee 'n' Tweedledum questions. There's no difference between being a mountebank and robbing a bank, between being a shod friar and a bold-faced liar. Same thing. My shirt looks like garlic skin. And where did you find such a scrofulous coat, doc? On the beach. Snapping at flies, watching the ships go by, twiddling my thumbs, crucified in the air, I throw my ostrakon across time and I get mad, I fuck myself in the ass, laughingstock, shuttlecock (which everybody knocks around but nobody enters). The Turkish woman cries for a bowl of soup, hum-dee-dum, lickspittle salamander emolument Epsom salts. Hello, out there in Radioland! My glasses are two Coke bottles. But I can see the future. Hey! Hey ditches, hey latrines, garbage cans, piss-stained sheets, scabs, hey bedbugs, old chamber pots, dog carcasses, sewers, and workers, listen to my prophecy:

> I see a lion in a cap
> blowing
> on the rich man's ass
> and a horse standing up
> flogging
> the poor man's ass.

La-de-da! It's night and it's day, it's here and it's there, it is and it isn't me, the change, the passage, the trans, I'm going and I'm already there, I go through the window but I'm not moving an inch, me in the middle of the tree, my arms open (two or four?), my hands open (four or two?), my heart open, what did I just say? come on, everybody! I protect Maria de França, I save Maria de França, I make the birds smaller: Maria's frightened heart beats confidently within my lucid shadow. I join left and right, near and far, here and yesterday, I am him and you too, sister, little sister, being who you are, you're still the same as before, we are who we appear to be and also who we are in another numinous place, shoo, big clumsy birds, creatures of the sad and piercing beak, shoo, this is Maria, her passage a rainstorm that comes quickly as it goes, brief ballad, embroidered pillow. Come, now, Maria, be once upon a time, open my tattered cape, my fly without a button-hole or button, the drawers I inherited from the victim of a work-related accident, my balls made of stockings, crack my wee little nuts, wheee! I pop out of the little nuts like a little bird, I come out small and soft, a little maizena cookie, a little china doll, la-de-da, and I grow, la-de-da, she gives me her arm, we are once upon a time, we go in, we go in on the leg of a duck and come out, come out on the leg of a chicken, there we go, she and I, the Báçira, toward the impossible limitiferous, to the onceuponatimiferous, to the Reciferous, to the open dooriferous, to the suckling piggiferous, to the axis of the universiferous, to the point of no returniferous, to the ampliferous, to the sonofabitchiferous, to the immensiferous, to the iferous, to the Báçira-baciferous.

Osman Lins was born in Brazil in 1924. After graduating with a degree in economics and finance from the University of Recife in 1946, he entered the banking profession. Shortly after he began writing fiction, which can be divided into two main phases: the first one, in a more traditional and realisric vein, includes the novels *O Visitante* (1955), *Os Gestos* (1957), and *O Fiel e a Pedra* (1962); while the second phase, with *Nove, Novena* (1966), *Avalovara* (1973), and *A Rainha dos Cárceres da Grécia* (1976)—translated into English as *Nine, Novena, Avalovara,* and *The Queen of the Prisons of Greece*—is characterized by formal innovations reflecting the evolution of his poetics. Lins was the recipient of three major Brazilian literary prizes, including the Coelho Neto Prize of the Brazilian Academy of Letters. He died in 1978.

DALKEY ARCHIVE PAPERBACKS

FICTION: AMERICAN

BARNES, DJUNA. *Ladies Almanack*	9.95
BARNES, DJUNA. *Ryder*	11.95
BARTH, JOHN. *LETTERS*	14.95
CHARYN, JEROME. *The Tar Baby*	10.95
COOVER, ROBERT. *A Night at the Movies*	9.95
CRAWFORD, STANLEY. *Some Instructions to My Wife*	7.95
DOWELL, COLEMAN. *Too Much Flesh and Jabez*	9.95
DUCORNET, RIKKI. *The Fountains of Neptune*	10.95
DUCORNET, RIKKI. *The Jade Cabinet*	9.95
DUCORNET, RIKKI. *Phosphor in Dreamland*	12.95
DUCORNET, RIKKI. *The Stain*	11.95
FAIRBANKS, LAUREN. *Sister Carrie*	10.95
GASS, WILLIAM H. *Willie Masters' Lonesome Wife*	9.95
KURYLUK, EWA. *Century 21*	12.95
MARKSON, DAVID. *Springer's Progress*	9.95
MARKSON, DAVID. *Wittgenstein's Mistress*	11.95
MASO, CAROLE. *AVA*	12.95
MCELROY, JOSEPH. *Women and Men*	15.95
MERRILL, JAMES. *The (Diblos) Notebook*	9.95
NOLLEDO, WILFRIDO D. *But for the Lovers*	12.95
SEESE, JUNE AKERS. *Is This What Other Women Feel Too?*	9.95
SEESE, JUNE AKERS. *What Waiting Really Means*	7.95
SORRENTINO, GILBERT. *Aberration of Starlight*	9.95
SORRENTINO, GILBERT. *Imaginative Qualities of Actual Things*	11.95
SORRENTINO, GILBERT. *Mulligan Stew*	13.95
SORRENTINO, GILBERT. *Splendide-Hôtel*	5.95
SORRENTINO, GILBERT. *Steelwork*	9.95
SORRENTINO, GILBERT. *Under the Shadow*	9.95
STEIN, GERTRUDE. *The Making of Americans*	16.95
STEIN, GERTRUDE. *A Novel of Thank You*	9.95
STEPHENS, MICHAEL. *Season at Coole*	7.95
WOOLF, DOUGLAS. *Wall to Wall*	7.95
YOUNG, MARGUERITE. *Miss MacIntosh, My Darling*	2-vol. set, 30.00
ZUKOFSKY, LOUIS. *Collected Fiction*	9.95

DALKEY ARCHIVE PAPERBACKS

FICTION: BRITISH

BROOKE-ROSE, CHRISTINE. *Amalgamemnon*	9.95
CHARTERIS, HUGO. *The Tide Is Right*	9.95
FIRBANK, RONALD. *Complete Short Stories*	9.95
GALLOWAY, JANICE. *Foreign Parts*	12.95
GALLOWAY, JANICE. *The Trick Is to Keep Breathing*	11.95
MOSLEY, NICHOLAS. *Accident*	9.95
MOSLEY, NICHOLAS. *Impossible Object*	9.95
MOSLEY, NICHOLAS. *Judith*	10.95

FICTION: FRENCH

BUTOR, MICHEL. *Portrait of the Artist as a Young Ape*	10.95
CREVEL, RENÉ. *Putting My Foot in It*	9.95
ERNAUX, ANNIE. *Cleaned Out*	9.95
GRAINVILLE, PATRICK. *The Cave of Heaven*	10.95
NAVARRE, YVES. *Our Share of Time*	9.95
QUENEAU, RAYMOND. *The Last Days*	9.95
QUENEAU, RAYMOND. *Pierrot Mon Ami*	9.95
ROUBAUD, JACQUES. *The Great Fire of London*	12.95
ROUBAUD, JACQUES. *The Plurality of Worlds of Lewis*	9.95
ROUBAUD, JACQUES. *The Princess Hoppy*	9.95
SIMON, CLAUDE. *The Invitation*	9.95

FICTION: GERMAN

SCHMIDT, ARNO. *Nobodaddy's Children*	13.95

FICTION: IRISH

CUSACK, RALPH. *Cadenza*	7.95
MACLOCHLAINN, ALF. *Out of Focus*	5.95
O'BRIEN, FLANN. *The Dalkey Archive*	9.95
O'BRIEN, FLANN. *The Hard Life*	9.95

(continued on next page)

DALKEY ARCHIVE PAPERBACKS

FICTION: LATIN AMERICAN and SPANISH

CAMPOS, JULIETA. *The Fear of Losing Eurydice*	8.95
LINS, OSMAN. *The Queen of the Prisons of Greece*	12.95
SARDUY, SEVERO. *Cobra* and *Maitreya*	13.95
TUSQUETS, ESTHER. *Stranded*	9.95
VALENZUELA, LUISA. *He Who Searches*	8.00

POETRY

ANSEN, ALAN. *Contact Highs: Selected Poems 1957-1987*	11.95
BURNS, GERALD. *Shorter Poems*	9.95
FAIRBANKS, LAUREN. *Muzzle Thyself*	9.95
GISCOMBE, C. S. *Here*	9.95
MARKSON, DAVID. *Collected Poems*	9.95
THEROUX, ALEXANDER. *The Lollipop Trollops*	10.95

NONFICTION

FORD, FORD MADOX. *The March of Literature*	16.95
GREEN, GEOFFREY, ET AL. *The Vineland Papers*	14.95
MATHEWS, HARRY. *20 Lines a Day*	8.95
ROUDIEZ, LEON S. *French Fiction Revisited*	14.95
SHKLOVSKY, VIKTOR. *Theory of Prose*	14.95
WEST, PAUL. *Words for a Deaf Daughter* and *Gala*	12.95
YOUNG, MARGUERITE. *Angel in the Forest*	13.95

For a complete catalog of our titles, write to Dalkey Archive Press, Illinois State University, Campus Box 4241, Normal, IL 61790-4241, or fax (309) 438-7422.